The Collis Valle Saga

BOOK 1: THE SALT MINE

A J GILLHAM

authorHOUSE®

AuthorHouse™ UK
1663 Liberty Drive
Bloomington, IN 47403 USA
www.authorhouse.co.uk
Phone: UK TFN: 0800 0148641 (Toll Free inside the UK)
*   UK Local: (02) 0369 56322 (+44 20 3695 6322 from outside the UK)*

Published by AuthorHouse 10/26/2021

ISBN: 978-1-6655-9338-0 (sc)
ISBN: 978-1-6655-9348-9 (e)

Print information available on the last page.

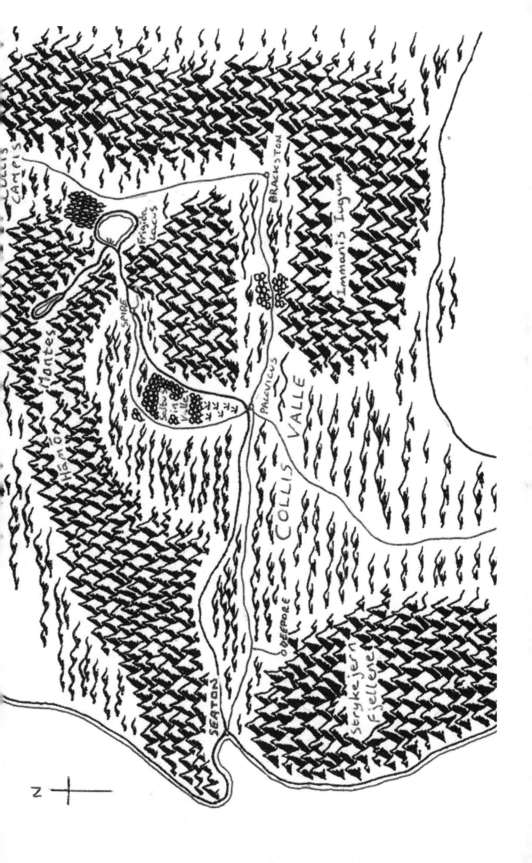

CHAPTER 1

The Settlement of Seaton

Seaton is the largest settlement in the region of Collis Valle, supporting over three hundred souls - not only Humans, but Elves and perhaps half a dozen Half-Orcs with their slightly pointed ears and bad tempers. They have stripped most of the surrounding trees to build their single-level wattle-and-daub roundhouses, and farming supplements their main resource: the oil-rich fish from a sea which, in the full force of winter, freezes over for more than half the year.

Much to his father's chagrin, Conn Bruis, a lean young Human of fifteen summers, has become Initiate Bruis to the Temple of Unda, Lady of All Waters. He walks happily down the and bronze-tooled planks of the docks. Inhaling the salty air, Conn's blue-eyed gaze rarely leaves the port and sea beyond, where the midday sun plays hypnotically across the waves.

"Get out of my way!" bellows a burly figure, carrying woven crates of pollock from one of the boats.

A quick sidestep saves Conn from being bowled over and soiling his freshly laundered initiate's tabard of powder blue.

Conn watches the robust figure continue towards the stone-and-wood dockside warehouses and realises fearfully, *He's a Half-Orc.* These dusky-skinned people with their pale-yellow eyes have extremely low emotional tolerances. He thanks the tempestuous spirit of the Lady of All Waters for his lucky escape.

Conn flicks his wavy brown hair from his face and hastens on to the temple. It is his privileged duty to perform the Blessing of the Water before the fisher fleets return for the Thanksgiving for the Day's Catch the evening service, a duty usually reserved for the older, more experienced Initiates. He hurries past the warehouses with a light breeze blowing off the sea, increasing to a chill wind holding the threat of the fast-approaching autumn. Further north, near the larger settlement of Windown, the sea ice closes the shipping lanes for the greater part of the year. Mountains to the north shelter the bay into Seaton, allowing the people to get their sewn, plank-built boats into the water earlier each spring and stay out longer.

Why, Conn wonders, does Windown do so well being so far north, while Seaton is only half the size with closer trading opportunities with neighbouring settlements and the Lakeside Settlement to the south? He does not understand how commerce works. Maybe that is why he is drawn to a more religious calling, despite his father's wishes for him to join the family business with the fishing fleets. Perhaps his brother, a couple of years younger, will follow in their father's wake, but by joining the Temple to the Lady of All Waters, Conn believes he still answers the call of the seas.

Conn reaches a large square with a great fountain dedicated to the Goddess Unda in the centre, cascading water into a deep pool, and the temple which faces the port on the far side.

A woman, perhaps a few years older than Conn, stops him. "Hello, young sir." Her voice is husky with a trace of a southern accent, placing her from beyond the coastal Strykejern Fjellene Mountains, perhaps from as far as the Southern Continent.

Conn shuffles his feet when she appraises him with dark, piercing eyes.

"May I talk with you? I've been considering religion of late and am in need of advice."

He finds her golden complexion and face, framed by long black hair enchanting. "That is difficult right now," he answers politely, anxious not to upset her. "I need to prepare for the ceremony at dusk." When she looks crestfallen, he quickly adds, "but I will be pleased to meet you after the ceremony."

"I would love to hear more about your faith," she responds coyly, running a warm finger along the V-line of his tabard, barely touching his chest. She gestures to a tavern behind. "I'll meet you there when you're done?"

Conn feels himself blushing furiously. "The Bawdy Sailor?" he chuckles. The tavern, appropriately named, is the hangout of sailors of both genders after the early evening ceremony, where a convivial drink or two and comparing their daily catch often degenerates into a brawl. "Very well," he tells her. "As soon as we finish."

"That will do," she answers huskily in his ear. She holds her body against his wiry frame, firm breasts crushing against his chest, causing another deep blush.

Head reeling, Conn heads to the temple. *Who is this woman with her long skirt and blouse akin to the gypsy travellers who sometimes come to town? She is well-groomed and with her floral perfume does not smell like travellers normally do.*

Conn tries to focus on his preparation for the ceremony, his mind wandering back to the mysterious woman. *I don't even know her name.* With the ceremony at last concluded, Conn cleans up quickly and leaves for the Bawdy Sailor.

In the smoky tavern, he scans the room. She is in a wood-partitioned booth near the door and greets him with a smile, sweeping a drink from a tray carried by a passing serving girl. Focusing on the exotic woman, Conn is oblivious the glances curious about the rare presence of an initiate at the Bawdy Sailor. He slides into the seat opposite her.

Her slender hand is over the top of a tankard as she passes it to him. He notices a ring has twisted around the wrong way and points it out to her.

"A gift from my father when I was a little girl," she explains. "It is too large for my finger." She twists the ring to its correct position, revealing a miniature pyramid ornament.

"May I know your name?"

"I am Lusha, from the Southern Slaver States near the Scorched Barrens. Please drink, before you tell me about your faith?" she encourages. Her eyes seem to pierce deep into his soul.

Conn drinks before speaking enthusiastically about worship and the Temple of the Lady of All Waters.

Lusha keeps up her intent gaze and replaces his empty tankard with another drink.

Conn's speech begins to slur, the sounds of the tavern growing more distant with a sensation of sailing away.

Lusha smiles but no longer with any warmth.

Conn's head hits the table; the wooden tankard falls to the floor, spilling the remains of the locally brewed beer.

Rising, Lusha easily lifts the boy in her arms and carries him out of the tavern. "Poor boy," she explains to those close by. "The lad simply cannot hold his liquor."

CHAPTER 2

The Settlement of Brackston

Brackston is the fourth settlement to be founded in Collis Valle. Their quarry, supplying stone to Windown in the Collis Campis to the north and to the settlements of Collis Valle to the west, helped Brackston quickly grow to be the equal of Seaton. The first major stop from Windown to the other settlements, Brackston is also the most culturally diverse, with Humans making up merely half the population.

One of these Humans, a tall athletically built man with dark greasy-looking hair, enters the warmth of a bread makers that he knows Glynis owns with her husband. The scent of the baking bread wafts up his Romanesque nose.

Glynis knows that she is starting to become a little more rotund with each passing year, "on the wrong side of forty" as she calls it and keeps her light-brown hair pulled back in a tight bun.

She looks at the visitor, her hazel eyes absorbing every detail about the man from his charcoal-grey shirt and trousers to his midnight-blue boots and long cloak. She also notes the outline of a short sword on his right hip, the vaguer outline of a dagger on his left hip, and the daggers poking out of each boot.

"Greetings, sir," she says with a smile, though she fells unable to convey any warmth behind it. It is as if this man drains the usual warmth from her voice with his very presence. She has an inkling that he is one of these Guildsmen - the polite term for the rogues operating under the official-sounding banner of the Guilde Kallun Trade Regulators.

The Guilde Kallun started around thirty-odd years ago.

While the settlement has a militia to keep order and defend it from the odd Goblinoid raids, the Guilde Kallun are supposed to maintain the merchant caravan movements between Windown and the other settlements.

Glynis wishes that they never lasted their formative years, not after their failed attempt to take over the militia's role too. It was the Brackston Council, made up of the people's representatives, the quarry masters, the militia, and the spiritualist leaders who stopped their plans. There was a merchant representative but when they mysteriously disappeared, the Guilde Kallun were there to take over from them.

The customer glares down at her coldly before deigning to speak to her. "I have come to ensure that the flatbread order is ready," he finally says.

She notes the slightly nasal tone to his quiet voice but puts that down his having a slightly larger nose than most people.

"It is, though the recipe that we was given was not easy. We are afraid that the bread did not rise like we expected it to," she tells him with a disappointed tone and a shake of her head.

"That is why it is called 'flat bread'," he tells her slowly and clearly, with the emphasis on the last word before fuming on. "It is **not** supposed to rise. It's not like they have an abundance of yeast in the Southern States."

"Well, sir," she huffs. "There's not much call for that attitude." She then realises that she has been sharp with a potentially very dangerous man and continues more quietly. "Bread that don't rise. It's unheard of, that is."

"Oh, give me strength," he groans quietly to himself. He then looks askance at her with a frown. "Let me see the order before I agree for it to be sent off."

"Well, I never," Glynis declares, glancing through the doorway where her husband makes the bread. "Reuben! The customer wants to see the flatbread order!"

"Coming, Aunt." A young man in his late teens with wavy ginger hair almost touching his shoulders and light grey eyes walks out, carrying the flatbread on three woven trays.

The Guildsman almost stops breathing as the boy enters the front, but he manages to recover, not quickly enough for Glynis' sharp eyes though.

He looks at the perfectly cooked and cooled bread. "Adequate," he sneers before taking one to rip off a piece and tasting it. He barely manages to cover his surprise. *These do not just look excellently done but taste good too.* When he finishes eating his voice is back to its deadpan tone. "Just as I thought. Adequate. Have them delivered to this address … Reuben … is it?" He drags out the young man's name while handing him a slip of parchment to the lean but strong-looking youth. *This boy strikes familiar. What is it about him?* The Guildsman's thoughts are disrupted by the youth's stammering acknowledgement after looking for his aunt's confirming nod.

Reuben then realises that she has not taken her eye off the customer since he came through the doorway. Without another word, he leaves and quickly heads up the street. He does not know why; he just has a feeling that he does not want to be near that man.

With the boy gone, the Guildsman returns his attention back to the woman behind the counter. "Who is that boy?" he demands slowly, coldly, and quietly.

"He's family he is." She then starts arranging the freshly baked bloomers around a woven basket to avoid the man's cold dark eyes.

"Don't give me that." His voice takes on a completely new level of coldness that would rival the ice floes of the northern sea. "He looks nothing like you so do not try lying to me again. Who, is, he?"

Glynis catches the man's eyes despite her best efforts and sees the promise of death in their depths. She has a terrible sinking feeling that if she tells him the truth, then it will bode extremely ill for the boy.

"He's a nephew from my sister's side." She silently prays to whatever Gods are listening to allow her bluff to work. "He's here to learn the family -"

The rest of her words are choked off when he abruptly vaults the counter, slams her against the wattle-and-daub dividing wall, a dagger to her throat in one fluid motion.

She tries to struggle against him who stands a good head and shoulders over her until his dagger pricks her throat. She then stops moving, knowing the futility of her efforts.

She whimpers a little and has to swallow hard at the lump in her throat. "We found him out back some years ago," she finally confesses. "He was injured almost to death, so we brought him in."

"And?" His hand tightens on her coarse woollen tabard for emphasis.

"While he healed in body, the only thing that he could remember was his name. So, we gave him a job and a home here." Glynis feels dejected and fears that she has just doomed the boy she raised as her nephew for the past ten years.

"Reuben."

She nods slowly so as not to prick herself again. A tear falls down her cheek. She closes her eyes where the pressure against her chest disappears. Breathing deeply a couple of times, she then risks opening them to see that she is all alone, and a pouch of bronze axe heads lies on the counter.

Reuben, quickly forgetting the incident back at his aunt's, is enjoying the late summer sun that falls on the half stone and wood buildings or fully built stone chunks that make up the main street here. All of them have either the farmers supplied thatch or wooden shingle covering the single-level buildings, with homes still following the roundhouse design while the traders have opted for a more squared design, like his aunt and uncles.

There is no organisation to Brackston. No two buildings join, providing a myriad of pathways and cart tracks of varying widths, which still fascinates him. It was the Council who finally decided to keep some routes clear of buildings so the travelling merchants could move their wares through the settlement. However, much of the trees were cut down to make the initial buildings, but some effort has gone into cultivating new trees on the outskirts. Mainly redwoods.

He is on his way back breathing in the various odours of woodsmoke and cooking food from the homes and businesses blending with the rank smell of animal manure. He just passes a Healer's half-stone and wood rectangular building when he hears someone call out from between the Healer's and a drinking house. Looking into the shadowy area of the alley, he soon spots a Hauflin on the ground in a faded green dress corded at the waist, though part of it is pulled over one diminutive knee as she clutches her leg.

"Young sir?" she calls plaintively. "I've had an accident. Can you help me? I'm having trouble standing up."

"Sure," he says leaning the trays against a wall. He enters the alley to help the auburn-haired woman when he suddenly stiffens as something tickles his mind. More like a sensation or an abrupt awareness. He hesitates to try to figure it out when his head explodes in a shock of pain, dropping him unceremoniously onto the Hauflin's legs, his head in her lap.

"Nicely done Emlyn," she says to the blonde-haired man who lifts the boy's head long enough for her to roll out and standing up. "You're doing better at moving quietly for a Human since I've been teaching you. Almost didn't hear you that time."

"Well, that's some praise from a master rogue like yourself, my dear Salvia," he responds with a twinkle in his azure blue eyes and a bow. He then grabs Reuben and carries the boy over one shoulder before continuing in a more serious tone. "Now let's get out of here quickly before the flaming Guilde Kallun catches us."

"Damn straight." They head down towards the other end of the alley and away from the main street both thankful that Brackston is not a walled settlement. Though if the rumours are true, that could soon change.

A person slips out of the shadows behind them and observes their passing. His face creases in thought. Should he stop them or go straight back to report to his superiors. When they reach a simple two-wheeled cart and load the boy, he then makes up his mind. He slips back out into the street and heads in the opposite direction.

CHAPTER 3

The Following Morning

The Guildsman finally gets out of the subsequent meeting around midnight. It does not surprise him in the least that it took virtually the entire day after their picking through every single detail that was raised. Nor did it surprise him that the Headsmen of the Guilde Kallun were especially scrutinous over the Guildsman's observations of this Reuben boy.

He has nothing definite. It is more of a gut feeling. Seeing the boy, the ginger hair, the shape of his face, and the way he moves with such a fluid motion is most unlike what other young people usually are like normally. It was all these factors that caused his indecision initially when he saw the boy being taken away about whether to track them down immediately or to report the incident to the Guilde Kallun Headsmen first. Also, this has not been the first disappearance from Brackston not controlled by the Guilde Kallun and it is becoming a bit of an embarrassment to them, though this could be the one closest to them if he is correct. At least one person has been taken every thirty days or so for quite a while now without any discernible rhyme or reason.

In the end, he had decided on the meeting to let the Headsmen decide what should be done and risk the trail going cold. Then, if anything does not come of it or goes wrong it will take a second meeting to ascertain who was at fault but only after he has a chance to speak in his defence. That is one of the first rules he learnt well when he was about Reuben's age; always ensure to cover your own back to lessen the risk of finding a dagger in it. The dagger being metaphorical and literal.

Now he is finally out of that protracted meeting, the Guildsman immediately goes to work on the necessary preparations before he takes a short nap where he will be awakened by the crowing of the many cockerels that call Brackston their home too. If he left immediately then it would be extremely difficult to find and follow the right tracks before the sun rose. The only way he could do so would be to fire up a torch to light his way but that presents itself with a whole new set of problems.

The first being that it would affect his night-sight. He is only Human after all, and trying to pierce the gloom beyond the light of a torch would be virtually impossible. Now, if he was an Elf, then he would have no problem following the tracks.

He could have called on one of his acquaintances where some of whom are Elves and Half-Elves but if he is right then he would then have to split the final part of the reward. If he is wrong, he could be the one who winds up dead in a ditch for his failure. Soon after the Traitor's Hunt nearly a decade ago several other Guildsmen were discovered that way. Some of those were suspected of assisting the traitors.

The second problem and an even more dangerous one to his mind is that a burning torch will be like marking a target on his back for predators, for rival Guilde members, or any one of the other Races who called the wild their home and love to roam at night looking for unwary victims.

The cockerels wake him up before the sun peaks over the Immanis Iugum mountains to the southeast of Brackston where their mined stone comes from out of the quarries. Even though it is still early, there are already some people out running errands or going to work. Many of the businesses are also preparing to open like the Bunner's, who will already be up to start preparing their dough for baking into round or long loaves. The Guildsman thinks back to the flatbread they gave him yesterday and how good it tasted. It is a pity that he does not have a couple for the road.

He gets up and washes his face with cold water held in a clay bowl. Just one of the tasks he set up before he put his head down. Once he is dressed in his charcoal grey shirt and trousers and his midnight blue boots and cloak, he pulls out two daggers from under a folded up thick woollen blanket he used as a pillow and slides them into his boot sheaths.

From under the sleeping cot, he pulls out his belt already loaded with a couple of filled belt pouches, one behind his sword scabbard, the other behind a sheath for his third dagger before buckling it around his waist tightly to prevent it moving too much. He then grabs the saddlebags from beside the only door into his roundhouse and leaves for the Bay horse-tied round back that he acquired last night. Once he is certain that everything is secured, the Guildsman leads the Collis horse back to the alley where Reuben was taken before the sun even rises over the south-eastern peaks properly.

It is as he thought. Finding the cart tracks on this chill dewy morning is not difficult. Fortunately, the light rain from a couple of days ago kept the ground good and soft enough to maintain the impression. If there was a heavy downpour instead, then the tracks could have easily been destroyed. With these people pulling the cart along the soft ground, well, one of them since the Hauflin will not be able to do much, it should not take him more than a couple of days to track them down. He turns his horse back west and starts out at a trot.

Calamity. *Oh great. This is going to take a lot longer than a couple of days now.* The last building out of Brackston is a rest stop for Merchants. There are signs of a struggle and a partially built round earthen mound to the north of the road nearer the Hamo Montes range just large enough for a Beaker burial. From what the people tell him, a blonde-haired man the Hauflin had called Emlyn, killed their husband who was trying to stop them from stealing a couple of their spare horses.

The people of the rest stop use the spares to switch out for the Traders own horses after the long seven hundred and fifty-odd mile road from Windown where the Guildsman knows much of the land is flat interspersed with hilly areas and truly little tree cover. The trees around Windown were used at the start of settlement and were never replaced. But despite all that the largest settlement in the area thrived and Brackston sent much of their stone trade to them.

Now he knows that those he is chasing are using horses to pull their cart. It is possible that was their plan all along. He squeezes his knees to his mount's flanks to spur it on into a run. His only hope now is that he can get to them before they disappear, a hope that is heightened by the simple fact that they should have to change horses more often than he will.

He believes that he is making great time over the next couple of days, the only problem is that he cannot spot them ahead of him. That is not surprising since the trade route winds through the hills that cover the passage between the Hamo Montes to the north and the Immanis Iugum to the south. Then there is the odd scattering of trees, shrubs, and even lightly wooded areas along this part of the road, including the odd homestead.

CHAPTER 4

The Settlement of Deepore

That stupid snooty bitch should not have yelled at me the way she did! Soon shut her up though! Ghorza thinks vehemently. Even the shining sun does little to calm Ghorza down. While the sun does shine, the days often remain cool when the wind blows off from the mountain range to the south.

It still amazes her how these feeble folks can take so much punishment from the Orc tribes that live in the Strykejern Fjellene mountains, yet one punch from her and they drop like a chunk of ore hauled up from the settlement mines. The village has five such mines running less than an hour away to the south in the base of the mountains.

Ghorza was born into one of the Orc tribes that live in the Strykejern Fjellene, to the Wutarjini. She was the result of a raid by the settlers of Deepore after they became angry from the continued raids against them. So, they decided to return the favour causing some of the Orc females to fall pregnant while others raided their supplies or held off the Orc defenders. It would not have been so bad if she were born a male but being female and a half-breed just made her a target for the most brutal upbringing for the first nine years of her life.

Of the thirteen babies born around the same time only four survived. The other three had been males and, therefore had a use within the tribe. While Orcs are always harsh when raising their young, they used to target her especially, until she escaped from them under a bright midday sun seven years ago just like when the Deepore settlers attacked her tribe and gave her life. All the tribes prefer to operate at night since their eyes can see more clearly then, though the half-breeds can see just as well at any time. She does love watching the sunrises and sunsets. When she finally got free, she came across Deepore to discover that she was not the only Half-Orc in the stone-walled settlement and decided to stay here.

She quickly learnt that life in Deepore is just as hard as the mountains that they mined, and she had difficulty fitting in even amongst the other Half-Orcs living and working here. These Half-Orcs were the product of the Orc raids against the settlement. She soon developed a darker temperament, and her moods became increasingly erratic. This often led her into trouble, especially for brawling at the slightest provocation where that Annest Wiliams is just the latest.

Because of her temper, Ghorza has very few people with who she can truly get along with out of the couple of hundred residents who live here. Around a quarter of those being Half-Orcs. She would have left long ago via that single rough and stony road leading north to the east-west trade route, but something keeps holding her back from taking that trip.

When things get too much for her like now, Ghorza sits on a flat rock near the edge of the spicy-scented maple woods overlooking this rough road. She stares at it with her pale-yellow eyes like she is trying to garner some answers by doing so.

Across the road, on a small plateau to the west of the settlement in the encompassing mountains, she can see a smooth stone tower that belongs to some spellcaster. She does not know him except from hearing the village gossip and has certainly never seen him to her knowledge. The gossipers proclaim him to be a strange one, more so ever since his father mysteriously vanished a couple of years ago. Some even theorise that he had killed his own father but there was never any evidence to that.

Gwendolyn Pryde is sixty-odd years who moves as one half her age. She is out looking for herbs and roots for her potions and poultices when she spots Ghorza sitting quietly on her 'calming down rock' as the older woman likes to call it. Ghorza keeps telling her that is a very Human expression where Gwendolyn keeps reminding her that she is Human. The sunlight reflects off the young girl's warm beige complexion where the light green highlights and facial features belie her half-breed heritage.

"What's happened this time, young one?" she calls softly, her voice slightly croaky from years of leaning over cauldrons and pans with smoke and steam wafting into her face

Ghorza snaps her head round on tense shoulders before she sees whom it is that breaks into her thoughts. However, she should have guessed by the boldness of that tone. She thinks about ignoring the salt and pepper-haired woman, but Gwendolyn seems blessed with the patience of an Elf's lifespan. She relaxes slightly with a heavy sigh.

"That damned snooty bitch bumps into me and then has a nerve to blame me for being in her way," she growls in response. "That stupid bit-"

"That's enough of that child!" Gwendolyn scolds her. The old woman is the only one in Deepore who can ever get away with using that tone with her and Ghorza still cannot figure out why. If it were anybody else, then she would have just flattened them without a second thought no matter who they were. Ghorza also knows how Gwendolyn feels about harsh language but she is too angry to give that much thought. "I already heard some of it, but did you really punch four teeth down her throat?"

"Four teeth? Damn, I missed," Ghorza responds much more calmly than she has been feeling all morning. It seems that Gwendolyn only needs to be around for the tension to leave her and she has no way to explain that either.

"You missed? I don't understand. What were you trying to do?" wonders the older woman, confusion etching her lined face.

"I wanted to break the cow's jaw. Stopped that damned, shrill, screeching voice of hers though." That brings a brief smile to them both; Gwendolyn knows exactly what Ghorza means though she still frowns at the cursive.

Even Gwendolyn fears Annest coming into her workshop for some of her remedies, always moaning about the state of Gwendolyn's workspace and the constant stench from the heating ingredients. Never stops the Head of the Miner's wife from going in though when her servants are busy with other duties or, more than likely, if she does not want them knowing what she is getting. Usually, some tincture to prevent her from falling pregnant, not that her husband knows this.

Ghorza vaults down from the rock to land softly despite her large size on the short grass, kept that way by one of the herder's animals who come this way from time to time.

"She is going to be alright. Annest is at the Templum Meum de Terra for treatment," Gwendolyn tells Ghorza who just shrugs in response causing the apothecary to frown. "This one is going to cost you this time young lady."

"But I have nothing except what you have given me when I could not get anything for myself," whines Ghorza.

"There may be other ways," Gwendolyn begins but pauses to think through it. "Obviously, working off your punishment is not going to work this time. I cannot see Annest letting you anywhere near her for a long while."

"Wouldn't be seen dead in her company anyway," Ghorza scoffs.

"That's enough of that talk!" the woman snaps. "If you were ordered to wait on her hand and foot then you will do exactly that with a yes ma'am, no ma'am! Do I make myself clear?"

Ghorza falls silent and starts toeing the earth suddenly feeling very much smaller than her muscular six and a half stature compared with the older woman's who barely reaches her chest. She glances to the older woman who fixes her in place with one of her rare steely green-eyed glares.

"May I continue? Or do I just leave you to the tender mercies of a really hacked-off guard?" Ghorza wants to respond but finds that her voice temporarily leaves her, so she just shakes her head causing her long black hair tied high into a ponytail to flap from side to side. Gwendolyn continues more calmly. "That's better. Now, as I was saying, servitude to work off your debt to Annest is more than likely to be out of the question and they cannot fine you when you have nothing to begin with. Imprisoning you for the duration of the sentence is more than likely to be out of the question, especially after what you did to those guards and the cell last time. So, they may seriously look at the possibility of executing or expelling you, which I'm sure will please Annest to no end."

"So, what am I to do then?" she pleads starting to get genuinely concerned for the first time since she escaped from the Orcs in what now seems a lifetime ago. *I could try a make a run for it, though I doubt if I'll ever be welcome back again. Not even Gwen will be able to protect me if I did return, that's if she even wants too by then.* The older woman then sinks within her own introspection before glancing up at the quiet Half-Orc while she continues to work through the options.

"I believe that if you show that you are trying to raise the rings to pay off any possible fine, then it may go a long way for you to be able to call for a stay of execution, though you may still have to go, quietly mind, to the gaol for a spell."

"If you think that's best, then that is what I'll do. The only thing is, some of the traders barely speak to me anymore," Ghorza answers quietly.

"And whose fault is that?" Gwendolyn snaps. Ghorza looks back to the toe-gouged trench in the earth sheepishly. She then hears a deep sigh that causes her to look into those green orbs. "Okay. Okay. I'll have a word with some of them to try a give you yet another break."

Ghorza looks at her hopefully but then notices the steel back in Gwendolyn's eyes once again.

"But you must stop lashing out whenever someone upsets you, otherwise this is not going to work," the older woman reprimands her sternly. Words escape Ghorza at that moment, strange how that always happens when she is with Gwendolyn, so she just nods her head while chewing on her upper lip with her slightly elongated lower canines. "I seriously do not know why I am doing this but go and see Dyfri. I know he needs a strong courier for a delivery. Tell him that I sent you and that I will meet up with him later after I have finished out here."

This is the first time that Ghorza notices Gwendolyn's wicker basket containing some roots and herbs and the curved bronze dagger that she always uses. Giving the smaller woman a careful heartfelt hug, she races off to find Dyfri Parcel's shop while Gwendolyn quietly smiles fondly at the girl's disappearing broad back. "If she listens this time, then she might do well enough," she says to no one in particular.

It does not take long for Ghorza to reach the log-fenced, dung-smelling animal pen containing a good horse and a couple of pit ponies in front of Dyfri's premises. She heads straight into the rectangular stone shop where he sells his smaller pets and companions to realise that the portly Dyfri is expecting her all along. *Gwendolyn's a right devious little sod at times*, she thinks with a smile that Dyfri mistakes for one of greeting. Once she tells him Gwendolyn's message, he then lets her know what it is he needs delivering.

"Be careful of this one, its look will stone you and if anything happens to this one it will be a while before I can get another. Not, that this one was easy in the first place. Now, this needs to go to the Sorcerer in the tower," he rambles on quickly and looking rather anxiously as he heads towards the back door of the shop.

There is a cockerel-legged bird with a serpentine tail and a strong bag over its head chained to a metal post just outside in a second smaller stone-walled pen. The draconic winged creature tries to scratch at the bag to remove it every now and then but keeps falling over with each attempt.

"Be extremely careful that you do keep that bag in place, even when you hand it over to Treorai. That is the most important part. If you have any trouble with the Watch, then give them this note immediately," he says this last so emphatically that it gives Ghorza the impression that he already knows about her situation, including being one of the very few that she has got on with in the settlement. "If anyone else tries to waylay you, then just growl at them, keep them out of your way until you can make this delivery."

"Yes, Mr Parcel," she answers in total confusion about why he is going into so much detail.

"There is a pouch of twenty bronze rings for when you get back, as well as any possible bonus that that Sorcerer may give you. You will get both to keep upon your return."

Twenty bronze rings are a great start to getting the fine together. Astounded, Ghorza then nods and heads off with the struggling bird as Dyfri breathes a sigh of relief and counts out the promised payment into a pouch. He even adds a few tin rings for good measure knowing that the child will need it for something or other.

Main Street is the only proper road through the settlement from the wall to the mines where fallen stone from passing carts has been pressed into the ground forming a hard-packed surface. The buildings lining the road are either square or rectangular structures of stone and bronze with wooden plank roofs. Behind the buildings lining Main Street are more of the same though these are more scattered in small clusters.

When she tries to walk through Main Street, half the time dragging along and the other half pulling the bird back, many people suddenly find themselves stopping short, dodging out of the way and one or two even tripping over it. In the end, she picks up the increasingly aggravated creature while holding its head and scrawny reptilian neck in a firm hold until she can get away from the bustling crowd. Once she passes through the log gates in the settlement's protective wall after showing the guards Dyfri's note, she drops the thing on the floor whilst keeping a firm hold of the chain and heads between the wheat and corn fields to the tower without any further trouble.

She has never been this close to the structure but now she can see that it looks like it has been carved out of one solid block of stone, unlike the buildings of Deepore where they are made with rubble stone from the mines.

Before she even gets to knock at the door, it swings open to reveal a thirty-something man with black hair and a cropped beard wearing an indigo robe who waves her into the tower.

"Excellent. Dyfri has sent you with my basilisk. He said that he would be able to get it, though I was not expecting one for another month or so," he says excitedly in his baritone voice. He then takes the chain to pass it through an adjoining door where someone else collects it before reaching into a pouch as he turns back to Ghorza. He holds a single golden pendant about an inch across between his thumb and forefinger that he spins as he continues talking to the Half-Orc in a much softer modulating tone. "See this shiny gold rondure, how it glitters in the light; the refractive play across its surface …"

Ghorza's yellow eyes suddenly start to feel heavy as the Sorcerer babbles on. Distantly, she sees a darker complexioned Orc coming closer and reaching out to her before knowing no more.

CHAPTER 5

Continuing the Pursuit

It is on the third day when the Guildsman feels that he finally gets a break. During his afternoon run, he spots a horse lying beside the road with a broken leg and a bloody hole where its eye used to be.

Looking around the area more closely there is a scrape mark on the edge of the road where a cart had slipped. The way he reads the signs is that the cart caught a stone, some have such marks just off the road, which threw it off. This caused one of the horses to break its leg as it tried to counter for the sudden shift judging from the multiple hoofmarks. After unhitching the horse, they put it out of its misery. More than likely it was the one called Emlyn who did that by the looks of the clean strike. The Guildsman doubts that it was the Hauflin since she probably does not have the upper body strength to keep the horse's head still long enough to insert the blade.

He remounts his horse and gives chase for the remainder of the day before resting up for the night. He does not want to cause any harm to his own horse on the road during the overcast and chilly night, so he pulls off at a copse of birch and oak trees.

Halfway through the morning of the following drizzly day, his horse stumbles and throws the Guildsman to the ground. It is only his quick reflexes that land him on his feet without any injury. He looks back to the horse to find it is favouring a foreleg. He gently feels the horse's leg where it whinnies in pain at one point.

"It's alright. It looks like you have pulled or strained something there my friend," he says softly. *Damn and blast! Of all the blasted luck!* Despite

21

his mounting frustration, he feels no animosity towards the beast that carried him for the past four days. The horse did very well but now it needs time to rest and heal. He takes the reins and walks to the next farmstead, which takes half of the afternoon.

While he is at the farmstead, the Guildsman learns that their best horse was stolen just the day before. They never got a glimpse of who stole it. They only found that the horse was gone when the men got back from the fields. The Guildsman just nods in understanding. At least he now has a timeline of how far behind them he is. About a day still. He accepts their offer of a replacement mount though he can see that this one is not as good as his own.

He also learns of the Hauflin's name. Salvia. She was the distraction for Emlyn by approaching the farmer's wife and taking her into the wattle and daub roundhouse to barter for a few supplies for the road. The Hauflin gave truly little in exchange for what she got, and the farmer's wife is still furious at being duped by the diminutive woman.

Climbing onto the fresh horse after ensuring that his own will be taken care of while it heals, he speeds off in pursuit while there is a little light remaining.

It is still about two days to Palovicus where he spends most of the ride at a trot to preserve this horse. He also knows that keeping two horses at a run while pulling a cart will exhaust them quickly. He wants to catch up to them on a fresher mount to better chase them to ground when he catches sight of his quarry.

At least the sky is clearing up where he starts seeing a few stars appear in the night sky, though his fresh concern now is that it is going to be a cold night unless he can find some shelter soon. He eventually finds a dell in a lightly wooded area where he risks maintaining a fire to keep him warm. No use in freezing to death before the job is done.

He did debate to himself earlier about starting out so late in the day, but he also knows that time is of the essence. He must get that boy back. He plans to push this horse harder than he ever did his own to try and close the distance in the morning.

For the next day, he does push the new horse harder but by late afternoon he can see that the horse is almost blown. Resting up earlier that night and cursing his foul luck once again, he lets the horse get its wind back overnight to continue at a trot the following day.

CHAPTER 6

The Settlement of Palovicus

"Kali!" hollers an old, hunched man from behind his battered table. Scratches, ink spots, and cut lines mar any part of the surface not covered in sheets and rolls of parchment. Ink bottles filled with lampblack, ground lapis lazuli, cinnabar, realgar, and malachite. Reeds and wooden pens cut with different nib styles, and a jar of sand on a shallow tray with a hole in one corner. "What, in the nine Infernums, are ya doing out there girlie?"

"I am assembling those sheets you completed last week into the right order Lippio," comes a softly melodic voice prior to a fair-faced girl with grey highlights along her cheek bones popping her head round the door to his private workspace, a warm smile for the old Human. Her smile always affects him as does that of a child for her father though he rarely ever shows it except with a twitch of a smile at times.

"Ah, yes, thanks." When he looks up briefly to see her, one of those rare twitching smiles of his flickers across his jaundice cheeks before the almost constant pain kicks in again to make him wince. Grabbing another clove from an old ink pot, he starts chewing on it methodically before continuing. "They are due a day after tomorrow. Never mind that now though. That parchment yer mama wants quick as should be dry enough now. Ya had best take it to her."

"The arcane scroll or the map?" She looks at Lippio and worries. He always seems to be in so much pain every day. She often wonders how to help the wispy-haired man, but he just refuses whenever she offers and guesses that today will be no different.

"The map!" he snaps between chews on the clove before adding another one. "Though, why Rosaria wants a copy a such an old map, I have no idea."

"Is there anything I can do to help?" Kali knows it is a pointless question, but she still feels compelled to ask it if only to let Lippio know that she does care for him.

"When ya get back, ya can learn the damned cantrip to help ya understand the damned arcane script," he grumps at her. "Yer diligent enough in yer work and certainly smart enough. Now git going!"

"Yes, Sir," she answers eagerly, her light grey almond-shaped eyes sparkling at the opportunity before her. "I'll get going right away."

She enters the drying room, a room with bar shelves lining the walls where the freshly scribed works are stored until being dry enough for transport. She carefully picks up the map and looks at it. It is of Collis Valle and the surrounding mountains of the Hāmō Montes, Immanis Iugum, and the Strykejern Fjellene ranges. There are also some odd markings at different points. Checking it carefully, she is satisfied that the parchment is dry enough before rolling it up and putting it in a stiff leather scroll case.

Heading to the front of the workshop she remembers what she was told of the old man who has been her mentor and guide in the art of letters for the past eleven years. Seeing him now, she cannot comprehend how this man, so hunched and broken, was ever the Master Ranger and a friend of the Elves that her mother so often had adventures with. It was their last adventure that finished it for Lippio Korba. They were too far from clerical aid when they were caught in a landslide.

Brushing her slate-coloured hair over a slightly elongated ear, Kali decides to return to Lippio's room and quietly wait until he finishes what he is doing before he looks up at her to wonder what she wants now.

"You should really take more of that potion Marroc brews for you. Not just for when you sleep," she says cautiously.

"I don't want to get dependant to the stuff that that stretched Hauflin makes. Lustrum only knows what he puts in that damned concoction a his," Lippio grumbles. It does not help that Marroc's potion tastes foul. It was much better before he was half-buried by that rockslide around twelve years ago. While Rosaria would be collecting ingredients for her arcane spells, he could seek the necessary plants and roots for his own medicinal remedy that tasted so much better and lasted for more than the few hours that Marroc's brew does. That damned Hauflin refuses to even think about acquiring the mix that Lippio used to brew and now he is too old to go get the ingredients himself.

"How about seeing a barber then?" she persists even though she already knows what his response to that one will be as well. It is always the same. Lippio does not trust any of them, possibly since the only barbers within the wooden palisade settlement of Palovicus are those more inclined to be those travelling through with the merchant caravans. He just glares at the girl from under his thickened brow.

"Is there something else ya can be doing instead a badgering me with yer inane comments?" Kali looks to the scroll case in her hand and waggles it briefly.

"I will just get this to mother," she answers him with a slightly embarrassed grin. She finally leaves him, grabbing her mottled brown cloak from just inside her work area before heading out of the shop front while clasping it around her slender shoulders and heading for the east gate. She passes several squared wooden buildings belonging to other tradesmen and homes down the currently dry and rutted mud road for the gate in the ten-foot-high wooden palisade.

The palisade has a five-foot deep stone and bronze-tooled wooden walkway about seven-foot up where leather armoured men with stone-tipped spears move around and keep watch beyond the settlement, mainly on the bog to the north in case the Lizardmen there decide to make another incursion. She passes the two guards at the gate who watch her leave, then across a wooden bridge over the dry ditch that surrounds the settlement just beyond. When Kali comes to a leucothoe shrub she turns north off the main east-west trade route for the Hamo Montes range. Since all the farms are to the south of Palovicus where the woodlands there were cleared for the settlement and farmland, she knows that there will not be anyone around on her journey to her mother's, something that she does at irregular intervals. These walks allow her to relax and enjoy the sounds of the birds in the red larch trees, the wind blowing through the leaves, and the smell of the sweet grass that takes over from the militaristic hurly-burly of the settlement.

While the day is warm enough for her, she can feel that the seasons are about to change, though she does not worry about the sudden drop in temperature that will follow. Her Half-Elven heritage allows her to continue normally when the other Races either stay indoors by a fire or wear warmer clothes. While she walks, Kali starts to remember what Lippio has taught her about the immediate area.

A Southerner called Kuede Simba who died only a few years ago and his last surviving wife, Chagina, chose to settle here after they fled north to escape the slaver gangs roaming around the region where they used to live. Finding the bogland just to the western edge of the Hamo Montes point, they decided to rest in the forest under the stars. It was while Kuede slept when he was visited in a dream by his goddess of all moisture, Oevu, who told him that the time to stop running had passed. He could pick up where he left off due to the richness of the earth for the growth of his crops. He awoke the following morning and started to make this area his home, clearing some space for a home and the land for tilling. When Kuede and Chagina nearly completed their crop fields more farming folk moved into the area. The settlement of Palovicus was then born to make this the youngest community of all the settlements along the east-west trade route, though the road was not called that at the time.

Kali loses all track of time until she stumbles into the middle of a campsite consisting of a wagon and a cart, a freshly made burning wood fire, and five places set out for the unknown occupants who do not seem to be around at this time. Four horses are tethered to another tree that are content to munch on a lavender bush.

Looking over to the cart, a twitch of movement catches her eye. She walks over to investigate passing a wide red larch tree. A large Half-Orc steps round and quickly slams a great meaty fist into her face, throwing her back down the slope several feet where she falls into unconsciousness. The scroll case is sent flying from her hand.

"That was harsh Krilge," comments a blond-haired man.

"Shut it Emlyn," the Half-Orc growls back.

"That's enough boys. Krilge, put her and the boy in the back of the wagon with the others. We'll just take the one with us for now," interrupts a close-cropped bearded man in a deep purple woollen shirt and trousers, a staff in one hand.

"OK Treorai," Krilge answers while the others go about settling down for the night.

"Any sign of your pursuer?" Treorai asks of Salvia when she appears by the light of the fire.

"Not yet, but if it was one of them, then we had better move out tonight," she tells him. The others grumble, but soon the campsite is packed up. Krilge takes the wagon and pulls it along with their cargo on board after Treorai casts a spell on the occupants. She noticed their pursuer when he stopped to examine their crippled horse and periodically kept an eye on his progress when chance permitted.

The Guildsman finally arrives at Palovicus, with the settlement all talking about a young Half-Elf woman disappearing earlier in the day. A contingent of Grey Elves appeared at the east gates before he did to ask where this Kali Celaeno had got to. Apparently, even the settlement's old Penman is highly distraught that the young woman has just vanished. The only clue they found was a day-old campsite where four horses were tethered to a nearby tree.

The Guildsman curses his luck once again and decides to stay until he can garner further news and maybe have a look around for any clues.

CHAPTER 7

The Hunt

The Guildsman finally got some good luck soon after arriving in Palovicus during the evening after the earlier commotion. A sign is being hung up on the door in one of the taverns saying that a room is available to let. A Hauflin Trader called Fortinbras had vacated the room earlier that day according to the talkative landlord. That sign soon came down.

After securing the room at the back of the single storey tavern, he goes in search of the Penman. That proves easy enough since this Lippio Korba is well known. The old man draws and amends the maps given to him by the Rangers who prowl and keep watch around the settlement, primarily over the bogland to the north. He is also one of the very few non-Spiritualists who knows his letters.

The Guildsman heads for one of the few rectangular buildings that are completely walled in stone with a strange-looking timber shingle roof. Reaching up to the lower shingles, he discovers that they are individually covered in an oily-like substance. *Very handy for keeping the wet weather out, I believe. I wonder how that came about?* He looks around at the other single-storey wooden, or half wattle-and-daub and half wooden buildings and sees the similar oily substance on the walls that he initially took for coal-black paint.

Returning his attention to the task at hand, he ducks his head slightly to enter the Penman's door.

The Guildsman finds Lippio behind his table, just staring off into space. It does take the man from Brackston a while, but he finally gets the old man's attention. Lippio's face is extremely pale, which accentuates his jaundice cheeks.

When the old man speaks, it is haltingly, but the Guildsman learns how Kali left by the east gate and took a track up into the larch woods that takes her to her mother's home. It then takes a while, but he eventually learns from Lippio that Kali's mother is a Grey Elf who lives in their mountain citadel. To get much more out of the old man proves extremely difficult for the Guildsman. To try and force him to say more would be liable to kill him and the Guildsman figures that the Penman is a too prominent person to be able to get away with it for long. Especially if he decides to stay at the settlement for a while pending on how his search for the boy goes. He does not know how, but he just knows that the abduction of Reuben and Kali's disappearance are somehow related.

Then Lippio surprises him by looking the Guildsman dead in the eyes. "Bring her home to me. Please?"

By the time he leaves the old man, he is on a promise of a reward if he can return the girl alive and unharmed. This is a new experience for him, and he ponders this while returning to his room. Normally he takes payment to use his deadly talents to permanently remove people. He has never been asked to bring one back alive.

The Guildsman gets up to the crowing of the cockerels and splashes water on his face from a clay bowl of cold water on the small table. He hopes he still has time to catch them up, for he knows that time is of the essence and feels that too much time has been lost already. Despite that and his deadpan face, he is in reasonably good spirits.

Soon after returning to the tavern, he had already decided to have a good horse ready for the morning, trading in the old windbag nag that brought him here. Heading straight round to the small stabling area, the young lad leads an excellent horse to him. An Ó Thuaidh breed. *Well, that was the weight in silver well worth spending,* he thinks while stroking the horse's silvery/grey neck and flanks.

He mounts the steed and throws a copper ring to the lad before racing down towards the east gate where the guards barely manage to open them in time. Flying over the bridge of a dry moat he eases into a trot and only just sees a shingle track leading up into the red larch woods. He then realises that it is not so surprising he missed it before. With the wagon traffic between Brackston and Palovicus and the farmers requiring supplies and hoping to trade some of their crops, the tracks are a mishmash of criss-crossing traffic. It does not help that there is also a thick leucothoe shrub to the east of the track.

Riding the horse up the track, he can pick out the wheel ruts once again. Cringing inwardly that he had made such a novice mistake in his haste to find Reuben, he now estimates that he has lost a second day on this Emlyn and Salvia.

The first thing he notices soon after starting up the track is the peacefulness of this area. The birds are singing in the trees, flying in and out of the branches of the conifers. And the heady scent of honeysuckle catches in his Romanesque nose before he even has a chance to see the ground-sprawling plants growing just in front of the treeline. He finds the smell of the shrub in the cool air rather too sickly for his taste.

Following the tracks further between the larch trees, the wind moves the thick, hawthorn bush to reveal a leather tube. He dismounts and picks up the hidden scroll case and takes the lid off. Carefully removing the contents reveals a map of the Collis Valle region.

He sees the immaculate drawing of the Immanis Iugum mountain range though there is no Brackston at the elbow and no Palovicus. Seaton is mainly a wooded area, as is much of the valley except for where the settlement of Spire is located. *What is going on here? A kidnapping from Brackston, a disappearance from Palovicus, and an early map of Collis Valle?* His normally deadpan face creases. Returning the map in the scroll tube and resealing it, he then places it in a saddle bag to continue up before he loses the cart tracks amongst the myriad of footprints. He knows that he is not the first to examine this area.

He stops near a cold campfire. Looking through the confer branches towards the sun, he estimates that this will be a good place to stop for some lunch.

After tethering the horse to a low-lying branch with enough slack to munch on the nearby grass, the Guildsman gathers some wood and rebuilds the campfire to heat some water in a clay bowl from the nearby stream. The stream comes out of the Hamo Montes mountains and heads west down the hill towards the larger river that skirts the bog.

He mixes in some dried leaves, stirring with a dagger until his tea is ready. Using two daggers to lift the bowl out of the fire, he puts it to one side then eats some salt pork with a bread roll he traded for in Palovicus. The roll is not as good as that flatbread the Bunners made. In fact, the roll is partially stale, but it does enough to stop him from feeling hungry. It is then he notices something on the bark of the nearby tree.

Getting up, he moves closer. Something has splashed against it. Scraping some off with a dagger, he looks at the gathered flakes in his hand and the dagger edge. He sticks a finger into his tea, then mixes it in the dried flakes. When the flakes absorb the water, it turns into a reddish liquid. *Blood?* He looks near the base of the tree to find the distinct shape of a heavy boot print. Not so much a heavy boot, but someone heavy wearing boots.

He thinks about what he has learnt. The kidnapping in Brackston, this Kali disappearing. *Of course! She stumbled onto the kidnapper's camp. She was just in the wrong place at the wrong time. But who made these heavy impressions? An accomplice?*

The Guildsman looks around some more before finding intermittent wagon tracks. The difference between a cart and a wagon is that the first only has two wheels. Wagons have four to carry heavier loads. But why would they need a wagon in the first place? He already learnt that the cart and some horses have been taken to Palovicus after they were first discovered. *Why would they need a wagon for just a Human boy and a Half-Elf female?* He would have thought 'girl,' but Elves are an extremely long-lived Race and most Humans often see a full generation being born and die before an Elf leaves their people. He does not know if the same applies to the Half-Elves, even though there are some in the Guilde Kallun.

He leads his horse to follow the distorted tracks heading west down the hill from the base of the mountains. He would have ridden down the hill, but he is worried the horse will stumble. It takes him the rest of the day to reach the treeline to look out across the hilly land where the sun begins to descend below the Strykejern Fjellene mountains, turning the peaks to gold towards the south-south-west.

About half a day away is the old Dwarven Road heading north for the dying settlement at the end of the box canyon created by the Hāmō Montes. The road crosses the river between Palovicus and the bog via an old stone bridge. The wagon tracks are clearer further down, heading for that bridge. Wildflowers dot the grassy hills like multicoloured stars. The shadows are already elongating with the sinking red-gold sun.

The Guildsman knows that he is not going to be able to move towards his quarry much more this evening. Not without the risk of hurting his mount over the sporadically stony ground in the dark. The days are shorter living amongst the mountainous region of the valley. With a sigh, he turns and walks back under the shelter of the conifer woods a little way to make camp for the night. He only hopes that he can make some headway on the lost time chasing these two in the morning.

The Guildsman jerks awake. He does not hesitate. He throws off the thick woollen blanket, grabs the daggers from his saddlebag pillow, and rolls into a crouch from his pine needle bed. His dark russet eyes scan the area. His ears listen for any abnormal sounds. He even sniffs the air. He moves slowly, daggers leading the way. After a couple of minutes, he frowns. Something disturbed him. He rejects the idea that it was just a dream. *Too many die quickly that way.*

He glances among the trees, the branches, but still, he sees nothing. Hears nothing. The sky is brightening, though there is still plenty of dark shade beneath the conifers. Then it strikes him. He hears nothing. Where are the bird sounds from before?

He cautiously packs up and returns the saddlebags to his horse, keeping a wary eye out for anything unusual or threatening. *There is something out there.* He is ready to snatch a weapon at a second's notice. The last thing he does is to kick earth over his campfire, then stamp on it to prevent any smoulders from reigniting, though he doubts anything will now. He remounts his horse and cautiously works his way down the hill in the general direction of the bridge he saw last night. The threatening sensation he felt upon waking starts to evaporate. Then the birds begin their morning songs.

After the stranger leaves, the trunk of a large larch seemingly expands into a Human female, her trunk-like complexion alters once clear of the tree to reveal a tanned, well-muscled woman with long black hair. She watches the retreating rider silently while a huge grey-furred wolf pads over to her from the other side of the stranger's camp. The wolf watches him go too. Once the rider is out of sight, they head into the mountains, along the path Kali would have taken to visit her mother.

The ground starts levelling out, though continues down towards the river. The Guildsman studies the ground carefully and watches the stones diminish where he then picks up speed in the growing light. The wagon tracks are much clearer and now he can see large, deep boot prints between the wheel ruts.

He slips down briefly to study them. *Just like those by that tree. Too large for the Hauflin and the Human.* The Guildsman remounts. Then realisation hits like a mattock. *Orc! Their accomplice is an Orc!*

He does not get halfway from the treeline to the bridge when a light breeze wafts the stench of the bog towards him. He decides to ignore it and focus on getting across the river before he loses any more time. Though whatever it was that woke him up earlier is still bothering him.

The sun is high in the pale blue sky when he arrives at the old Dwarf Road. The Orc pulled wagon certainly came this way, since the muddy wheels left a trail a child could follow. The trace continues to follow the road. *Could they be heading for Spire?*

He kicks the horse into a gallop and lengthens the reins to let it have his head even after the trail begins to disappear. The speed of the horse impresses the Guildsman. He even smiles at the powerful beast's play of muscles. Although he really is enjoying the charging mount's speed, he does not forget to keep an eye on the roadsides in case the wagon leaves it at any point.

The Guildsman sees a spruce forest ahead sandwiched between the road and the river on the far side of the bog. The horse devours the miles with every stride. It is not until the sun starts falling towards the mountains over his left shoulder when his beast slows to a fast trot.

With the bog soon behind them and the ground firming up under the trees, the Guildsman slows the horse further and heads into the treeline. While the horse seems quite happy to continue, he does not want the horse to become blown for that will do neither of them any good after covering so much ground since crossing the bridge.

He ensures that the horse is eating first then clears a space to create a shallow fire pit. Then he freezes. Something is rustling the shrubbery behind him. By slowly turning his head, he spies a twitching alum root plant. Slowly sliding out his dagger, he then snaps round to launch the blade. It strikes something. Walking over, a hare is lying and twitching behind the shrub where the Guildsman then ends its life quickly.

Nodding in deadpan satisfaction, he throws the dead animal towards the fire pit to grab some firewood. Once the fire is a light, he proceeds to skin and gut the creature, then creates a spit to roast it.

After he has eaten, he checks on his horse to make sure the magnificent beast is alright just before feeling a familiar sensation. A sensation he felt in the forest by the Hāmō Montes before his leaving. Looking around, listening intently, he tries to detect what has alerted him to something else out there. It is not the birds falling silent this time for he can hear the hoot of an owl, the grating, metallic kraak of the nutcrackers.

His spine-tingling, the Guildsman feels the need to move on quickly. It is not fear that drives him. He is wary of not knowing what he is facing, even if he must look for it first. But whatever is out there, they are good. Exceptionally good. He hastily throws the waste of his dinner into the fire pit and proceeds to bury it, finishing off by stamping it down.

Remounting his horse and keeping his head low until he clears the lower hanging branches, the Guildsman then continues northward, reflecting on the dangers of lighting fires. *Rookie mistake. Twice.* He cringes. *You just make yourself a target doing that.*

Iridescent green eyes blink. The smell of the cooking hare attracted him. The large black and brown-furred wolf pads out of the deeper shadows, paws the area around the firepit, then disappears back into the shadows to his waiting Human boy companion.

Apart from the gaps and cracks in the Dwarven road where random seeds have taken root or broke through the blocks, the road is relatively smooth. With his horse slightly rested, the Guildsman nudges the fine beast into a trot and lets him have his head again for as long as the horse wants it throughout most of the dampening night. He notices that the road is gently veering off towards the east.

By the time the sky starts brightening with the new dawn, the sun tinging the light clouds from the south-easterly direction, they have reached the northern edge of the forest. The Guildsman then brings the horse to a halt. Looking at the road edges, he catches sight of wagon tracks leaving the road a little way ahead. *But that will take them away from the settlement. Why are they avoiding it unless they are hiding from them too?* He dismounts to ensure that these are the same tracks he has been following while his horse wanders onto the grass to eat.

Sure enough, he sees the booted Orc foot tracks between the wheels, though now he spies three more pairs of more Human-like feet. Judging from the impressions, two are male while the third belongs to a female. He believes the female feet do not belong to the Half-Elf since even they can walk with little trace, though not as well as Elves and Hauflins, so this pair must belong to a Human. *What are three Humans doing with a Hauflin and an Orc? Why is a Hauflin even working with an Orc?*

He looks up to his horse who just stands there watching him. Nodding, he climbs back on and continues to follow the new track at a fast trot through the rugged hills that go round the dying settlement of Spire.

He stops for a late evening meal and takes the time to rub his horse down, the first chance he feels he had since leaving the Hāmō Montes. He prefers to look after horses better than he has and feels a twinge of guilt for not doing so. He even apologises to the horse who just nuzzles him.

The Guildsman feels that the horse understands him and accepts his apologises. Or even understands that speed is the order of the day and forgives the Human for his neglect. Even the Guildsman knows that he needs a proper wash. Especially his clothes. He then rests rough for the night, wrapped in his thick blanket.

The following morning, he quickly resaddles his horse and climbs back on despite still feeling tired. Fortunately, the chill air helps him to stay awake. They continue following the clearly defined tracks at a brisk trot through the hills. He spends the next day traversing the land, even riding up some of the gentler hills to see if he can find them ahead of him, knowing that they will be keeping their route level where possible through the rising rugged hills before he is forced to rest up again.

CHAPTER 8

The Settlement of Spire

He still finds it hard to believe that Spire was once the first and largest settlement in his grandfather's day. Looking over the poppy-strewn area, he can still see the scarring in the reclaimed hills encompassed in the arcing range of the Hāmō Montes mountains that create this wide box canyon.

His grandfather often told him stories of how Spire was the only prominent settlement for years due to the proximity of the Dwarf Hall of Spire. That was until they closed the mine, around a hundred years ago now, where Spire also fell from prominence. The tale of the Blackest Night is still told concerning that dark time.

Few buildings remain now and much of the ruin at the end of the glory days has already been used to repair and maintain the remaining dozen or so buildings.

The only clue of the Dwarfs ever being there is the long winding road that winds from the great doors in the mountain, across the stone bridge they built to skirt around the Saltus in Valle Forest. The road continues to a second Dwarf-made stone bridge to where Palovicus was to be founded, though why they stopped there, even his grandfather did not know. The old man told him that was a secret those Dwarfs took to their graves.

He is Trystan Gibbs, a large, heavy-set man in his late thirties who loves his goats, many of them being the offspring of his original herd almost twenty years ago when his father died of a fatal punch. He threw that punch.

That was a double celebration for Trystan since he not only inherited the herd, but he also got rid of his violently abusive father whose greatest love was the locally brewed rye whiskey after his wife died when Trystan was still a young boy. Only his best friend Mailse, now the local shepherdess knows what really happened since she helped him bury the body. All anyone could do was suspect what happened, but no one said anything due to Trystan being the only one who could provide their milk.

The irony of his situation is that Trystan was also fond of the rye whiskey and even got aggressive when drunk. He knows that the few remaining descendants would rather see him gone, but for his affinity for his goats. This would be the final death knell of Spire, so they had put up with it, or let Mailse deal with him.

Then something changed in the Goatherder.

It was sixteen years ago to the day when he last got really drunk. A traveller from the eastern lands came to the settlement to learn what happened to cause such an abrupt decline in the settlement's fortune. They had heard the stories but wanted to learn from more first-hand sources.

When Trystan got too loud and boorish for the other patrons in the three roundhouses converted into one larger drinking hall, the traveller stood in front of him, their head barely reaching his chest. Before he knew it, he was struck three times. Trystan woke up in his roundhouse with this strange woman working by the fire pit he used for his food and warmth. A year later, Hai Lifen agreed to marry him and now they have two wonderful children. He still gets drunk occasionally, but Hai soon snaps him back into line.

He is enjoying the brisk evening, thinking how much Hai has changed him as a man in the fifteen years they have been married almost to the day while contemplating taking the goats back home to their shed that she helped him build for their safety. Before, he would often lose a few to the night predators, but not so much now.

He turns to head back when he spots four people and a child with one of the larger adults pulling a wagon moving through the hills.

"'Ello there. Can I 'elp ya folks?" he bellows out to them, his brassy voice carrying clearly across the hundred and fifty feet or so distance. He watches the group stop before disappearing behind a hill to look in his direction. It looks to him like they are conversing amongst themselves before one of them heads towards him with his staff supporting his weight.

In the time it takes the man to get closer, Trystan can see that the man has a dark cloak over his narrow shoulders and lean build, his pale face accentuates his close-cropped black beard. Trystan thinks that this man may be slightly younger than his own thirty-nine years.

"Are ya lost, friend? There's naught that way but mountains," he offers, trying to be helpful. Hai has insisted that he do better about helping others. If she learnt that he guided them wrong or did nothing to aid them, then she would soon have a go at him. Despite being such a small person, she can be truly terrifying at times. *By the gods, 'ow I do love 'er.*

"I'm fine thank you, Sir." The man stops about fifteen feet from him before speaking in a baritone voice. A strange look enters the man's dark eyes as he begins to speak before continuing normally. *"Carmen persōna.* In fact, I believe that I can help you if you come with me my friend."

A strange sensation washes over Trystan's mind. He shakes his head and rubs his eyes before he can begin to answer.

"I would really love ta." *Ya can't,* his mind screams at him. *Think of yer goats and Hai is expecting ya back.* "But I 'ave my goats ta get back first."

"Oh, don't worry about them." The strange man is watching Trystan trying to ready an answer to refuse his request.

The voice in Trystan's head seems to be moving quickly away while still screaming at him that something is not right here.

"My associates will take care of the goats and return them to your humble farm for you."

Trystan looks behind the lean man to see a dark-skinned Half-Orc and a blond-haired man standing there. They both nod at him with a smile though with the Half-Orc it comes out more like a grimace.

He has heard of these Half-Orcs from Hai. She even drew charcoal sketches of them and Orcs which seem to be more common in her homeland.

For some reason that he does not understand, he feels that he should not go with this strange man. The screaming voice in his mind is barely a whisper now. Against his better judgement, he decides to go with them, though for the life of him he has no idea why. Maybe the answer will come to him later. That sometimes happens.

"Okay. If ya insist, Master." *Master? Master? Why did I just call this man, Master?* Confusion creases his rugged features. He can see the man looking at him with a cold smile in the failing light where bright stars are beginning to appear.

"There's a good fellow. Now come with me while Emlyn and Krilge get your animals home." With that, the man starts walking back to the wagon where Trystan can see the final two people.

One is a dark-skinned woman, and the child turns out to be a Hauflin female.

The man asks Trystan to pull the wagon for him where they set off once more to continue with their journey towards the mountains.

It does not take Emlyn and Krilge long to return. Their arrival being announced by a couple of thumps into the back of the wagon.

The others look around in surprise at how quickly they do return, where the blonde-haired man just says "sorted." Krilge immediately helps the goatherder, thus increasing their speed.

After a couple of hours, they arrive at a fast-moving river slicing through the mountain range where the man indicates for them to stop. He then bangs his staff twice on the ground to cause a bright flash.

Before Trystan can recover his eyesight, he hears the man say "*Magicus sopor.*" His brown eyes become very heavy before he drifts off.

CHAPTER 9

Close Encounter

Dusk has fallen like a blanket over the rugged hills the Guildsman is traversing when he spots something ahead of him. Goats wandering around aimlessly. It seems that the wagon stopped for a while here, and three pairs of feet, including the Orc tracks he is following moved south a little way to meet a fourth pair of large Human feet. He then spots that one of the Human tracks returns to the wagon with the person they met. *Another accomplice?*

He stops where the three pairs of tracks stopped, then finds that the Orc tracks and a pair of the smaller more Human-like footprints run around for a bit. He finds dark fresh blood splatters in a couple of places along their tracks before they return to the wagon where the Orc prints then assist the large Human to pull the wagon at a faster pace, judging from the spaces between each of their prints.

He remounts his horse and rides in the wagon's trail feeling remarkably close to his quarry now. Even his horse seems to agree with him.

Even though it is dark, he continues with the light of the full moon and a starlit sky to help keep him on course. It still means that he must stop every now and then to recheck where the tracks are going. Rounding a large hill, he then sees something ahead of him.

Is that the wagon I've been following? Dismounting once again, he makes his way forward cautiously interweaving a circuitous route through the hills. He carefully closes on the focus of his search while looking around intently to ensure that no one is planning to ambush him.

41

When he is beside the wagon, he looks inside to reveal fresh blood and little else. Touching one of the larger pools, he notes that it is still damp just like the pools he found near the footprints. He flicks his tongue across his fingers. *Goat. But where did the people go? None of this is making any sense.*

He looks around once again to ensure that there really is no one around, though he cannot understand where they could have got to either. There simply is nothing here except for a fast-flowing river to the south heading back to the settlement, hills back towards the west, and mountains to the north and east.

He decides to move away some distance and stop for a cold meal of dried fruits, nuts, and the remains of the hare from that brief stop at the forest while pondering what to do next. His horse munches on the leaves of a hawthorn bush growing near a solitary maple tree.

After they have both eaten, the Guildsman makes up his mind and climbs back on his horse to aim for the settlement by following the river. Maybe someone there can shed some light on his questions.

CHAPTER 10

The Meeting

Treorai and his four associates, he will never call them his friends, are sitting in a huge ornately commemorative carved room. Half pillars seemingly made from the walls rise to join in the middle of an arching ceiling approximately twenty feet above their heads. Despite the number of torches burning in here, the air is extremely clear, and the room is very cool. It is more than large enough to accommodate the long dining table and the eight chairs surrounding it. There is even enough space for the tall, large stone-looking manservant to move around the edge of the windowless room where he serves them their meals and drinks.

Treorai is sitting at the head of the pine table mentally planning on finding three more associates to bolster his numbers, preferably those with their own men that can be accommodated close by. The trouble is that these four associates do not have followers of their own, though it is surprising to the Sorcerer that it is the Half-Orc Krilge who may have the chance to get some soon. He would have thought it would be either Emlyn or Lusha who would have the better chance since they are both much more charismatic than the Half-Orc.

When they finish eating the roast dinner organised for them, the creature Treorai calls Hobbes, clears away the crockery and cutlery with surprising gentleness. The wide-mouthed creature then takes them to a table that stands between a set of double doors and a single door at the end of the room. A couple of Goblins soon appear from the single door to clear the table while Hobbes picks up a prepared tray of tankards and goblets.

Treorai is about to speak when Krilge lets out a mighty belch, drawing frowns from the Sorcerer and Lusha while Emlyn smirks and Salvia giggles. Krilge glances around each of them and just shrugs by way of an apology.

"As I was about to say before the interruption," begins the baritone voice of Treorai, which creases the Hauflin up to the point where she nearly falls onto the floor if not for Hobbes' timely arrival with the tray of ales and wine in one hand to stabilise Salvia in the chair with his other. Treorai waits for her to regain her composure long enough so that he can continue while Hobbes serves. "Now that Skarmazh is sorting the prisoners out with his Goblins, we have some very important business to discuss."

"Yer mean the goat herder?" Krilge grunts. "Still don't know why ya brought 'im along."

"Because he saw us you oaf," Lusha responds heatedly. "He would have dropped us all in it with those other slack-jawed wenyeji wa nchi from Spire."

"Don't yer call me an oaf ya Souther! I'll kill ya where yer sitting."

"That's enough from both of you," Treorai shouts over their rising volume. He then takes a deep breath before daring to continue. "We need to discuss this now as his absence will soon be noticed. Emlyn, Krilge, what did you do with his goats?"

"We did nothing with them, much," Emlyn begins nonchalantly, brushing a blond lock from his forehead until he sees the cold look from Treorai and Lusha. A cold shiver runs down his spine.

"Though we did bring a couple back fer dinner," grins the Half-Orc as he shares a conspiratorial look with the blonde-haired warrior.

"Oh, boys," Salvia responds quietly, shaking her head and causing her auburn locks to swish from side to side. "You were supposed to actually take them all back to his farm. We know the guy can be a lush, but he would never neglect his herd before he goes for a drink."

"Why don't you guys just hold up a banner saying that we have him here?" Lusha comments sarcastically, causing them both to glare at her.

"That's enough," Treorai breaks in quickly. *If they fall apart now, then everything that I have strived for will be for naught. I must get through that door first though. If it does lead to the Dwarven stronghold as I suspect, then its magic is powerful enough to resist even my strongest of spells.* "We still need to work closely together. What is done is done and now we need to move fast to rectify the situation."

He looks at each of them to ensure that he has their full attention.

He only needs them all to work closely together long enough to find what he is seeking and for the sake of the overall plan. He desires to unite Collis Valle under his leadership, starting with Spire as the initial test for his stratagem before embarking on those along the east-west trade route. After that, these associates will either be totally loyal to him, or expendable. They all look to him and wait for the Sorcerer to continue.

"Thank you. Whatever animosities that you harbour against each other will need to simmer over the campfire until we achieve our final objective at the very least." He inaudibly breathes a sigh of relief when they nod quietly after his gaze passes over each of them.

"So, what are we going to do, Tre?" Emlyn's silvery voice breaks the silence that descends.

"We could always go round up the rest of the goats and try to get them back before anyone notices," suggests Salvia.

"If we're not too late already," Lusha huskily answers the Hauflin cynically.

"There's no need for that attitude Lusha," she retorts. "I was just trying to help rectify the problem in part since the goat herder will probably be missed by someone. Even if it is only by his family."

"You're right Salvia," Treorai responds while giving Lusha a firm look to keep her quiet. "But we also need to make a move now rather than later. It seems that time will begin to run out for us if we do not." *In which case, all my planning could then be jeopardised.*

Treorai rubs a hand over his close-cropped beard thoughtfully. Looking at Krilge, he then asks the Half-Orc what his chance of recruiting the Strykejern Orcs are.

"It will be much easier to order 'em, but only the tribal chiefs can make sure such an order be followed, so a very large incentive will be required for 'em to even leave their homes, let alone join us," he grunts as he looks to the table thoughtfully. "Even then, they might decide ta wander off and do their own thing after receiving payment."

"Could you take control of the tribe yourself, big guy?" Salvia wonders aloud.

"There's only one way ta do that and that is killing the existing Chief in combat," he answers automatically. "There is no way that I can take ma father out, even if he would let me back in the tribe long enough ta make the formal decoration."

"You mean, declaration, don't you?" scoffs Lusha. Treorai cringes.

"Yeah. That one," responds Krilge gruffly, ignoring her tone this time. The Sorcerer looks to the Half-Orc, pleasantly surprised.

"How about poisoning the Chief?" Salvia asks eagerly, her normally well-modulated tone becoming tremulous in her excitement at the thought.

"That won't work either. All that accomplishes is the tribe would then fall into fighting amongst 'emselves as ta who will take the top slot which is very costly ta the tribe's strength an' leaves 'em weak enough fer other tribes ta take their territory," the Half-Orc grumbles by way of explanation. "No. The only way ta secure leadership of a tribe is ta issue a challenge ta the current Chief, where we will then have to fight ta the death. Then lead until another decides that it is their time ta make a challenge. It is the Orcan way."

"We could poison the Chief to slow him down some," Lusha offers. "Or even go after another tribe altogether."

"The Wutarjini clan are the largest tribe close enough for our needs as I understand it," interjects Treorai looking to Krilge who nods his confirmation. "We need that tribe for our initial plan to be successfully launched on to greater schemes. Especially since the tribes of the extensive Hamo Montes range were ousted by the Dwarfs first and then the Elves and the Giants afterward."

"Then we need to help our Barbarian friend to get ready for what he has to do as I see it," Emlyn's silvery tone cutting through the following silence. "Tre, Lusha. Can you use your magic to locate what it is that Krilge will need to take down his father or whoever it is who happens to be leading the tribe by the time he gets there?"

"I can most certainly do so, though location spells may not be that precise depending on the distance of such items," Lusha answers him.

"I'm going to be tied up here for a while, so I suggest that you had better set out immediately and see what you can do." Everyone agrees that it is the only possible solution left at this time. They need the Wutarjini tribe. "Take this stone amulet with you," Treorai continues as he places a rock disc threaded with a leather thong on the table. "It will transport up to three people touching the wearer activating it directly to this room once the goats have been returned to their shed."

"Why do I have to go Master?" Lusha complains sourly. "It was not me who messed up so badly with the goat herder."

"I need you there to ensure that it all works out properly and to offer support should anything go awry," Treorai says as he struggles to remain calm. "Good enough for you?"

Lusha grumbles quietly to herself though she cannot refute the wizard's logic.

"That's great," Krilge growls sarcastically. "But how're we supposed ta get there in the first place?" he finishes, glaring at the wizard.

"I will gate you to where we met the man!" Treorai snaps at him.

It is not the Half-Orc's fault so much. Krilge just likes to keep things simple and to know exactly what will be happening as much as possible, though even the Half-Orc clearly understands that not everything that does happen can always go to plan. What is annoying Treorai was the general enmity of the group when they are all together. Salvia and Emlyn can work pretty much with anyone, even the short-tempered and oft belligerent Krilge. Surprisingly, the worst of them is Lusha. She can get on nearly everyone's nerves at any time on any point. *Maybe I should not have bothered helping her out of the desert after the peasant uprising destroyed her slaver's caravan in the name of some damned god of theirs. I am still not even sure why I did at the time.* He had been having trouble with a local cult and their screeching shamans back then on his brief visit to the Southern Continent; maybe they had something to do with it.

"What are we to do if we meet anyone or they try to stop us?" Emlyn wonders. He knows that Treorai is trying to prevent anyone from finding out where they are while also wondering why he brought them here in the first place, though that is not a question that he feels will be answered to his satisfaction any time soon. Salvia did ask the wizard when they first arrived, but all Treorai said then was that time would tell. That was almost a whole season ago when spring became the summer.

"Try to get rid of them any way you can as discreetly as you can. If you do have to kill anyone, it will be unfortunate, but make sure that they will not be discovered anytime soon at any cost," Treorai answers him. "Lusha, will you try to locate whatever it is that Krilge will need to defeat his father and take control of the tribe while you're out there?"

She looks up, startled from her semi-private grumblings. "Urm, yes. Yes, Master, I will. I will see what I can learn while they take care of the goats." The Wizard nods his understanding at the enormity of the task before her in such a short space of time. If she has any luck, then maybe they can start out immediately.

"Emlyn, I'll need you back here soon after the goats have been returned and you have let me know how it went. Lusha. I have an incredibly special project for you once I have worked out all the details. Krilge and Salvia, you will both be required to continue scouting and mapping out the area in as much detail as possible after you both get back as well." Krilge snaps a look at him as if he has just been insulted. Treorai catches the look and suddenly realises why. "I know you cannot write very well yet Krilge, but your map drawings are of an excellent quality and you can tell Salvia anything that may need to be written down. Okay?" Krilge nods, mollified.

"You had better get off since the longer we sit here talking; the greater chance that we will be discovered," finishes Treorai. He stands up with his staff in hand and opens a mystical doorway with a double tap of his staff for them to pass through. He gives the four of them a nod and they each walk through the portal.

Krilge is the last to go through. He still gets awestruck by the glowing door-shape in the ornately carved wall with the rugged hills beyond, just like looking through an actual doorway, though even the Half-Orc knows that there is no way it can be possible from where they are right now without magic. Being underground is something that does not concern him; unlike the other three of his colleagues who prefer to be in the open air compared to this dungeon atmosphere with its generally still and virtually stale air. Salvia is more used to the open skies, even though her home used to be under a hill. Lusha and Emlyn, being Human, prefer operating above ground. Before coming north with Treorai, Lusha spent most of her life living in smoked animal hide tents.

CHAPTER 11

The Goats

Once they are all through, the portal disappears. Lusha immediately looks around for a sheltered area where she can prepare her spells to locate whatever it is that the damned Orc needs to take control of some damned Orc clan. She soon discovers a shallow cave by a shrub facing the southern edge of the mountains in a gully. There is a small stream passing the cave a few short feet away before disappearing into another hill. Emlyn, Krilge, and Salvia set off to locate the goats.

"And don't either of you try to kill any more for your supper," Salvia tells them with a smile on her cherubic features. "Though it was good," she finishes with a wink. Grinning back, they give her a nod and head out, only to find that the goats have wandered off in different directions.

Krilge begins rounding up part of the herd into one place when he suddenly realises that he is being watched. There is a Human female with almond-shaped eyes, black hair pulled back into a ponytail reaching down to her lower back, not twenty feet away. He freezes in place. She is standing on top of a hill with her arms behind her back watching him clumsily try to get the dozen or so goats to move in one direction.

"Hey!" she calls to him. "What are you doing to my animals?"

"I'm ... err ... trying to get 'em together. Caught 'em wandering around loose like," he tells her sizing up the little woman in case she decides to cause him any trouble. She cannot be more than four-foot-tall to his six nine, though her calm and relaxed stance troubles him more than he cares to admit. Even to himself. This admittance causes him to really worry, though he cannot explain why.

"Where's my husband? He should be looking after them," she says, slowly gliding down the slope.

Salvia is having only slightly more success than Krilge. She finds that they respond to clicks of her tongue, though she still finds it difficult to determine the correct click for each command. How that goat herder does it so easily amazes her. She watched him at work once, but there is no chance of asking him how now. The returning medallion that Treorai gave them is only a one-use item and Lusha has that.

She just manages to get half a dozen together at last when she hears a female voice call out, presumably to one of her companions since she cannot see anyone else nearby. Leaving the goats where they are, she heads up a hill to see if she can find out what is going on while hoping that the damned goats stay put.

Emlyn is having even less luck than Krilge after he comes across nearly twenty of the creatures. He keeps moving around in half circles with arms wide to guide them in the direction of the herder's farm when one or more decide to wander off in the wrong direction. He keeps stopping to get them back to the herd before trying to move them again. He wonders what that goat herder's secret is. He is a physically fit warrior, yet these goats are making him breathless. He even put his spear, short bow, and the shoulder-strapped quiver of arrows to one side to try to make it easier for his herding attempts.

He is trying to figure out an easier way to move them without killing the beasts when he hears a woman calling out. While she sounds close by, he knows that the voice could come from anywhere in these rugged hills. Then he hears Krilge's stammering response. Realising that the Half-Orc must be remarkably close. He decides to ignore the goats and see what is going on.

Snatching up his bow and arrows, he crests a hill and hides behind a scrub brush to see a small dark-skinned woman slowly moving towards Krilge. At first, he thinks that her slow walk which looks like she is gliding down the hill is due to the hill's slope until he sees the stance she maintains with each step. She seems to be readying herself for a fight despite her lack of weapons.

"What are you doing here and where is my husband?" the woman coldly demands once again. Krilge sees that she is nearer half a foot taller than his previous estimate. He does not realise that she knows these creatures very well from her homeland before her travels led her to settle in Spire.

"Oh, sod it," Krilge mutters, pulling a mattock from off his back and holding it in a two-handed grip. "Let me take ya to 'im, ya stupid bitch!"

She says absolutely nothing and moves with the grace of a dancer, sliding to the side and pirouetting around him, seemingly without taking his eyes off him. The look unnerves him more than her movements though he has never seen anyone move around in a fight so much as this one unless it is some weird ritualistic dance. He studies her slight build and knows that he will be able to take whatever hit she can throw at him, especially since she does not have any weapons. *I'm bigger an' stronger than 'er. Women can't hit fer goblin shit.* He brings his great club up ready with newfound confidence to bring it down on her skull when she stops moving long enough for him to hit her.

She seems to pause where he then strikes hard, burying his huge club in the ground. It takes him a second to realise that she is not a bloody pulp beneath his weapon. A sharp pain then erupts from his kidney region and he spins around, yanking the mattock with him in a low smash. Something connects with his jaw. He hears a very sharp crack, and an explosion of pain erupts throughout his skull. He feels his club dip briefly in the middle of his own retaliatory swing. Another explosion of pain from his back causes him to heave while fighting to regain his breath.

It takes him a couple of seconds to realise that he is on the grass struggling to breathe, but at least there is no new pain to add to his existing injuries. Krilge sees his mattock off to one side. He moves his arms beneath him to stand back up to destroy this woman. Then he realises that his legs refuse to move.

Emlyn watches the scene unfold beneath him. He can see Krilge say something quietly while pulling the mattock off his back. The Half-Orc then waits for the woman to stop moving before swinging in an overhead strike designed to smash the much smaller woman's skull. Watching the encounter, Emlyn looks on in amazement at the speed of the woman. She slips round behind Krilge to launch a double punch straight into his lower back and causing him to roar in pain.

Realising that the Half-Orc is in trouble and knowing Treorai will be extremely upset if anything happens to Krilge, Emlyn takes his short bow and readies an arrow while Krilge drags his great club round to bludgeon the woman in half. Emlyn divides his attention between loading the bow and the fight.

He sees the woman leap over the mattock and kick Krilge in the jaw causing him to yell in agony. She lands on the head of the mattock when he back swings and uses it to somersault over the Half-Orc to kick him in the middle of the back.

Seeing his companion go down, Emlyn takes careful aim on the woman and fires the arrow straight for her back. She moves. Cursing, he snatches a second arrow out and then realises that his first arrow has sliced through her throat which is followed by loud child-like screams across the way.

Salvia gets to the top of another hill to see an olive-skinned woman kick Krilge in the middle of the back, dropping him to his knees. Two children watching the scene below them catch her attention. When the woman calmly approaches the Half-Orc to finish him off, she suddenly jerks sideward with blood exploding from her neck. She staggers and falls to the ground, the dark liquid forming a pool beneath her head. The children, only a second ago watching with excitement, suddenly scream.

"Oh, children. What is happening here," Salvia asks softly, causing them to spin round in fright. When they see that it is only a solitary Hauflin female, they seem to recover from their surprise though they cannot stop crying. "Did you know that lady?" Salvia has a suspicion just by looking at the olive complexion of the girl.

"That's our mother." The boy answers between sobs.

"Can you help us get away?" the girl asks her in sheer desperation, like a drowning young lady grabbing at a straw of hope.

"I'll see what I can do Sweeties," Salvia responds and indicating for them to follow her away from the scene. Heading down the hill with the sobbing children following behind her, Salvia keeps checking over her shoulder.

Every time she does, the children also look, and then the boy screeches that there is someone following them. Salvia starts to run with the children following closely and dives around the base of the hill where a babbling stream passes by a shallow cave. She suddenly stops and crouches down inside, a scrub bush hiding the entrance. The children follow her in where she then tells them to be quiet and to stay put while she leads the man away from them with a promise that she will be back for them soon. She also wonders what happened to Lusha who was supposed to be here.

"No, please. Don't leave us," the boy calls between sobs.

"I need to lead him away, else he might come for you too," she says trying to reason with them. Then the girl starts crying again, holding tightly onto her little brother. Sighing, Salvia reaches into a pouch and pulls out a cloth wrapped in a ball with the ends tied together. Undoing the cord, she carefully opens the small bundle to reveal its powdery contents. "This'll help you calm down enough for me to leave you for a bit and lead that very nasty man away." She then softly blows the powder into the children's faces before getting up and walking back out into the night air.

"How are the kids?" Emlyn asks her as he leans against a solitary tree.

"Sleeping like babes," she responds calmly. "How's Krilge?"

"Lusha's with him now. She heard his bellow," Emlyn tells her, where she nods in understanding. Sharing a conspiratorial look between them, they walk back to where the Half-Orc fell to an unarmed female who was only a fraction of his size.

"He's going to be in a foul mood when he wakes up," Salvia sighs. Krilge is often in a bad mood at the best of times, but this is pure humiliation to the big guy's ego.

When they return to Krilge and Lusha, the Half-Orc is sitting up while Lusha continues to cast her magic on his jaw. Although he cannot speak, his glowering yellowish eyes screams volumes.

"How is the big guy?" Salvia calls spotting the arrow sticking through the woman's neck. She gives Emlyn an admiring nod for his handiwork. Emlyn smiles his thanks and retrieves the bronze-tipped shaft.

"He had a broken back, two severe bruises in his lower back and now I'm reluctant to heal his shattered jaw on the grounds that he's actually quiet for once." Krilge glares evilly at her. She then sighs loudly while Emlyn and Salvia smile in amusement. "I'm going to do it, if only to placate Master Treorai," she tells the Half-Orc in a resigned tone.

"*Ponya jeraha.*" They watch as Krilge's jaw begins to repair itself under the guidance of Lusha's hands and her magic.

They soon know the magic is working when he starts cursing up a storm at the woman who took him down so easily. They all know that it is more due to the embarrassment that a humble female did so than anything else. Especially by one who used nothing but her hands and feet.

"I bet you're glad that Orc women don't know how to fight like that," Emlyn jests, receiving such a hard glare in response. Salvia creases up in laughter.

"Never mind that now," fumes Lusha. "There is now a body to dispose of as well as four of us to get back to report in."

"Six," Salvia tells her. When the Spiritualist looks to the diminutive woman in query, the Hauflin finishes with, "the woman had two children with her."

Lusha looks to the stars in exasperation.

"How far did you get with your location spell for Krilge?" Salvia asks her in trying to refocus the young lady.

"South," she replies simply. Seeing the wondering looks in their eyes she sighs dismally before continuing. *If Treorai knows that I did not give them as much information as I could gather, then he will not be best pleased with me.* "What you seek is beyond the Immanis Iugum, if I remember the mountain range correctly from the maps."

"That's ten days away to reach them as the Sparrowhawk flies," Emlyn breathes incredulously.

"That is only the direction you need to travel to help you fulfil our master's instructions. It does not mean that he will have to travel that far at all," she responds haughtily.

"From what you said about that only being the direction, it could also be further. Am I right?" Salvia interjects. Lusha's lips twitch at one corner. *Was that in agreement?* Salvia wonders: though she decides to keep that thought quiet.

"Oh, flaming wonderful," grunts the Half-Orc.

"The way I see it is that the amulet can only get four of us back, so you and Emlyn take the children since Treorai has got more immediate jobs for you after your return," Salvia says working through her train of thought carefully. A difficult thing for her to do at the best of times since she is more prone to follow whatever course takes her at a whim. "Me and Krilge will head out to start our search now and get back soon as we are able."

"Sounds like a plan to me," Emlyn replies before being unable to resist adding that it will also save Krilge some embarrassment, drawing another revenge-promising glare that causes him to smile widely.

"We will get a message to you somehow when I learn more. What about the whore?" Lusha asks indicating to the dead woman.

"Oh, don't worry about 'er," Krilge says with an evil smile. "I know some Bugbears that will love to have her in their company. She'll be a pile of shit down the mountain by the time a week's out." Lusha suddenly feels so queasy at the thought that it looks like even her golden complexion turns green. She is really glad that it will probably take them nearer fifteen days before they even get to the Immanis Iugum mountains, just so she can get some space from that vile half-breed.

CHAPTER 12

The Wakening

Kali awakens to realise that she is lying on a cold stone floor with her cheek resting in something soft and wet. While the sensation is disgusting, she remains where she is to prevent anyone realising that she is awake while trying to regain her bearings. She tries to take time taking stock of herself, but the dull pounding in her head along with the numbness in her face makes it exceedingly difficult to concentrate. She focuses on just listening. A rumbling snore reverberates through her head antagonising the pain she is already suffering. There is a smell of burning pitch from somewhere tickling her virtually blocked nose. The air feels dank and still; and there are other odours here that she does not even want to dwell on, wherever she is.

She opens her eyes very slowly to see some dirty metal bars with a bar gate of a metal she does not recognise a few feet away. The explanation for the burning pitch reveals itself to be a single lit torch in the middle of the rough-hewn wall just beyond the bars in the other half of the room. At the end is the outline of a sturdy-looking wooden door. *It does not seem to have been made by stone or bronze tools like those made in Palovicus,* she grasps. *Those are not the usual marks that such tools leave behind.*

She then tries to move into a sitting position where something drops from her angular cheek causing her to shudder, and then catch her breath when someone close by speaks to her.

"Hello there. Wondered who would be the first to wake up," he says softly. Looking up, her grey almond-shaped eyes glance upon a young man with shoulder-length brown wavy, dirty-looking hair. "Do you need a hand?"

If she were just a Human, then it would have been unlikely that she would have ever heard him above the rumbling from the broadly built person lying with their back to her. Kali thanks her mother quietly to herself for that part of her Elven heritage.

Looking around slowly, the young man who spoke to her sits against the roughhewn wall. Half of the cell would be in complete darkness if not for another Elven gift of being able to absorb the ambient light to see further than the surrounding shadows would normally dictate. She realises that there is a fourth person, another Human, in the cell lying on his back as if he is asleep at home, breathing quietly and regularly from what she can see of the rise and fall of his well-defined chest. He may be snoring quietly, but she cannot tell considering the noise from their other cellmate.

"Who are you?" she says to the patiently waiting boy.

"I'm Conn Bruis. Initiate to the Temple of Unda from the settlement of Seaton," he answers her question first after seeing her panda eyes and reddened nose dimly lit from the torchlight. His voice is becoming clearer the more he speaks, but the furriness in his mouth is still there from when he came to. "Would you like me to check you over to see if you have any more injuries, Miss …?"

"Kali Celaeno," she responds automatically.

"Pleased to meet you Kali," he says smiling warmly. "I may not be able to do much, but I can ensure whether you have any worse injuries than the nasty bruising on your face."

"Nasty bruising?" She gently touches her face where she then sees a line of blood across her delicate fingertips from catching her nose. "Oh, I'm bleeding. You can if you want." She only decides to make that decision since he seems nice enough and is willing to talk. She might be able to learn something, anything from him. She already knows that the settlement he claims to be from is over five hundred miles, about fourteen to seventeen days walk west of her own settlement. While she has never been to Seaton, she has seen it on the maps that Lippio draws.

Conn slowly walks over to her, ensuring that he does not catch the behemoth's feet, to kneel beside the Half-Elf. He then carefully starts his examination of her injuries and to see if she has any others after double-checking where she is obviously hurting, talking gently with her at the same time.

"Your name is very interesting," he says distractedly, beginning to look at her visible injures. "That's an Elvish name, I believe."

"That is very astute of you," she says in her melodic tone before wincing at the soft touch against her nose where he apologises immediately. "Very few people would even take note enough to realise that. My mother is one of the Gray Elves from the Hamo Montes range near Palovicus. What are you doing to my nose? That really hurts."

"I'm just ensuring to see if it is only severely bruised or if it has been broken." He then gently lowers her head forward to feel the scalp at the back as he continues speaking softly. "Do you live with your mother?"

"Oh, no," she answers with a shake of her head that she immediately regrets when a flash of pain erupts before Conn even starts his examination there. Groaning briefly, she continues. "Well, I used to, but now I live with Lippio. He is a master Penman in Palovicus where I am learning the trade as his apprentice."

"That sounds interesting, tell me more," he mutters as he moves his hand through her slate hair and checking his fingers from time to time.

"So, are you a healer?"

"Top of my class," he replies casually.

By the way he touches her head she can see that he is not actually bragging. He is so much more careful and gentler than Marroc. For a Hauflin, Marroc Mugwort is extremely heavy-handed when it comes to examining his patients who often feel worse afterward than they did before. Though she does suspect that his approach is to make them feel that they need to trade for more healing remedies than they really need.

"There is some severe bruising and nothing worse. Give it enough time and the headache should cease on its own, along with your injuries."

"Thank you, Conn," Kali says softly. He is right, even though he never really did anything more than examine her, the headache is easing to a dull ache, despite their snoring companion. She then starts to look around the room with a feeling that something is different. It takes a few seconds to realise that it was the change of tempo in the boy's breathing who is lying on his back.

"How touching," he says caustically, sitting up slowly due to suffering from a headache from lying on the floor. "In case you haven't noticed, we're in a jail cell. Now is hardly the time to cosying up to each other."

"And who, in the nine hells of Infernum, are you?" Conn's heart feels like it just jumped through his rib cage and demanding an answer of their companion is more like a reflex action. Kali chuckles briefly, drawing a confused expression from him. "And what did I say that was so amusing?"

"I apologise," she begins with a smile. "But you just remind me of Lippo when you curse."

"How charming," the young man sneers. Kali virtually shoots daggers at him with a glare. He notes that her complexion has grey tinged highlights to her ivory colouration. Ignoring her further, he then turns his attention back to Conn. "Reuben."

"Greetings. A pleasure, I'm sure. I am Conn Bruis, and this is-"

"I *can* speak for myself altar boy!" snaps Kali, due to Reuben's continuing rudeness. She is not angry with Conn, but this Reuben is really rubbing her up the wrong way. The unknown of their current situation is getting to her too. Conn shoots her an incredulous look as she continues to glare at their companion and fumes, "Kali, and it is most definitely not a pleasure to meet such a rude, obnoxious piece of Human trash. You may deserve to be here, but I definitely do not."

"Greetings to you both," Reuben smirks. "Sharp tongue you've got there, Kali."

The snores from the last person in the room cease much to Kali's and Reuben's relief. When the person rolls onto all fours and gets up, Kali looks up in surprise. This individual turns out to be possibly the ugliest woman she has ever seen. While the woman looks around at her immediate environment, the Half-Elf and Conn start taking notes about this person.

Her jaw is quite broad, her nostrils are slightly too far apart, her slightly pointed ears and small tusks are revealed when she lets out an almighty yawn, causing her hair to fall back.

Oh, by the goddess. She is a Half-Orc, Conn suddenly realises, causing a chill to run up his spine.

Kali has never heard anything good about these brutal people either. They are aggressive and quick to vile tempers. Then something else strikes her. She is just a girl, despite her size and build, with muscles rippling across her bare arms.

The Half-Orc continues to look around until she catches Kali's gaze. "What are you looking at bitch!" she verily growls at the apprentice Penman who promptly looks away with a brief apology. She then mutters a "whatever" to herself and approaches the bars that divide the room in two while Conn looks from Kali to this other person.

Unlike Kali, he has seen Half-Orcs before. Back in Seaton. "Hello there. I'm Conn," he says holding his hand out as he approaches the Half-Orc to see if she will respond in kind, though his stomach feels like a bowl of jellied eels.

She looks at the boy, down to the offered hand, then back to his cherubic face, eyeing him suspiciously. With a brief shrug as if deciding on something, she decides to slap her much larger hand against his, making Conn wince as his hand grows hot and stings from the impact.

"Ghorza." Ignoring him further, she then turns her attention back to the bars and tries her strength against them only to learn that they are not going to move in a hurry. *Better made than the cells at Deepore, blast it. I would wind up stuck in a place with some damned fools asking stupid questions. This must be the 'coming to a bad end,' Gwen warned me about.* Slamming her hands against the bars, she then throws her back to them and slides down to sit on the floor.

"Are you OK there?" Reuben asks from the darker end of the cell.

"And you are?" she responds, glaring at him.

"Reuben." He then indicates to the Half-Elf. "This is Kali."

Conn looks on, waiting expectantly for the sharp retort against Reuben, which never materialises to his surprise. It is then that he realises that Kali is trying to remain out of the Half-Orc's notice.

"So, the rude bitch does have a name then," Ghorza snarls. "Don't like others staring at me. It's not right."

"No, you are right," Kali begins hesitantly, more because she knows that she was in the wrong and her mother would be so disappointed in her if she stays quiet. So would Lippio. "I do apologise but I have never actually met one of your ..." She stops abruptly as Ghorza glares at her. "I ... ah ... mean ... erm, that I have never actually met a Half-Orc before," she finishes rapidly. Ghorza just grunts. Kali tries again. "You are from the Strykejern Mountains, are you not?"

"Only born there. What's it to you?"

"Just curious is all," Kali replies quickly to try and not annoy her anymore. *By the gods, talking to this one is hard work. She is as hostile as Reuben is plain rude.*

"We're in a cell that would make the Deepore gaol feel inferior and all you're concerned with is where I'm from? You need to get your priorities right bitch," Ghorza fumes.

"There's no need for the attitude. We're all stuck in the same boat, as the saying goes," Conn starts when Ghorza quickly rises and glowers at him. Before she can say anything, Reuben moves towards the annoyed Half-Orc.

"That's enough, all of you," he says standing toe-to-toe against Ghorza's taller stature. Conn and Kali look on in surprise while Reuben and Ghorza try to outstare the other.

After what seems like an age, with Conn and Kali watching with bated breath at the contest of wills taking place before their eyes, Ghorza eventually smiles.

"I like you Rude Bin. You show no fear," she says with a gruff chuckle.

"What just happened there?" whispers Kali to Conn.

"I don't know. A meeting of the minds?" he whispers back.

"I heard that altar boy!" Reuben calls out while still facing Ghorza. "And, as for you, that's Reu-ben. Not, Rude Bin."

"And my name is Conn Bruis. Not altar boy!" he fumes as he glowers at Kali.

"What did I say?" Kali bristles, wondering why Conn suddenly turns on her.

"You're the one who started it by calling me altar boy in the first place!" he yells back at her.

While Ghorza smiles at the exchange, no one notices the door to the passage open to allow a large, heavyset man through.

"Settle it down in there!" a rough voice bellows from beyond the door, silencing everyone in the cell.

CHAPTER 13

New Assignments

With a sharp crack and flash, Emlyn and Lusha appear in the dining room with the sleeping children in their arms. The stone amulet they used, crumbles to dust. Lusha removes the leather thong and drops it on the table. When they look around, the room is empty except for Hobbes who is standing in his usual place half-buried in the wall.

"Hobbes. Get Master Treorai," she orders the grey-skinned creature.

"Yes, Priestess." Hobbes' voice sounds like stones rolling down a mountain.

The creature seemingly peels away from the wall without leaving an impression and heads through a set of double doors where his head almost catches the door jamb. Ten or so minutes later, Treorai returns with Hobbes close behind him.

"What happened out there? Where are Salvia and Krilge?" he demands without preamble.

"They are fine, Master," states Lusha, making it clear that she has said all that was needed. As Treorai looks at her quizzically, Emlyn decides to fill him in on all that happened.

"As we had these two to bring back after killing their mother, Salvia and Krilge headed south after Lusha's location magic said that that was where he needed to go." Lusha nods in agreement when Treorai looks at her with raised eyebrows.

"I see," the Wizard, says slowly looking thoughtful for a minute or two. "Hobbes, have Skarmazh brought to me and then bring us some refreshment." Hobbes ambles away without a word.

"Where is the woman now?" he asks.

"Krilge's taking her to the Bugbears before continuing on," Emlyn answers.

Treorai nods in understanding and turns his attention to Lusha. "Are you able to narrow down your search for what Krilge needs if given the time?"

"I can, Master. But I am not sure what use it will be since I have no way to tell them what I find," she explains hurriedly. *I cannot disappoint him again. He already seems to be annoyed with me for some reason. If it was not for that oath, I made in my fear of dying alone to feed the Malomortis' vultures, preventing me from dying honourably in the service of my goddess, then ... I do not know what I would have done otherwise.*

"I have that covered." Treorai stops abruptly as a greenish-yellow-skinned humanoid enters the room, followed by Hobbes who immediately begins serving the drinks before returning to the wall. "Greetings, Skarmazh. We have two more for you to put to work immediately. See to it?" He was not really asking the tall human-sized creature. "Then introduce our guest to our new arrivals."

"Don't ya want 'em softened up a bit first?" the creature wonders.

"They are children. I think the guards will do the softening up for us, don't you?" chides Lusha. He goes to ask them another question, but she stops him immediately. "Throw a bucket of water over them to get them awake. The louts look like they could do with a good wash anyway."

He nods and scoops them up without another word, one under each arm as Treorai makes a motion in Hobbes' direction. Peeling himself from the wall, the grey sentinel strides across to the double doors in the middle of a long wall and opens the door to allow Skarmazh to leave. When Hobbes begins closing the door, they hear him shout at someone beyond, "Puo n'uzo obara tupu m gbanye gi..." as the door closes. The double door opens again briefly to allow two scared yellowish-green Goblins into the dining room before disappearing through the single door in the corner.

"Anyone would think that he hates Goblins," jests Emlyn, drawing a tight smile from Lusha. Her reaction causes him to cough into his tankard when he is about to take a drink. Treorai grins, though Emlyn is hard pushed to know whether it was the jest or that he nearly choked. *He does have a twisted sense of humour in that regard.*

"Back to the business at hand," Treorai continues. "Since Krilge and Salvia will not be continuing their mapping of the surrounding area, I will need you to continue with your search for the aid Krilge needs. I will then ensure that word gets to them."

Lusha nods and asks if he wants her to start immediately. He holds his hand up to her briefly before looking to Emlyn. "More importantly right now, I need you to begin searching for any Spears that we may be able to hire, though try to avoid the more moralistic groups. They will only quibble if we need them to do something that infringes on their ideals." *If we are to take dominion over these lands as they have in the south, then we cannot have those idiots questioning our every decision.*

"As we have agreed. Sell Spears with loose morals," Emlyn answers with a nod and a sneer.

"Quite." Ever since Treorai returned from the old country in the south almost a year ago, he held the dream of ruling the north along similar lines as they do in the southern regions. But he also knows that these people are more resistant to the idea due to their strong principles and self-sufficiency.

Those on the Southern Continent are divided into falme and watawala, or kingdoms and lordships, as he understood it. The Northern Continent has no such leadership, and every settlement has their own form of law and some sort of government whether it rose from the chapels, which seems to be the most common of late, a local council, a mayor, the small number of choice people or even a combination of these, but they were reluctant to cede any power over to Treorai when he initially spoke to them. Then there are the Races other than the Humans that he also wants under his rule with his chief advisors and leaders being those that Treorai has chosen. To accomplish this, he plans to take one settlement at a time and then expand on his holdings. His first objective is a small out-of-the-way place as a practice run before moving onto the next settlement since it is more easily defensible should anyone choose to raise an exception to his expansionist plans.

Another reason and the focus of his plan was the recent discovery of an ancient Dwarven stronghold abandoned over a hundred years ago where, rumour has it, that a vast wealth remains virtually intact in the hidden vaults. Some of the complex he now occupies may have even been an extension to that stronghold or even a part of another one sacked about around the same time or earlier. Not only will it bring him wealth, but there are supposed to be powerful artifacts that could aid in his scheme. If he can get in there, then he will not need this paltry mine to gain the wealth he feels that he needs, especially if he must buy the loyalty of those serving under him.

"I'll get right on it, Tre," Emlyn says before finishing off the last of his ale and then leaving Lusha and Treorai to their own part of the plans. If they are successful, he is sure that they will fill him in later, but now is not the time. He has much to do for his part. *After all, if this all falls through, then I can always go back to my home of Lakeside.*

He first met Treorai and Lusha about three years ago when he tried to ambush a small caravan heading north that the Wizard was riding in. While most of his cohorts died during that attack, Emlyn and three others all agreed to serve the spellcaster for ten years in servitude as his henchmen. That was three years ago, though his cohorts died from one cause or another. This left him as the only survivor and, by proving his loyalty very quickly, earned more leeway than other indentured servants.

"Lusha, as I hinted at before, I have a very special task for you," Treorai says as soon as the door closes behind the fair-haired warrior.

"You have watered my appetite, Master," Lusha says as she struggles to keep her mounting excitement internal. It is an extremely rare opportunity for Treorai to let anyone else near his special assignments, trusting very few to be successful with them.

"Simply put, after you find the information to help Krilge, I need you to locate some Changlings in the area."

"Changlings?" Lusha blurts fearfully without thinking. "Oh, Master. They cannot be trusted."

"I know very well their treacherous natures. By the time we need them, I hope to have enough to even quell those desires of theirs," he admonishes a little more sternly than he intends, wincing at the thought that he may have exposed his most secret agenda concerning his latest find. Treorai knows that Lusha has watched him studying the door in another part of the complex. He continues more calmly, realising that Lusha has not grasped his near slip as she sits there looking at her sandaled feet. "But in this case and with the right incentive, we will trust them long enough for them to do as they are told." Lusha nods without looking up.

"I'll get right on it, Master," she says quietly, getting up and leaving to make her preparations without a backward glance.

Chapter 14

New Arrival

The burly man shoved through the open doorway, his hands tied with a piece of hemp rope in a double handcuff knot behind his back, yells in a brassy tone at his captor. "Watch it! Nearly 'ad me over that time, ya idiot!"

"Jest shut ya jabber, Slave!" An equally large, greenish-yellow-skinned humanoid creature says in its guttural voice as he follows the Human into the passage. He is wearing little more than a dirty, coarse woollen tabard and carrying a hazelwood switch in one hand. Dark reddish-brown hair grows thick on his muscular arms and head. The creature pulls a large metal key from a belt pouch and places it in the lock while forcing the bound man against the bars with the other hand holding the whip. He gives the current occupants of the cell an evil glare with his yellowish feral eyes. "As for you lot, you can move ta the back o' the cell one an all."

Ghorza, standing close to the bars, returns his glare with her own, yellow-eyed glower full of hostile promise for their gaoler. While holding the man against the bars, the slightly pointy-nosed creature quickly belts the key and uses the switch, flicking it to catch Ghorza through the bars just under her chin and making her flinch.

"Move, Slave! Back o' the cell. Now!"

"Ghorza, please," Reuben calls quietly. Without taking her eyes off their gaoler, Ghorza slowly backs up to the wall. Reuben quietly thanks her.

Ramming the handle of the whip into his wide belt, the creature then unlocks the door and shoves the man into the Half-Orc when she launches herself at the cell door. The gaoler then slams the door shut and relocks it before moving back a few steps from the cell where he then smirks at the Half-Orc and Human entanglement on the floor before leaving them all alone again.

"Get off of me, you bastard!" Ghorza growls as she starts breathing rapidly and knees him in the gut, causing the man to grunt in pain and roll off onto his side. Now free of the man's weight, she gets up and slams her hands against the cell door once again in sheer frustration.

"Easy there, girl ..." Reuben starts, but then falls silent as she snaps a vile look of pure hatred on him, her breathing coming in ragged gasps.

"Ghorza? What's wrong?" Conn asks quietly, carefully approaching her with his arms kept loose beside him and his palms forward. He breaks out in a cold sweat just approaching the Half-Orc, but his instinct to heal drives him forward.

"Gotta ... get ... out of ... here," she gasps throatily, clutching her chest.

"Has this happened before?" He keeps his tone soft while getting closer. She puts a hand out to stop him, her face creases and she clutches with her other hand all the tighter at her chest. As he watches her struggling to catch her breath, he then works through the possible theories.

"Ghorza, is your chest hurting?" She nods again. "Ghorza, I think know what is happening here."

"And 'ow would ya know that, Boy!" erupts the brassy voice of the man in the far corner where he receives three looks of annoyance and/or hatred.

"He's a healer," Kali cuts in. "Now leave him be."

"Ghorza, you are over-breathing," Conn tells her softly, deciding that it was best to ignore the abhorrent man. "You need to slow your breathing down."

"Snippy little girlie, aren't ya," snipes the man.

Ghorza tries to do as Conn asks her, but he notices that she is glaring at the old windbag who is still slightly hunched to favour his stomach. "Ignore them Ghorza. Just try to focus on me, on my voice."

"Quiet you," snaps Reuben quietly at the man who stands a good head and shoulders over him. "Whatever Conn's doing, it seems to be working."

Conn is gently holding Ghorza's head to help her to focus on him. "Take it easy and talk to me Ghorza. Has this happen before?"

"Deepore settlement," she gasps.

"What was happening at the time?" Conn makes sure he keeps his tone low, forcing her to concentrate on him.

"They put me into a … a cell … for fighting."

"And that is when it started?" Ghorza nods. "What happened next?"

"Not entirely sure. I just had to get out of there."

"Keep going."

"They said that I hurt several people. When they tried to stop me."

"Have you noticed anything right now?" She shakes her head, nonplussed by his question. "You're breathing much easier now, as well as looking a little calmer."

Ghorza looks at him quizzically and then begins to take stock of herself. When the realisation sets in, she then looks at the boy.

"Thank you … Conn, is it?" He nods with a warm smile.

"Ah, goats' crotch!" bellows the man.

"Oh, shut up, you oaf," Kali snaps back at him.

"People, can we keep it calm and low for a while?" Conn rapidly interjects to the room in general and drawing their attention to him.

"What's up with Ghorza?" Reuben wonders quietly.

"It seems that Ghorza suffers with a severe restlessness, possibly brought on by enclosed spaces which may be aggravated by the number of people in that area. It is this restlessness that is causing her muscles to rapidly flex, causing her breathing difficulties, which is then increasing her restlessness even further, and so on." He pauses to look at each of them in turn. "We need to keep it as calm as possible in here, for a little while at least, to help Ghorza."

"I'll be okay, Conn. We just need a way out from this damned place and soon," Ghorza responds throatily.

"Then it's about time that we find out about our newcomer," demands Reuben as he stares at the man. "What's your story, stranger?"

"Ya arrogant young pup! It's not like I know any of ya any better," the older man growls. "Ya kids are just as much strangers ta me!"

"Okay, Sir," Kali's normally melodic voice sounding stiff while she struggles to remain polite. "May we know your name at least?"

"Trystan Gibbs. Now, you want to know anything else; then you will have to barter for the information. Deal?"

"Are you an idiot?" Reuben wonders aloud. "I think that it is plainly obvious that none of us are carrying anything right now. We're just flaming grateful to be left with the clothes on our backs."

"Then, the sooner we can get out of here, the sooner ya can start paying me," he says with a smile that would make the fruit of a lemon seem sweet in comparison. "Oh, and someone untie my wrists."

"Oh, please. Give us a *particularly good* reason why we should bother," Kali sneers.

"Cos if one of ya don't little girlie, then what will yer chances be without my 'elp?" he responds with an evil-sounding chuckle.

With a sigh, Reuben walks over, indicates for the man to turn around, and then spends a few seconds studying the knot before untying the hemp rope. He voices his admiration for the doubling of a simple cuff knot. This elicits a growl before Trystan grunts and starts rubbing his wrists to help reduce the slight tingling sensation that he was starting to feel.

"You're one for showing your gratitude, aren't you?" Conn says tautly when the newcomer says nothing more.

"That's yer first question, boy," Trystan states smugly at his cleverness. "I'll mark yer slate."

"How about, we start with our congenial host. Who and what is he?" Kali demands irritably.

"Ha! Just because ya ask two questions in one, don't mean that ya can get away with paying only for one. I don't put up with such shenanigans like that," he says with a superior tone to his brassy voice. "That'll be two marks for ya girlie. But, in answer ta yer questions, our host is a mean-spirited gaoler is called Skarmazh." Ghorza looks into the Human's eyes and sees that is all he knows about their guard.

"Where, in all of the Infernum, are we?" Conn asks.

"We're …"

"If you say that we're in a cell, then I'm going to lump you right here, right now," growls Ghorza threateningly. Trystan looks back at her indignantly.

"We're in a mine actually, girlie," he huffs.

"What type of mine is it then?" wonders Ghorza aloud. "In Deepore, we have a coal and ore mines and one with loads of natural chimneys littered with crystalline deposits, or so Gwen tells me."

"Salt," Trystan states abruptly.

"Salt?" exclaims Kali in surprise, echoed by her angular features.

"More precisely, rock salt," the man gloats. "Or so Skarmazh tells me. Has so many uses, such as preserving and flavouring food."

"I do not mean to be rude, but bay salt is much better," Conn chimes in. "It's so much more flavourful."

"But I did not know that salt could be mined," Kali says to clarify her confusion.

"Where did ya think it came from? Sprouting from trees?" Trystan remarks sarcastically, prompting the Half-Elf to look incredulously at him. "All I know is that the people who captured me were heading for some virtually impassable mountains with a foul-smelling wagon pulled by an 'alf-Orc as well as any 'orse wiv you lot in it. If we're in those mountains, then there is a lot of water that flows down the mountains to the river and, I guess, can seep through the rocks where the salt can then be mined. Oh, and I'm still tallying the marks ya'll owe me."

"Who cares," snipes Ghorza. "Here's a question for ya. Who runs this place?"

"Ah," Trystan nods knowingly. "It's run by a Sorcerer."

"Do you have a damned name for this damned Sorcerer?" growls Ghorza, getting thoroughly annoyed with the stupid game he seems intent on playing.

"As a matter of fact, I do," he smugly nods.

"Who is it then?" Kali shouts at this stupid man and his mind games.

"Okay, okay. His name is Treorai." Ghorza's legs seem to disappear from under her as she suddenly drops to the floor, stunned. Conn races over to her and gently moves her head to look into her eyes, wondering what has brought the Half-Orc down this time.

"Ghorza? Ghorza. What is it?" he asks softly.

"Treorai," she breathes.

"What about him?"

"He's the bastard I had to make a delivery to," she says, her breathing becoming shallower. "He's got a tower at Deepore."

"Did you actually make that delivery?" queries the young Initiate.

"I don't know," Ghorza answers slowly. A puzzled expression creases her forehead as she struggles to remember. "I remember seeing his tower with a connecting house, but then it becomes darker after that. Like, it's more of a dream?"

"It's going to be okay, Ghorza. It may come back to you, eventually. From the sounds of it though, you may have been enchanted," he continues softly. She looks at him quizzically. "Someone, possibly this Treorai, has cast a spell on you. As to what type, I cannot tell as yet." He then looks to Trystan. "A foul-smelling wagon? That we was in?"

"That's right, boy. Why?"

"Where was this?"

"North of Spire. Why?"

"Because, from Seaton to Spire is about seven hundred and fifty miles as the Eagle flies," Kali chimes in distractedly. "That is approximately twenty-five days away."

"That smell you noticed?" Conn continues, "was something to keep us asleep. Of that, I'm sure of."

"How come we don't feel any weaker if we haven't eaten for that long?" Ghorza wonders.

"Of that, I don't know, I'm afraid," Conn answers her.

CHAPTER 15

The Escape

The door to the room beyond the cell opens and they immediately move to the back of the cell apart from Trystan. Their large, green-yellow gaoler enters with a tray containing five small wooden bowls. With a vile chuckle, their gaoler slides the tray beneath the cell door with his foot. Focusing on moving the tray under the door, he does not see the burly man launch forward to grab the Hobgoblin behind his head to smash his face into the bars.

Trystan makes a grab for Skarmazh's key tucked in his belt, but winds up with a punch in the face, forcing him to lose his grip on the gaoler.

"Oh, that's the way of it?" he sneers at the man. He really hates it whenever his 'guests' start causing him problems since any failure in controlling the captives always falls squarely on his shoulders. *It would not be so bad, except for that last prisoner caught trying to escape only thirty days ago.*

Even though they did manage to recapture her, they found that it was safer to keep her locked away from everyone. The fact she escaped the first time round still came down to his failings as a gaoler and he was damned well going to make sure that it never happened again. *Not on my bloody watch at least.*

Glaring at the red-faced and angry Trystan, Skarmazh quickly comes to a decision. "If that's the way it's ta be, then ya bloody well going ta get it, Slave! All o' ya!" Without another word, Skarmazh storms off, slamming the door closed behind him. *If they want ta cause me grief, then let the bloody mines have 'em!*

"Now ya bloody done it! He's off ta get the rope ta take us ta the mines now!" he grumps loudly at the other four who just stare at him.

"Us? It was not *us* who decided to attack the gaoler," Kali explodes.

"Oh, shut ya yammer child and help ta figure a way outta this mess instead," Trystan orders.

"You want us to figure a way to avoid being sent to the mine after you got us into this mess in the first place?" accuses Reuben. Then a thought just struck him. "Did you set this up so that we'd be forced to do something?"

Trystan goes quiet for a few seconds as he mulls the accusation over in his mind before answering the boy more calmly. "He ain't stupid but Skarmazh can be angered easily enough. That's when he's liable ta make a mistake."

"Are you an idiot? You may have just got us all killed," snaps Ghorza. She cannot believe what she is hearing.

Before another word can be said, the door is yanked open and Skarmazh storms in leading some smaller yellowish-green-skinned creatures, almost like a childlike version of the gaoler, though with slightly longer noses and pointier ears.

They are half the size of the Hobgoblin and each of them carries a set of rope bindings in one of their tiny claw-tipped hands. All dressed in outsized clothing from Human shirts to Dwarf-sized tabards. There are five of them standing in a line either side of Skarmazh.

"Face the wall, all o' ya!" he growls.

"Goblins," Trystan grumps quietly to himself, though Conn only just catches what he says.

Kali and Trystan comply with the Hobgoblin's guttural order.

"Goblins?" the young initiate repeats, turning slowly so he can eye them a little longer. He has heard of them but never seen one. Let alone five of them.

"Quiet slaves! Jest face the bloody wall!"

"I'll tell you later if we get the chance," Trystan answers him when their backs are to the gaoler.

"Oh, a smart arse are ya, or jest plain stupid?" Skarmazh growls.

The occupants look over their shoulder to see who the Hobgoblin is upset with now.

"You want me to face the wall," begins the throaty response. "Then come make me," she finishes in a dangerously quiet tone.

Skarmazh slams the key into the lock and yanks it open so hard that it catches one of the Goblins by surprise. He snatches a set of bindings from another of the creatures who fails to let go in time.

The Goblin is then dragged into the cell by the gaoler. He finally releases the figure-of-eight looped rope before Skarmazh swings the binding at Ghorza.

She blocks it with her forearm where Trystan spins round to plant a fist to the gaoler's jaw.

Skarmazh drops the binding, stunned by the blow.

Conn and Reuben launch themselves at the cell door before the other Goblins realise enough to shut it again.

Kali launches herself at the one dragged in the cell that is struggling back to his feet.

Its eyes go wide, and it tries to bolt for the door when Kali crashes into his back.

The Half-Elf snatches up the fallen binding and swings it across the Goblin's throat. He tries to fight back until Kali jams her knee into the back of his neck while she pulls on each side of the rope and leans back.

Skarmazh spins on Trystan where Ghorza snaps her powerful arms around the gaoler's muscular neck to keep him in a chokehold.

Reuben leads the way to the passage, using the top of the cell doorway to vault over the Goblin heads, putting himself between them and the room's sole exit.

Behind the agile Human, Conn throws himself forward when the Goblin Skarmazh stunned recovers enough to start closing the door. Conn crashes through to catch the unfortunate creature a second time, where it flies back to smash its head against the hard floor.

Skarmazh slowly drops to the floor under Ghorza's increasing pressure, his arms waving weakly before dropping to his side altogether.

Kali releases her Goblin once it finally stops struggling.

Trystan races for the other half of the room to help the boys with the remaining creatures. By the time he gets to the cell door, only one of them remains.

The last Goblin looks between the two mad-looking Humans and begins backing away. He does not realise that there is a large man behind him. It continues to slowly retreat when his yellow eyes fly wide open at the pressure it feels on the back of his neck. He frantically grabs and claws at his assailant's hand.

Trystan flicks his wrist. A loud snap resonates from the Goblin's neck, and he ceases to struggle. Trystan then casually throws the body to one side into the cell.

The whole fight only took less than a minute before it was all over, where Trystan begins to search through their unconscious gaoler's belt pouch while Ghorza pokes at the limp Goblin.

"He's dead," she says to Conn, where they then look at the older man. "Why did you kill him?" She is just not sure how she feels about this one's death.

"Get used ta it, girlie. If ya want ta get out of here alive, then yer going ta have ta kill or be killed," he answers, finding some vials containing an amber liquid. He opens one and sniffs it before looking over to Kali.

She is sitting quietly by her unconscious Goblin, her nose bleeding from where the struggling Goblin caught her to accompany a new persistent headache. She is supporting her head in her hands, her elbows on her knees.

He recorks the vial and gives her a nod when she looks up at him. He continues to hold it out to her, pocketing the other one. "Hey, kid. Drink this. It'll help ya."

She takes the proffered vial, which is no larger than the more exotic inks that come in four-ounce measures. When she removes the stopper, a mild flowery odour wafts her nostrils.

Conn puts a hand on hers to take the vial gently from her.

Kali had not even realised that he was there. After her initial surprise, she then looks at him with raised eyebrows.

The young man sniffs the liquid, then thumbs the narrow neck to upend the bottle briefly. After licking his digit, Conn looks at the vial in puzzlement and is then pleasantly surprised. He hands the vial back and nods.

"What is it?" her soft melodic voice barely carrying.

"It's a healing potion. Don't worry," he softly answers her before looking to Trystan. "How did you know what it was? The only similar potions I've seen had no colour."

"Skarmazh gave me one when I kept complaining of a headache and blurred vision. I thought that it would help her."

Kali drinks the potion and smiles at the sweetness that trickles gently down her throat. Soon after, she feels a faintly warm sensation spreading throughout her slender body, where it then localises in her head, easing the throbbing ache, the congested sensation of her angular nose, and the numbness of her jaw where the Goblin caught her. In a short space of time, she feels no more pain at all. She looks up at Trystan and nods her thanks.

Ghorza and Reuben are dragging the remaining Goblins into the cell. They then use the rope bindings to secure the Goblins and Skarmazh to each other. Once they are finished, they close the cell, locking it behind them.

As a final insult, Trystan leaves the key, dangling from the torch sconce.

Ghorza opens the door to hear a surprised squeak from the other side.

CHAPTER 16

First Blood

There is no light in the connecting passage. When Ghorza plunges ahead, her eyesight automatically adjusts to the darkness, allowing her to see a greyscale view of the passage and another door at the end.

In front of this door, there is another Goblin guarding it who squeaks in fright at seeing her. Wasting no time at all, she charges the creature, which turns on its sandaled feet, snatches open the door, and sprints through.

The Half-Orc proves to be faster and soon catches the small creature in a foul-smelling room beyond. Her eyes automatically shift back to see normally in the solitary torchlit room. Grabbing it by the back of the neck, the small humanoid's dull yellow eyes widen in fright before being face-planted into a door it was racing past with a squelching thud. Ghorza releases the creature, where it falls like a rag doll onto its back, its face a bloody mess.

Reuben, the next one through the door, slides to a halt on the filthy floor next to Ghorza and looks from the creature to the Half-Orc and back to the creature in surprise.

Trystan, following closely in the boy's wake, twists out of the way to avoid crashing into him and collides with a bunk bed against the far wall.

Conn and Kali arrive next to see what has happened. The Half-Elf screeches briefly in fright and the young Initiate looks sidewards at Ghorza fearfully while lowering himself to examine the creature.

"Is that a Hobgoblin child?" Kali says, her melodious voice sounding thick before continuing in a low tone. "Ghorza, what have you done? You've hurt-"

"Killed," Conn interrupts softly. Ghorza and Kali look at him in surprise.

"You killed a Hobgoblin child," Kali finishes.

"Goblin," Ghorza states quietly. Conn detects a sad tone in her voice.

"What was that?" Reuben asks, not really catching what she just said.

"She said that it was a Goblin. No 'arm no foul," Trystan answers him blithely.

"No harm no ...? A what?" Kali stammers as she trips over her words.

"A Goblin," Conn replies in hopes of distracting her before turning to face Kali. "We learnt about them at the temple. After the world was created, during the Creation of Second Life, there were only a few Races. These were the Ahborhominīs, the living trees; the Terrestres, the nature dwellers; and the Saxums, those of the land. After the Splintering of the Races, some of the cursed Saxums became what we now call Goblins who then forced themselves on the Elven folk, splintered from the Terrestres, which produced the Hobgoblins, which-"

"Yeah, yeah, yeah already," Trystan breaks in, glancing around the torchlit room and finding little enough to catch his eye. "Enough of the sermon kid an let's get going shall we?"

Looking around the room, they see by the light of a single low burning torch in a sconce between the door they came through and the one that Ghorza used to kill the Goblin. There is a third door at the end of the room and five bunks spaced along the length of the room. A brief search yields only a solitary chest below the torch sconce containing a single fresh torch that Trystan grabs. After a hurried discussion, they decide to go through the bloodied door until Conn realises that Ghorza has not moved from the Goblin's side.

"Are you alright?" he softly asks the Half-Orc and drawing everyone's attention. When she does not reply, he asks Reuben to fetch him the torch from the sconce and bring it closer. It is only then that Conn realises that her usual warm beige complexion has paled, diminishing the green-tinted highlights. Her yellow eyes stare fixedly at the bloody creature lying at their feet. "Ghorza, look at me? Are you okay?"

"I killed someone," she answers, her throaty voice sounding distant.

"So what?" Trystan breaks in abruptly, his frustration putting an edge to his tone. "It's just a damned Goblin. Who cares?"

"Who cares?" Kali snaps at the overbearing man. "We are not hardened killers like you seemed to be, *Mr. Gibbs!*"

"Can you two just calm it down while I help Ghorza right now?" Conn calls out, trying to appeal to their good sense. "Ghorza, talk to me."

"I am no hardened killer girlie," he replies in that brassy tone of his. "I've just done what I've had ta, ta protect my farm an' animals!"

"Will you two just shut the nine hells up?" Reuben bellows, drawing surprised looks from the pair of them. "By Umbra, you two just sound like a father and daughter I know in Brackston!"

"Ghorza, come with me and sit down on a bunk at this end," Conn continues to try and help the Half-Orc from her stupor whilst ignoring the others. As he tugs at her hand, she automatically follows him to the far end of the room and sits her on a lower bunk, which creaks ominously. He then realises that he is not so fearful of this Half-Orc which surprises him. He relishes in that thought briefly, then feels guilty at his joy at such an inappropriate time.

"You just invoked the shadow goddess' name," Kali shrills fearfully. "Why would you do that?"

"Oh, by the gods, heed this boy not," Trystan says by way of a quick prayer. Invoking the goddess of shadows by name is normally only done by evil rogues and spell-casters. To do so otherwise is to invoke bad luck upon yourself or even death upon another.

"It was an accident Ghorza," Conn continues softly before glancing at the others. He decides that there is only one thing he can do if he is to help Ghorza. "Kali, can you bring the torch over here while Reuben stays with Trystan?" If he can separate her and Trystan, even for only a short space of time, he might then be able to focus on trying to get the Half-Orc responsive enough for them all to escape wherever it is they are. He wants to leave the stale air of this room, which is worse than the cell they were in quickly before they are discovered. *I'm just amazed that nobody has turned up already.*

Kali walks over with the low burning torch and kneels in front of Ghorza, placing a small delicately fingered hand upon one of the Half-Orc's broad knees.

"What's it with ya boy?" Trystan demands from Reuben while trying to keep his brassy voice low. "Calling that much ill-luck down on us before we even get outta 'ere."

"Conn is trying to help Ghorza and you two just kept on bitching at each other," he answers angrily while trying to remain sotto voce. "What, in all of the Infernum, is that all about?"

"Ya really want ta know boy? That girl needs ta grow up an fast if she wants ta get out of 'ere in one piece. I ain't no killer, but when I was growing up on the farm, we were infrequently attacked by some of those creatures and others besides. Those Goblins breed like rats and are just as much vermin. As a result, I don't have a problem with killing one every now and then," the larger man says by way of an explanation. "Now it's yer turn boy."

Conn finally gets Ghorza talking some. She admits that she has never killed anyone before even though she does have a quick temper. Conn is just relieved that calling Kali away from Trystan and Reuben has put an end to their shouting match. For now, at least. When he looks further down the room, he spots Reuben and Trystan sitting together on another of the bunks talking amongst themselves. Trystan looks almost fatherly at Reuben, but Conn cannot see Mr. Gibbs as a fatherly figure at all. It just does not seem to be in that man. While he can still hear what they are saying, he is grateful that they are trying to keep it down and allows him to focus on helping the Half-Orc.

"It's just a phrase that I heard from somewhere in my past," Reuben tells Trystan, who sits quietly with his elbows on his knees as he listens to the lad. "It sounds so distant in my mind, more like an old memory, a dream that continually evades me when I try and focus on it. Never said it before today but when you two were arguing, I had to stop you. It was the only thing that came to mind."

Ghorza looks at Conn's round face, which reminds her of the cherubs that the merchant caravans carried to the Deepore Settlement to decorate their buildings with. "Gwen always said that it will be my temper that will get me into trouble," she tells him quietly.

"Gwen?" Kali asks softly, trying to help. Conn smiles at her, grateful in her attempts to distract Ghorza from the Half-Orc's current problem.

"Gwendolyn is a herbalist who looks out for me at Deepore," she replies with a brief wistful smile. "She is never afraid of telling me when I did bad and will often find ways for me to repay my debts." The smile falls away as she continues. "She even said that if I was not careful, then I will kill someone eventually."

"Is that why you killed the Goblin? Because you were angry?" says Conn getting to the significant part and drawing a stern look from Kali. He shakes his head briefly at her as he awaits Ghorza's response.

"No. I was just scared. Scared that he was going to raise the alarm." Tears start to sting her eyes as she resumes. "I don't want to go back to that cell, not to the mine either." She looks to the cherubic-faced boy beside her. "I'm scared, Conn. For the first time ever since I left my birth tribe, I am truly frightened."

He looks into her eyes and he can see that fear reflected in them. "I know you are Ghorza. We all are. As for that Goblin, you did the right thing. If he had raised the alarm, then we might all be in the mines or even dead by now." He pauses for a second or two before continuing. "In fact, keep that thought as your focus in your mind. None of us are going to blame anyone for doing what we need to do to get out of this place and, I am sure, that even your Gwen would agree with me on this. Okay?"

Ghorza smiles weakly at him and nods. She then gives him a big hug where he is pleasantly surprised at how gentle she can be despite his initial concerns for her size and strength. When she pulls away, he is relieved to see some of her pallor returning when she looks intently into his blue eyes.

"I will do my best to remain as calm as possible and to not get too angry," she promises while swamping Kali's more diminutive hand beneath her own.

"Nonsense girlie," Trystan's brassy voice cuts through the air as they look up to see the large man and Reuben calmly coming over to them. "Just like yer strength, ya use yer anger ta yer advantage. Besides, it doesn't 'urt none ta let rip once in a while!"

"Now this is going to be a rarity," Kali responds in her soft-spoken melodic tone. "But I am actually going to agree with him. If any of us are in trouble or you find yourself in grave difficulties, then you have every right to '… let rip …' as Mr. Gibbs puts it."

Ghorza snaps a look at Reuben and Conn who both nod their ascent in turn.

"Now, I for one think we should get going to find a way out of this place," Reuben bluntly states to get everyone moving again.

They enter another room via the bloodied door after moving the Goblin onto one of the bunks and covering him with a filthy blanket, looking like he has just gone to sleep. All the next room contains is a single cot and a fairly clean mattress with a small split to reveal the straw contained within, a blanket folded at one end; a chair behind a table with a couple of sheets of parchment, a wood stick shaped into a point with a split nib beside a half-empty ink bottle at one end of the room. There is a small well with a bucket tied to a long length of rope beside it; a sodden table with a washboard inside half a barrel on it; and a second chair with a damp tabard hanging over the back.

They look at the sheets of parchment. It is a list of Races, where they were taken and where they are working written down in a smooth flowing script. A second less artistic marking by the script has a second date beside some of the Races, though others are included to the bottom in the artistic writing, each with a similar date. These latest additions include a Human male from Seaton and a Half-Elf female from Palovicus for the mine, a Human male from Brackston for the crushing room, a Half-Orc female from Deepore Settlement, and a Human male from Spire for the slave quarter kitchen.

"Oh, how delightful," quips Kali as she reads the sheets. "We are to be split up to different locations."

"We 'ad best get outta 'ere soon as we can then kids. Else it's the shutters for us." Even Trystan seems slightly cowed by what Kali has just read out. "What are those numbered entries 'ere and 'ere by the names?"

"Some of those only have one entry while the others have two," adds Reuben quietly.

"I presume these are the dates that these were brought into the mine or captured," Kali answers them. "It is these double entries that concern me more. Half of these people only lasted less than ten days in this place for whatever reason."

"I know the mines are a dangerous place to work in," Ghorza tells her. "Gas pockets, cave-ins, and so on." She looks around to see everyone looking at her. She shrugs before adding, "Gwen told me."

"But at least a third of these people who died were not even placed in the mines to begin with." Kali shudders as she looks at the large Half-Orc.

"I agree with Mr. Gibbs. Let's just get out of here like now," Conn says, nervously looking over his shoulder to the door, expecting to see someone there already.

Reuben heads straight out with the others following him, where he then heads to the door at the other end of the room. He presses his ear to the rough wood before lifting the latch to open it and peer through. Beyond the door, all is in darkness, so he closes it again before facing them.

"It's a tad dark out there," he tells them before looking to Trystan. "I'm going to need that torch lit.

Trystan nods and puts his torch to the one from the sconce for a brighter light. After a second or two, the second torch takes, and the room suddenly brightens to show them the disgusting state of the bunks and the floor. Conn surreptitiously wipes his hands on his trousers at the thought of moving the dead Goblin and covering him over.

CHAPTER 17

Moral Dilemma

Reuben reopens the door to find a corridor with two doors along one side. Opening the first one, he sees a room with piles of leather, some metal, and a lot of cloth in the middle of the room. There are some partially assembled pieces of protective garments on hanging racks against the wall with sawdust below them, and a sturdy door in the wall at the end of the room.

"Well, well, well, well. What 'ave we in 'ere?" Trystan wonders aloud. When they start to look through the pile, he looks at the items already hanging up. "Well, what do ya know, we 'ave armour." Not seeing anything in his size, he joins the others near the pile, though he does note that Kali has not joined them.

"They probably belong to someone else," Kali proclaims. "Since I never had any armour when they kidnapped me, I am not touching it. That is just thieving."

Looking from Kali to Trystan and back again, they all stand back up as the large man continues pulling out some choice pieces and trying a few on.

"Kali's right," Conn says with a sigh. "We should just leave it where it is and continue on."

"Only if ya don't want ta make it out alive," Trystan snorts at her before pulling out a toughened leather breastplate. Trying it against himself, he then discards it and pulls out a second. "This should fit me better," he says as he pulls it on over his head and letting it fall around his body with a nod of satisfaction before tying it up.

"But it is wrong to take things that don't belong to you," Reuben says, continuing to puzzle things through. "That's what my Aunt always said."

"When someone comes at ya with a pig sticker or something larger, then ya'll wish that ya did 'ave something more solid than that shirt on ya back," Trystan tells him. "Now stop yer bleating and put something on that'll 'elp protect ya!"

"Maybe we can get out of here without the need to rob those that came before us," Conn says hopefully, as he goes to stand by Kali.

"Well, I ain't taking that chance," declares Ghorza as she pulls out several pieces that look as if they will fit her size. After asking Reuben to help her, she settles on some hide tabard-style armour that is slightly too large for her except for perfectly fitting around her chest. It appears to have been made for a broad Human male.

"But this is wrong," Kali tries again to appeal to their better sense of judgement.

"Sorry Kali, but Ghorza and Trystan are right. I'm going to use it if I can find something half decent amongst this pile," Reuben tells her kneeling to where Ghorza also helps him. "Besides, I'm not stealing it, just borrowing it for a while. I believe even my Aunt would agree to that."

Eventually, they find Reuben a suit of leather that so accommodates his stature, it is like the armour was made for him.

"Okay, if we're only borrowing it, then help me find something for myself please," Conn asks them. After the fifth attempt, they find a leather cuirass for him, and, nearer the bottom of the pile, there is a small wooden shield though the leather covering has long since disintegrated to leave the boards bare.

"Well, even if it is borrowed, I'm still not taking any of it," Kali tells them just before the door opens to allow two averagely built Humans and a fat-faced Goblin to enter.

The older Human is carrying a wooden box with a cord handle filled with an assortment of carpentry tools in one hand and the other has some lengths of wood under each arm. The Goblin's yellow eyes go wide, and he bolts.

"Ah'll be glad ta git this 'ere room done, Ilias. Ah suren does not like that Sorcerer that hired us," the one with the toolbox says to his companion.

"Ah totally agree," Ilias replies as he then sees the room's current occupants. "Er, Tarild. What did he say if we 'ave a problem wiv intruders?"

"Stop 'em," he replies, realising their escort has gone.

Tarild turns around after shutting the door. He then snatches a hammer from the toolbox before he lets the box fall upon seeing the group. Ilias, following his older friend's cue, drops everything but a length of two by four as he prepares to attack as well. "Now people, 'ow about you stop what ya doing an' return ta ya nice cosy cell," the virtually bald man tells them condescendingly. His accent betrays him as one of the more northern folks to Kali's and Reuben's ears. The only hair he has is long brown and greasy looking over his ears and round the back of his head.

"Like 'ell are we going back there," Trystan growls as he advances on Tarild with Reuben right behind him.

Ghorza moves with Conn towards the puny-looking Human called Ilias.

The younger man brushes his long brown hair over his head before taking a two-handed grip on his length of wood, looking worryingly up at the half breed who stands a good head and shoulders over him. In the lands he is from, such people are found among the nomadic Barbarians that follow the herds north of the Hāmō Montes mountains.

Ilias looks at the two against him and decides to swing at the 'more normal' of his opponents, cracking Conn in the ribs. Conn's newly acquired cuirass absorbs the worst of the impact. Then Ilias realises his mistake when Ghorza grabs the two by four out of his hands and brings it down squarely on his head. The bar snaps in two before she drops it next to the fallen man.

Tarild swings at Trystan, who manages to step back before retaliating to crack him on his jaw. This seems to have little effect since the Northerner goes to swing at him again.

Suddenly, an arm lances around Tarild's throat. He jerks, colour drains quickly from his face. When the arm disappears, Tarild drops to the floor to reveal Reuben standing there, a bloody chisel in his wet hand. He pales at what he has just done without even thinking about it.

"Well done!" Trystan praises him before noticing how he looks. "You okay boy?"

Reuben nods his answer, walks over to a corner, and empties what little contents of his stomach were remaining. That is the first time he ever did that to his knowledge, and he is still uncertain as to how he knew to use their own fight as a distraction while slipping behind Tarild to scoop up the fallen chisel. Let alone where to stab it for the best effect with the supporting arm around the man's neck. The only people he has ever heard to do that were a very few select members of the Guilde Kallun back in Brackston. And those few people were the ones to avoid at all costs.

Trystan turns away from the boy in the corner with a wince to see Conn looking over the one called Ilias before nodding with a smile to a much-relieved Ghorza.

It appears that she did not kill him this time, though she does rip up a piece of armour into strips to bind the unconscious one's wrists and ankles. She also makes a thick wadding tied into place with another strip to gag him for when Ilias wakes up.

"You okay boy, after taking a hit like that?" Trystan asks Conn walking over to them.

Looking up at the large man, he nods and confesses to only some bruising.

Kali looks on in stunned disbelief, though she is uncertain whether that is because at how fast it happened or that it happened in the first place.

When Conn answers the man, Kali recovers enough to scoff. "What's up with you?" he asks her bluntly, receiving a filthy look by way of an answer. "I can return the armour later. I'm just lucky not to wind up with a couple of cracked ribs after a hit like that," he snaps at her.

"You okay boy?" Trystan smiles at the interaction between Conn and Kali while he speaks to Reuben. The young man nods his head.

Ghorza hands him a partially filled water skin that she found on one of the workers. She did find a second one, but that one had burst.

Reuben takes a swig to rinse his mouth out and then thanks her, handing it back.

"If you have all quite finished, then we should carry on getting out of here before anyone else turns up," Kali says without even looking at Conn, still being terribly upset by what she considers a betrayal after he refused to forgo the armour. *Being a worshipper of Unda, he should know better.*

Conn, with a wave of his arm at her, storms off through the door the workers came through back into the corridor and on the room next door with Reuben frantically and futilely calling him to stop. Though, once through the door, Conn does stop when he looks around.

CHAPTER 18

Armed Escort

"Conn. What is it?" Reuben calls out, his voice almost bordering on fear. He then moves to the side of the doorway before looking through.

"We now have weapons," Conn whispers to him, the smells of cleaning oils and abrasive powders mixed in with the stale air tickling his nose. "Though I think I also just heard a hinge squeak from somewhere close by."

"What ya got in there boy?" Trystan booms joining them and then marching into the room. He sees that two-thirds of the long room have various melee weapons, while the far end has missile weapons.

"Quiet," Reuben admonishes the large man. When the goat herder glares at him, he hurriedly tries to explain. "We may have company soon."

"Well, let us get prepared fer what comes then I say," Trystan says with a nod. Kali and Ghorza are right behind him to hear the concern in Reuben's voice.

They enter the room to see freshly made racks along the wall and more racks reaching out into the room half-filled with various weapons, those with metal blades and hilts are all made with bronze. A table against the opposing wall contains a wooden-handled weapon with a single-edged slightly curved blade on one end where the handle is two-thirds the length of the bronze blade, a rhomphaia, with cleaning equipment and sharpening stones beneath two lit torches. The only other exit is in the opposing wall. Sawdust swirls around with their movements.

"We cannot just help ourselves," the Half-Elf starts to tell them.

"Then don't and die," Trystan snaps at her grabbing a bronze-headed spear and testing its weight.

"But they are not ours to take," she persists.

"Sorry Kali, but if it is a matter of them or us, then I'm taking these," Reuben tells her strapping a sword scabbard with a short bronze sword and a dagger in a sheath to his waist and then hesitates when putting a dagger in each boot. There is something about equipping himself in this way. He finishes what he is doing and decides that now is not the time to dwell on it too much,

"Take this for now," Ghorza tells her as she gives the flustered Half-Elf a staff. Kali looks at her disapprovingly before Ghorza finishes speaking. "Even if it is only until we get out of here. Staffs are a tin ring a dozen back at Deepore. I'll buy you your own then if you really get on with this one." Kali nods quietly in surrender to the Half-Orc's surprising logic.

Ghorza then spies the weapon on the table. She used to love watching it in play when she was still in the mountain settlement. It was one of the exceedingly rare fond memories she has of her birth home. She reaches out for the two-handed weapon as if in a dream, even though no female Orc was ever allowed to wield any weapons beyond that of a dagger in any of the tribes around where she was born. She did watch the men wield it to great effect and with surprising grace for such a naturally brutal race.

Conn picks up a heavy bronze-headed mace and tests it before choosing a lighter version. He theorises that while he may cause more damage with the heavier weapon, it would soon prove useless if he is not strong enough to be able to keep swinging it. He knows that he is not as strong as Ghorza or Trystan who could probably keep using it till the fish came in.

"You might want to grab something smaller in this room," Reuben points out to Ghorza while taking cover behind the weapon rack arm closest to the maintenance table, while Kali steps back into the corridor with Conn. Ghorza looks at him quizzically where he then whispers harshly for her to get down, hearing the voices start growing louder. It seems that they have heard some people approaching before she did. She ducks beside the young man, noticing Trystan crouching behind another rack with a spear in front of them.

The door opens to spill a bright light into their room and allow some more Hobgoblins with torches into the room when the first one stops and sniffs the air upon entering. He mutters something to his companions, where Ghorza recognises it as a more guttural version of the goblin tongue. The first one is warning the others to be wary. The creatures each ready a club as they begin to move through the room.

Trystan is the first one to stand up and stabs at the first creature, catching it in the stomach. Growling in pain, it brings its club straight down on the spear shaft to try to break Trystan's weapon, only to push the weapon down into its dark reddish-brown hairy abdomen, causing more harm to itself. A second of these nearly six-foot-tall creatures jumps Trystan's hiding place to crash into the big man, causing him to lose his grip on the spear. Another one shoves the injured creature into the brawling pair to continue past, not caring that the bronze-tipped spear punches straight through the howling creature's upper spine, ending its life.

The third creature glances round with his pale yellowish eyes briefly to ensure that Trystan is entangled enough to be unable to prevent his progress. He fails to notice Ghorza. The last Hobgoblin follows him in.

She jumps up from behind the second rack arm and slices with all her strength to take the creature's head straight off its shoulders, burying her weapon deep into the door jamb beside her.

Reuben spots the immediate problem with Ghorza struggling to free her weapon. He slides his slender build straight under the rack to get a boot to the ribs from Trystan's struggle for his effort. The fourth creature, shoving his beheaded companion into Ghorza, then slams his club straight onto her shoulder.

Conn steps into the room from the armour store to swing his newly acquired bronze mace up between the creature's legs at the same time Reuben thrusts his short sword straight into its lower back to angle up into his lungs.

Trystan finally manages to elbow the heavier creature in the side of the head and then grabs its club to bring it down on the back of its skull with such force to cave it in. When he finally struggles back to a standing position, they see that one of his eyes is closed and blood is pouring from his nose, Ghorza nurses her left shoulder and Reuben, his ribs.

Ghorza then notices the beheaded creature and looks around quizzically. "Who took the Hobgoblin's head off?" she asks the room in general.

"Hobgoblin? Erm, you did," Conn answers hesitantly.

"Right before you buried your weapon in the door jamb," adds Reuben.

"Oh, I know my rhomphaia got stuck. I had to open my eyes to find out why it wouldn't move anymore." They all look at her, stunned. "I didn't really do that, did I?"

When they nod, still shocked at her reply, she races back into the corridor and throws up.

Kali picks herself up from the floor where she only just dives out of the Half-Orc's way to avoid being flattened.

Conn follows Ghorza and tries to help by rubbing her back till she finds herself dry heaving. He is thankful that none of them have eaten at this point.

When she returns to the room wiping her mouth, it is apparent that Reuben and Trystan have gone through the Hobgoblins belt pouches and found some more vials of amber liquid. Trystan downs one and Reuben hands one to Ghorza for each of them to take now. Within a minute, their injuries and pain evaporate as if blown away on a summer's breeze, as Trystan describes it.

"How do you know that these are Hobgoblins?" Conn asks Ghorza after she finally frees the weapon from the door jamb and locates the cradle to strap it across her back. The Half-Orc looks around the room and then belts a short sword to her waist as a secondary weapon while she answers him.

"Used to see them every now and then. Trading with the tribe, usually forcing Goblins to carry their wares, then more after I fled before living in Deepore Settlement. They're vicious bastards."

"Better we finish this lot off now then," Trystan says flippantly. He then checks them over, using a knife to slice the throats of those struggling to breathe.

"If everyone is ready, then I suggest we get out of here soon as," Kali says irritably. From the goat herder's oh so casual comment, his even more casual action to the dying and to distance herself from their odour which proves repellent to her sensitive nose. *Would he treat any of us with as little regard if any of us fall?*

They head straight to the freshly made racks at the end of the room that hold missile weapons of various designs with a shelf above them holding different types of ammunition and smaller weapons.

There are wood and bone bows, and half a dozen throwing spears with flint or bronze heads carefully constructed for optimum balance. On the shelf above the weapons rack, are a dozen throwing knives, three quivers holding a dozen bronze or stone-tipped arrows in each, and a sling with a small pile of rounded stones next to it. The one weapon that draws Kali's eye is a solitary harpoon.

When she draws the weapon from the rack, she can see that the weapon originates from the southern territories just by the designs carefully etched along its length. She has only ever seen one such weapon like this and that belongs to her settlement's founder, Kuede Simba, before he passed it on to his only surviving son. Turning around, she then notices the others looking at her with expressions ranging from smugness to bewilderment.

Conn just looks accusingly at her. *After all her speeches about not stealing other people's property and she goes and takes that. The hypocrite,* he fumes to himself.

"If I am right, this harpoon belongs to the family of our settlement's founder who came from the south to settle at Palovicus. Before he died, he gave this to his son," she tells them rather defensively. "I mean to find his son and take Kito and his weapon back."

"Wherever he is," Reuben says with a snigger and drawing a murderous look from Kali.

"Whatever," Conn mutters, though Kali's sensitive ears still catch it.

"I don't know what any of ya are doing, but I'm taking a bow," Trystan bluntly tells them, grabbing a quiver of arrows at the same time. As he intends, he manages to focus everybody's attention to their predicament and where they are right now.

Reuben also picks up one of the short bows and ensures that he has a quiver of bronze-headed arrows; Ghorza takes a short spear and gives Kali a couple of throwing daggers with a, just borrowing explanation.

Kali just swallows and nods her head in thanks.

Conn, thinking back to his multiple failed attempts at the throwing games he used to play when he was growing up, decides to remain with the mace and shield. He knows that he is not the strongest person of the group, and he feels that he will probably do more harm to his new friends than he would to any others if he starts using them.

Once they are ready, they head for the next door out of the room.

CHAPTER 19

Ambushed

Kali feels so upset that she is being dragged into the others' attempt at petty thievery while being judged by them for wanting to do right by her settlement's founders that she just pulls open the door. *As soon as we get out of this place the better, and the sooner I can return these-,* she staggers back a couple of steps, a sharp pain erupts from her stomach. Looking down quizzically, she sees an arrow protruding from her abdomen, the shaft still quivering as she falls to the floor. A second arrow shatters itself on the door near where she was standing.

Trystan leaps for the door to slam it shut again before turning round to face the others. "We are under attack!" he declares with a curse.

"We sort of figured that one out for ourselves!" Reuben snaps at the man while he, Conn, and Ghorza move swiftly to Kali.

"I need you all to keep her as still as possible while I get the arrow out," Conn tells them all in a calmer tone than he truly feels. His heart is beating so fast it feels like it is trying to bash its way out through his chest. He looks to Trystan and the others in turn. "I need you to hold her shoulders down and keep her there. Reuben, you hold her legs and pull her straight. Ghorza, I need you to keep her waist as still as you can."

The pointy-nosed Goblin nudges its larger brute of a cousin to look down to him. It then points two fingers of one hand to his eyes and then points down the hallway. When the Hobgoblin nods and waits until a clear shot presents itself, the Goblin darts off in the opposite direction. Another Hobgoblin with their bow is similarly hidden halfway down the corridor.

"Okay, Boy. What are ya going ta do while yer busy throwing orders around," Trystan demands. His brassy voice almost deafens Conn due to the proximity of their heads. The older man forces Kali's shoulders down to the floor and causes her to scream in agony where she tries to roll on to her side back into the foetal position.

"Getting out the arrow and covering her wound," he answers almost distractedly.

When the Half-Elf settles down again to a whimper, forced into this uncomfortable position, tears trickling down her now much paler face. It does not help that Reuben has her legs pulled straight out and Ghorza presses her waist to the floor. Kali cries out at the fresh spasm of pain erupting from her injury, but she cannot move to make herself more comfortable.

Ignoring Kali's cries of protestations, Conn wipes his forehead with his sleeve. He then presses down on either side of the wound with one hand and gently tugs on the arrow shaft with the other, testing to see if the head is catching on anything internal. Feeling no hindrances, he carefully eases the arrow out, readjusting his grip around the bloody shaft until all that remains is the arrow's head.

All the while, Kali moans and her eyes stream while he works.

Taking a deep breath to steady his nerves, Conn gently pulls the stone arrowhead out, causing Kali to jerk hard enough for Ghorza, Reuben, and Trystan to lose their grip, allowing her to return to the foetal. He is surprised that the arrowhead looks intact, knowing how notorious they are for shattering on impact. Breathing a sigh of relief, Conn then tells Ghorza to push Kali onto her back and to place her hand over the freshly bleeding wound. He races back to the workbench and grabs a handful of rags, then returns to Kali's side.

"Mr. Gibbs, can you make sure that no one comes through that door while we bandage her wound?" he asks, sorting through the rags for the best ones. He then lifts Ghorza's hand long enough to shove one of them over the entry wound before returning the Half-Orc's hand to maintain the pressure for a moment longer. Trystan looks at him in surprise, nods, and places his back against the door while they finish helping Kali.

Folding up another rag several times and placing it to one side, Conn then begins to tear the rest up into wide strips with Reuben helping him. Through Ghorza's help, Conn gets the Half-Elf into a sitting position, causing her to whine weakly. Replacing the sodden rag with the folded piece under Conn's directions, Ghorza holds the wadding against Kali's wound long enough for him to wrap the strips around her, where Kali finally passes out.

Conn looks fearfully at the ivory-toned girl whose complexion has become a more porcelain quality, her grey highlights paling into virtual obscurity.

The Goblin returns to continue its vigil beside its larger brute of a cousin with a quick nod to it and waits to fire its own stone-tipped arrows at the door.

"Are you OK Chara?" Reuben asks him, anxious at seeing Conn's complexion pale.

"I really need some herbs or poultices to help her right now," he answers quietly. "Or, I fear, that we may still lose her. She's lost a lot of blood."

Trystan then jerks with a start, causing the others to jump in fear or surprise and making them think that someone from behind the door has attacked him. He pats a pocket and then shoves his hand in to pull out a tiny vial filled with an amber liquid. "I just remembered that I still have this. Can she still use it, or would it be better to hold on to it for now?"

"Where did you get that from?" Conn demands.

"Don't get snippy with me boy! Skarmazh! Where else do you think I got it?" he snaps back. "When we knocked 'im out! It's not like any of ya remembered that we 'ad it!"

"May I have it to help Kali?" Conn says, suitably abashed and apologetic at the same time. He thought he saw Mr. Gibbs pocket something back in the cell, now he knows what it was. Right now, he is only too glad that the man is coming through for Kali.

Studying the boy who is still holding the Half-Elf's hand, he finally hands the precious liquid over. "That's better. 'ere you go and be careful with it."

He watches the young lad open the vial and carefully lifts Kali's neck slightly to cause her head to drop back and open the unconscious girl's mouth. Keeping it slow, he trickles the amber liquid in where her throat reflexively swallows it down until the entire potion is gone. Within a few heartbeats, her breathing comes much easier and steadier, gaining strength with each passing second.

"Now that she's on the mend, do ya mind if we think of a way past the 'idden bowmen?" While he is relieved that Kali is healing, all Trystan wants to do is to move forward. He knows that they will not leave her behind, even if that leaves them all at risk, but standing still getting nothing done is just driving him insane. *It's as if they do not realise, that the kind of danger they're in is liable ta get them all killed.* But he also knows that he is not brave enough to try it on his own; even if that means that he may have a chance to see his wife and children that much sooner.

In answer to Trystan's request, Reuben gets up and asks to look through the door to find out what he can see.

"Yer nuts boy. It's dark as night out there and they are liable to shoot you with their arrows!"

"I can see in the dark," Ghorza chimes in, her throaty voice calm and steady. "Could I look for you and tell you what I see?"

"That's inspired Ghorza," Reuben tells her with a broad smile. "But keep your head low and they will have a better chance to miss you if they shoot."

"Yer all-bleeding nuts," Trystan says with a frown as the Half-Orc nods and lies on her front near the door.

The instant he opens the door again, three arrows come flying out of the darkness to strike the sturdy door. Ghorza uses her arms to slide across the floor enough for her to lookout. Several more arrows shower her in feathered shafts and shattered stone. Her eyes automatically shifting into the greyscale sight, that all Orc breeds have, to reveal a long corridor. She sees some movement about halfway down and two more at the end, all in partial cover. Three more arrows strike the door, one of them almost catching her. Convinced that she has seen enough, she quickly scrabbles back into the room where Trystan quickly closes the door. There is an accompaniment of squeaking hinges louder than before, though it does not come from their door.

"That was strange," Reuben declares.

"That was not this door, but another from further on," Trystan answers him. "Someone else is out there, probably more of what is shooting at us."

"Never mind that now," Reuben says with a shake of his shoulder-length ginger hair. "What did you see Ghorza?" While she describes the passageway, a plan starts to form in his mind. "What we need is a shield," he says once she finishes.

"Here, take mine," Conn tells him. When they look to the young man, he offers the round wooden shield he took from the pile of armour.

They notice that Kali is looking much better, even getting most of her colour back in her cheeks. She has not woken up just yet, but Conn is not so worried now since that could be because she did lose a lot of blood. Much of it now decorating the front of her dress.

Trystan is about to take the shield and thanks Conn, but Reuben tells them that it is too small for his plan to work.

"What is it that you're planning to require a larger shield fer then?" Trystan demands.

"I'm thinking of a shield tall enough for us to hide behind so we can move down the passage without the fear of arrows hitting us."

"What you need is a door or a table," Ghorza says quietly.

"Exactly," Reuben mumbles and then suddenly brightens with the realization of what she has said. "Exactly," he says excitedly. "Ghorza, come with me."

He races back to the weapons maintenance bench where he up-ends the table to spill the contents onto the floor before she realises what he has in mind. They carry it to the door and try to angle it through without exposing themselves, but the table catches in the doorway. They twist and turn it but after a few close calls from the arrows, Reuben curses that the legs are getting in the way.

Ghorza drags it back into the room, then breaks off two of them from one long side, taking the supporting braces out binding the legs together.

It proves no problem to get the table through now, though it will never be able to be used as a table afterward as it is.

He then gets Ghorza to stab a dagger through the table about halfway down the side where she broke the legs off and declares that they are ready. Reuben then explains his plan.

"You're nuts," a sleepy Kali tells them.

"That's what I keep telling them," snaps Trystan.

"Are you sure that this is going to work?" Ghorza wonders hesitantly, looking to the excitable young man.

"Trust me. I know what it sounds like, but of course it will," Reuben answers with more confidence than he actually feels. Then the doubts start creeping in. *It had better work now; else, none of them is liable to speak to me ever again.* The irony of his thought does not escape him.

"OK," Trystan breathes opening the door whilst keeping well behind it.

Ghorza works the table through into the dark hallway. More arrows strike the door and the tabletop before she gets it properly into position.

Conn guides a waking Kali out of the way of the door and removes the bandages to check on her wound. All he sees now is an angry red spot which is fading while he looks at her smooth ivory stomach. He then rolls up the makeshift bandages and tucks them into the waistband of his trousers.

"Might need them again if this does not work," he whispers to Kali when she looks at him in puzzlement. She then nods in an understanding of his meaning.

Ghorza lifts the table by the leg nearest her shoulder, and the dagger enough to allow her to walk and to see over the top without exposing her head too much at Reuben's suggestion. Progressing down the hallway slowly, more arrows thud into the tabletop, many of the stone heads shattering against the surface judging from the fragments left on the floor when Trystan's low burning torch illuminates them.

"Just remember kid. When we reach our attackers ya aim ta kill. **Not** to injure, but ta kill them," Trystan whispers harshly to Reuben while they follow close behind Ghorza and the makeshift shield. Reuben nods solemnly, adjusting his grip on his short sword and dagger.

More arrows strike the table where one of the heads manages to punch through near Ghorza's face. She jerks the table up enough for a stone arrow to skitter off her shin, nearly causing her to lose her grip. The Half-Orc's quick reflexes allow her to rapidly catch the falling table just in time to prevent another two arrows from striking into them. Readjusting her grip on the wedged dagger and the leg, she continues forward at a slightly quicker pace.

Reuben is wondering if they will ever get anywhere any time soon when the doorway to his left suddenly appears.

Trystan drops the torch and launches in, knocking Ghorza forward in his haste. He thrusts his spear into the Hobgoblin's gut hiding there, forcing it against the back wall of the room. The creature does not even have time to cry out. "Damned Hobgoblin!" Trystan curses, stabbing it twice more for good measure. He then hears a human and a husky roar from further down the hallway. Looking out, he sees that Reuben has his dropped torch and they are charging. Ghorza crashes straight into the wall at the end where the passageway turns sharply.

The Half-Orc crushes a Goblin with several of the broken arrow shafts and the protruding dagger piercing the creature.

Reuben withdraws his sword from a second Hobgoblin.

Ghorza looks at the crushed Goblin and the ruined table. She shrugs and drops it on the floor.

"You okay?" Reuben asks her with some concern.

"It'll never catch on as a body shield," she answers him flatly. "Too damned heavy."

The young man laughs clapping her on the shoulder. "You're beautiful Ghorza. Don't you let anyone tell you different," he says with a chuckle, making her smile at her new friend.

One of her own age at long last?

"Oh, 'ow bloody sweet," Trystan comments; provoking murderous glares from Reuben and Ghorza when he joins them. "Ah just meant on 'ow ya took out those two," he lies hastily. They both seem to believe him when they return to Conn and Kali at the new room they just passed. They note that Kali looks much better after using their last healing potion.

"So, what 'ave we found now?" Trystan calls out as they regroup.

"It is just a storeroom. Nothing more," Kali answers him with a shrug.

"A storage area for additional torches and outdoor clothes, by the looks of it," Conn clarifies, giving her a look.

"OK, let's see what we can pick up here," Trystan says with a smile. He notices Kali shaking her head disapprovingly, but just ignores her condescending look.

"What have we got here?" Reuben calls when he and Ghorza reach them.

"Clothing," Trystan calls out from inside the room. "'ey! I found a few cloaks in 'ere. Including me own," he says with a glare at Kali, stepping out as he put his well-used brown full-length woollen cloak embroidered with a Golden Dragon on. "I'm glad I found this again. Me wife made it me for our wedding day. Worn it ever since."

"You have a wife?" Kali looks at him incredulously. He just glares back at her like she was a bit of goat's dung on the bottom of his boot.

"I guess you won't want this then," he snarls as he holds up a full-length mottled brown cloak he vaguely recognises. He grins evilly as he sees her face drop in stunned silence. She takes it from him with an embarrassed quietness. He notes that she cannot even meet his gaze at all now.

She just puts her cloak on quietly.

Conn finds a pale blue cloak that drops to his knees and a pair of surprisingly clean brown trousers making him feel warmer soon after putting them on. He had not realised how cold he was feeling

Ghorza discovers a pair of wolf fur boots to replace her sandals and a cloak that hangs down to her knees, though on a Human it would be full-length. She wears it with one shoulder exposed so that she can still get to her rhomphaia and short spear should she need to.

Reuben finds a pair of soft boots to replace his own ruined pair and a charcoal grey three-quarter cape with an additional piece to cover his shoulders.

"Right, let's go before anyone else turns up," Trystan orders when they are ready.

CHAPTER 20

Trapped

They return to the corner where the Goblinoids met their brutal end. They are about to turn the corner when Reuben frantically calls out. "Stop, Ghorza!" before she rounds the corner. He takes the lead and listens once again. Breathing a sigh of relief, he nods to the others that it is safe before snapping his head back round. He cannot see anyone there, though he is sure he hears a faint chuckle from the far end of the corridor when the others join him.

"What is it?" Ghorza whispers at seeing his distraction. He just holds up a hand for silence where even Trystan remains quiet for a change.

"*Obtestor laqueus tendicula.*"

"Move it!" Reuben calls loudly leaping forward with Ghorza close behind, albeit briefly.

An indigo glowing net erupts from the walls on either side of them catching everyone except Reuben. He looks up to where the voice came from to see a close-cropped bearded man in an indigo cloak holding a staff shimmer into appearance standing beside another door. Looking back, he sees that Ghorza and Trystan have the best chance to escape the magical snare trap, but there is no chance for Conn and Kali to get out so easily. He also catches the confusion in Ghorza's expression when she looks at the spellcaster.

"Ghorza! Just concentrate on breaking out of it," Reuben calls, drawing her attention to him. She gives him a quick nod and continues to struggle at the conjured mesh. Reuben returns his gaze to the man and draws his short sword. "Release my friends. Now!"

The man looks at him and smiles thinly. *"Carmen persōna,"* he says calmly.

Reuben feels a strange sensation wash through his mind. Shaking his head, he returns his attention to the man and continues advancing on the Sorcerer.

"You really do not want to hurt me, my friend, do you?" Reuben lowers his sword as he looks upon the man. *He does not seem so bad to me. Why am I trying to attack him?*

"Sorcerer!" Trystan's brassy voice cuts through the noise of Ghorza, Conn, and Kali struggling against their magical binding. He has managed to get his arms free. "I'm going ta kill ya!" he calls, raising his short bow to take aim.

"Will you defend me against your friends? That bellicose man is trying to hurt me," he says to Reuben. The young man turns to face Trystan, drawing his dagger, though he just stands in front of his new friend.

"Outta the way boy! I don't want ta hit you!" Trystan calls out to him. Reuben refuses to move, drawing a curse from the man as he lowers his bow slightly.

"Treorai! What have you done to him?" Ghorza yells, pulling her leg free of the strands at last.

"They are a feisty lot. Would you not agree boy?" comments the Wizard. "Still, needs must I suppose." He draws one hand up over Reuben's shoulder as if holding out a gift. *"Alacritas iacula,"* he whispers.

Two glowing bolts of pure energy appear in his hand before directing one towards Trystan. The other at Ghorza who seems to be the closest to escaping his magical net.

As the bolts strike unerringly on their targets, Reuben screams out, "No!!!" He spins on Treorai with murder in his eyes but finds that he can make no move against the man.

The battering from the bolts Ghorza receives leaves her severely weakened but does virtually release her from the magical net. Launching herself forward with the last of her strength and snapping the last of the strands, she knocks Reuben aside and falls beside him as the Sorcerer taps his staff on the floor twice. Trystan raises his bow once again and shoots when he sees Ghorza strike Reuben. As the arrow flies towards the Sorcerer, a glowing portal shaped like a doorway appears just in front of Treorai.

With a self-satisfied smile, he calmly steps through and disappears with the portal closing just before the arrow is about to strike home, only to splinter against the wall at the end of the hallway.

"Damn it!" Trystan curses as the last of the magical lattice eventually starts to dissipate.

"What did he hit us with? That bloody hurt," Ghorza exclaims with a wince.

"It looked like an energy bolt," Kali says thoughtfully. Watching Lippio work on sheets of parchment for another arcane wielder, she learnt something about the magic they use.

While he cannot cast them himself, he does have the rudiments to allow him to write the scrolls for Sorcerers too busy to do their own. Those very few that trust him too at least. Her mother being his primary client. It was also her mother who taught him how to read and inscribe the magical runes, though he never really got to grips with the arcane arts. When she got back, he said he would teach her what he knows so that she can help him with them. *Though, when that will be, I have no idea.*

"Well, it bloody well hurt," she tells the Half-Elf vehemently.

"I can have a quick look, if you want me to," Conn offers.

"Are ya alright boy?" Trystan asks, looking to Reuben and drawing everyone's attention to him.

"I think so, just not sure what happened," Reuben answers with a frown. "I'll be fine. How's Ghorza?"

Conn looks to the Half-Orc who just nods her ascent for him to have a look. He carefully pulls her Hide jerkin aside to reveal a circle of severely dark bruising on her chest near her ample cleavage. He then turns his attention to Trystan to find that he has a similar bruise centred on his chest. He then tells them what he finds, but there is nothing that he can do right now.

"I suggest we keep going then," Ghorza says tiredly.

"We really need to rest," Trystan comments drily.

"I agree with you, but that Sorcerer knows where we are now," Reuben tells him. "So, I agree with Ghorza. We go on." With everyone nodding in agreement, he catches Ghorza's surprised look that someone should agree with her about anything, and he smiles at her. Reuben then listens for anything beyond the door and whatever surprises await them there.

CHAPTER 21

Supplies

After a few seconds, Reuben is satisfied that there is no one beyond the door that may jump them upon entering. He then checks for any traps. He still has no idea how he knows these strange skills, but at this moment in time, he does not care either. Once he is satisfied that he has checked out everything thoroughly, Reuben then opens the door to the sound of squeaking hinges.

"I guess that explains the sound we heard way back in the weapons store," Reuben winces, knowing that if anyone is nearby then he has just alerted them to their presence.

They enter a room and even Kali stops to look on in amazement. The room has shelves and racks containing everything anyone needs from those residing in settlements to merchants and other travellers, from packs to the thick blankets typical of this region. Near another door leading out of the room, there are half a dozen small sacks holding nothing but rings and axe heads of copper and bronze, and silver nuggets of refined ore. One silver nugget being the most valuable ever mined in the area, two ounces being worth twenty-one tin, thirty-five bronze or seventy-seven copper rings, with each axe head being equal to four of each. Though the tin, bronze, and copper rings are the most used for trade exchanges.

When Reuben looks at the sacks, he estimates that each one could hold a hundred and fifty rings and axe heads of any denomination. *With just one sack full of bronze, I could leave Brackston and just travel or settle down with my own bakery business in another settlement. Maybe as an expansion to aunt and uncle's business to begin the Bunner name as a brand in all homes. Now, that would be something.* He suddenly has a feeling intruding on his mind and turns round to see Kali glaring at him like she can read his thoughts. He looks away to see Ghorza looking worriedly about something. Ignoring Kali entirely, he walks over to the Half-Orc. "Are you alright there? You do not seem so taken with the room as the rest of us." He glances at Kali who is still looking at everyone in the room in that accusing way of hers while Trystan and Conn discuss how best to divide up the room's contents. "As most of us are," he finishes.

"It was that Sorcerer who we met in the hallway," she says with barely a whisper.

"Yes. Nice bloke. What of him?" *Nice bloke? He nearly killed us!*

"Nice bloke? He nearly killed us!" Ghorza suddenly fumes at him and drawing everyone's attention to her sudden increase in volume.

"Hey, hey, hey. What's all this about?" Conn says moving swiftly to intervene.

"Sorry, Ghorza. I, I, I don't know why I said that?" Reuben stammers, alternately looking fearful and confused.

"I'm sure Reuben did not mean it that way Ghorza," Conn says, quickly catching the gist of what he overheard and stepping between her and the perplexed young man. "From what I saw, it looked like Reuben fell under an enchantment of some sort, wouldn't you agree Kali?" he says, looking desperately hopeful to her for confirmation.

"What?" she snaps at him for disrupting her disgruntled thoughts. "Oh, yes. I suppose it did," she spits out sharply.

"What is it with you now?" Conn wonders aloud, confused by her response.

"You lot are unbelievable. You're asking me what's wrong when you're the ones who are dividing up the room for your own personal gain like common thieves and you expect me to be fine with that!"

"You're the one who's unbelievable!" Conn snaps back. "You're stressing out over what we are doing for our own survival to get out of this place and what comes after, while one of our friends are about to rip another's head off! By the gods, you really need to sort your priorities out."

"My priorities? My priorities are simply fine! We do not stop for anything until we are out of this place for once and for all. After all, it cannot be that big a complex, but it does seem to be taking an awfully long time to get out of here."

Trystan, while he is enjoying their argument, decides that it is high time he took control of the situation before they wind up with every creature and beast within a day's march turning up to kill them all. "I really 'ate ta interrupt yer fight ..."

"You do not hate it," Kali snipes.

"Well, no, actually I don't," he responds honestly with a nonchalant shrug. "But we ain't going ta go anywhere at all if we do not pick up the essentials ta 'elp us on the way outta 'ere. That also includes being prepared for whatever is ta come. Now if ya don't mind, let's get what we need so we can then get the flock outta 'ere. I do 'ave a farm that needs attending ta."

Everyone looks at Trystan in stunned silence at hearing him say so much in virtually a single breath, which also makes him feel uncomfortable. He turns his back on the kids to start gathering what he thinks they need in a pile.

"He's right," Reuben says, just to break the silence that suddenly descends on the room.

"Since you put it that way," Kali begins slowly and quietly. "I guess it would be okay. We could always try to return it to the rightful owners-"

"Kali," Conn says warningly.

"Fine. Let us just do this already," she sighs while going to see what Trystan is gathering in the middle of the room.

"Ghorza, I didn't mean to upset-" Reuben begins until she holds a hand up to him.

"Forget it. We need to get out of this shit hole first," Ghorza sharply tells him before joining Kali and Trystan.

Reuben looks to Conn who just shrugs with a sympathetic smile. He taps the young man's shoulder before joining the others.

"What have you got here to help us get out?" Kali asks Trystan tartly while he kneels to look through everything.

"We 'ave six packs; five belt pouches, two large and three smaller ones; seven candles; firewood ta last us a couple of days each; two cooking pots; two lanterns with three flasks of oil; a map case; two lengths of rope; seven sacks, five of those 'alf the size of the other two; seven tinder boxes, all partially used; three more water-skins; four sharpening stones and three good blankets," he itemises briefly. He then looks directly at Kali. "Some of these are what we'll need ta 'elp us get out of 'ere and back to the nearest settlement. The rest, cos we 'ave no idea where we are afore we find us a settlement."

"Do you have any idea where that is?" Conn asks him.

"I can't be certain, but that might be the settlement of Spire. That's where I met that spellcaster while tending my flock at any rate."

"How did you get in here then?" Ghorza wonders.

"I believe he used his magic ta get us inside."

"Us? Who else was with you?" Reuben begins to have a nasty suspicion that he does not like. Is this man possibly being in league with the Sorcerer? Though, whatever the reason is that he is working with them totally eludes him right now.

"There was an 'alf-Orc the Sorcerer called Krilge, much darker skin than you," he says looking to Ghorza. "Then there was a man called … what was 'e called?" Trystan's face creases up for a while. "Damned if I know now. Then there was a childlike woman and a dark-skinned woman."

"Lusha." The simple statement draws everyone's incredulous look to Conn. He then feels the need to explain. "She is the one I met back in Seaton. I think she drugged me."

"Wow," comments Reuben.

"Interesting friends you keep Conn," says Kali scathingly.

"As it seems to be about time for openness," Reuben interjects before another argument ensues. Conn just glares at Kali. "A Hauflin woman seemed injured when I went to help her before someone else struck me from behind. That was in Brackston. Could she be the same one as you saw?" This last question he directs to Trystan.

"I couldn't tell ya either way kid." Bored of the conversation already, Trystan starts dividing the pile he made in the middle of the floor, throwing the worst-looking backpack to one side.

"Alright then. Let us try and put this all together," Kali suggests. More focused on sorting through their individual encounters. Trystan practically ignores her, preferring to work through the tinder boxes for the best ones, then using the others to supplement the flint, stone, and tinder of those he has selected. She carries on unperturbed. "Conn meets this Lusha woman, ridiculous name if you ask me, in Seaton which is on the west coast."

"That's just over seven days from the Deepore settlement where you met Treorai, Ghorza," Conn offers helpfully.

"I do know. Deepore trades often with Seaton," she sharply responds. "The traders have to make rest stops at the various homesteads on the way, just as they do from Palovicus." Trystan just keeps loading the backpacks.

"I was only trying to help," he responds defensively.

"I do have ears that work-" she starts to retort before Kali cuts in quickly.

"And Reuben was at Brackston which is another fifteen days from where I was taken just north of Palovicus." Kali falls silent for a while as she thinks about what she has just stated. "Where was it that you were taken again, Sir?"

"Spire," he says distractedly, starting on the belt pouches.

"That's about ten days walking distance north of Palovicus," Kali exclaims almost excitedly. "And we were all together when you brought us here?" she persists, her excitement escalating slightly.

"Yes," he sighs.

"Then we must be somewhere in the middle," she breathes. "Or, at least, some way north of your Spire."

Trystan gives a snort. "In all honesty, Spire is nought more than a struggling Thorpe girlie. The glory of Spire died years afore I was born." He says with a sigh as he starts handing out packs and pouches to the others. "There's bugger all there ta be of use ta anyone now," he grumps.

"What has got you so excited?" Reuben asks her.

"When I was taken, I was on my way to my mother to deliver a copy of an incredibly old map about this area. She wanted Lippio to redraw this map with additional information included that she had gathered over the years relating specifically to a specific region surrounding the Hamo Montes range. This was in a time when Brackston and Seaton were humble settlements, Palovicus did not exist and Spire was the largest community in the region, though no one could find out why or how this one town could do so well for a long time until the Dwarfs of the Hamo Montes declared themselves openly as the protectors of Spire. Suddenly, the region begins to die, and the Dwarfs leave after being driven off by a flight of Dragons. This is all extremely exciting from a historical point of view. However,

Lippio and I still never knew why mother was so insistent on having him draw this map. The region has changed much in all that time."

"But not the geographical features," Conn added.

"But why would that still be important?" Kali says in confusion.

"The Dwarf kingdom beneath those mountains," Trystan answers her.

"If there was a Dwarf kingdom beneath those mountains somewhere, then there may still be a Dragon's worth of treasure there," Reuben suggests. "But how would you start to look for a hidden kingdom?"

"From the front door," Trystan replies. "But that is pointless since those doors 'aven't been opened in a 'undred years."

"You know where the front doors are?" Conn asks him incredulously.

"Look, right now this is absolutely pointless kids," he admonishes them. "We are going ta be enslaved or killed if we don't get the flock outta 'ere as soon as we can." He then notices that Kali has stopped paying any attention to what he is saying but is just staring at a wall instead. "Kali!"

Jumping, she looks to him, but not at him. "Does that wall look strange to you?"

"What are ya blabbering about now girlie?" he fumes.

The others start looking at the wall she has pointed out and then Reuben looks quickly around the room before returning his attention back to the first wall. "The other walls are all hewn whereas that one looks like more care has been taken on it."

"Exactly," she replies as she walks over to examine the smoother wall.

"What are ya doing?" Trystan demands. He begins to feel even more frustrated with her and her continuing delays. *What is it with this child? It's like she's not right in the 'ead.*

Kali studies the wall very closely for a minute or two and then starts pushing against sections until one part gives a little before popping back towards her briefly. "I think I have just found a faster way out of here," she says looking back with a smile. Pulling the door open, she grabs a torch off the wall and steps through with the others close behind her, carrying the packs and pouches Trystan has given them. Conn takes Kali's pack for now.

"No, you haven't," Ghorza begins.

"You've found another room," Reuben finishes. They both smile briefly.

"But why would anyone think that this room is so damned special?" Trystan gripes.

"Because of what it contains," Conn tells him, watching Kali step up to the shelves lining the far wall of this room. Trystan looks at him in confusion and then snaps his head round at the soft click that comes from behind him to see that the door has softly closed itself.

"Do not worry," Kali tells them distractedly as she begins to thumb her way through one of two tomes in here. "I know how to open it from the inside."

"What have you found there Kali?" Reuben wonders at the wood and parchment object in her hands.

"I've found some highly valued healing herbs," Conn whispers excitedly.

"This is the most exciting discovery of all so far," she tells him, her eyes sparkling. "I know what this is, but it is the first time that I have ever seen one up close," she says, excited once again. "This is a tome that a Sorcerer uses to cast their magic. Lippio has been contacted on the odd occasion, usually by my mother, to help write pages like these up. He is going to teach me how to do so myself once I get back to him, though a few of these spells I can actually understand now."

"So, what. We 'ave to be going and now!" Trystan demands, really starting to lose his rag with her now. *By the gods, if my girl acted like this, I'd 'ave slapped 'er already.* He then smiles in amusement to himself wistfully as another thought comes unbidden to him, though no one notices. *And Hai will slap me right back. If these kids don't start focusing on getting themselves out of 'ere, then I may even leave 'em ta it and take my chances.*

"I think we really need to rest for a while somewhere soon," Reuben says softly.

"I feel dead on my feet," Ghorza adds, rubbing her chest.

"How about we rest up here?" Conn suggests. "Kali, can we secure that door to stop anyone from opening up from the other side?"

"Hmm? Oh, yes." Kali moves over to the door and wedges a dagger under one side. Trystan and Ghorza look at her in confusion at the simplistic method. "We will be able to open it, but nobody can push it from the other side now."

"Well alright then. I guess that settles it," Trystan grumbles at yet another delay before they leave this infernal hole in the ground. He slumps down with his back against the secret door, not trusting the girl's theory. Though he is somewhat relieved to rest. For a short while, at least.

Conn goes to look at Trystan's injury from earlier, but a growl from the older man soon has him scampering off to check on Ghorza's instead. He mumbles quietly before telling her that there is truly little change in her injury and suggests that she takes it easy while she can.

Ghorza looks around and sees Reuben sitting against the far wall, using his pack as a cushion. She walks over and sits down beside him while Conn and Kali look over the shelves. "They could be at this for hours," she says quietly.

"I guess they could be," he mutters with a smile at her. He does not know how long they have been wandering around this place, but he suddenly feels tired now that they have stopped for a bit. "Trystan," he calls out. When the man looks up, the tiredness is also evident in his face judging from the drawn look he gives them. "What are in these packs and pouches that you gave us?"

"Why don't ya just look," he snaps. Trystan then takes a deep breath. "Well, since we're gonna ta be 'ere for a little while, I might as well tell ya." He says with a glare at Conn and Kali. "Oi, kids. Yer attention is required."

"This room has been ransacked already," Kali complains. "I would really love to know what else was here."

"Never mind that for now," Trystan says sharply. "I gave you each a pack and a pouch." He looks at each of them to ensure that he has their full attention and nods before continuing. "Good. Yer pouches all contain a tinder box and sharpening stone for yer blades." He looks to Kali. "Girlie, ya also 'ave candles since ya keep going on about yer precious Penman."

Conn and Kali nod at him, though they both decide not to disturb him since he seems so short-tempered right now.

"Now fer the packs," he continues. "We each 'ave a sack, though the boy and I 'ave a larger one as well," he tells them with a nod back to Conn. "Both of ya boys also 'ave a cooking pot. The 'alf-Orc and 'er friend over there also have a length of rope each, being the strongest members of ya all.

"The boys an girlie also 'ave an empty water-skin, though I 'ope to get 'em filled at the first chance we get. The boys and me each 'ave a blanket and Kali also 'as a map case. There is also a couple of days of trail rations and firewood in each pack. Use 'em wisely since we don't know 'ow long we're gonna be 'ere. Ya all happy with that? Good. Now keep it down cos I'm gonna get some shut-eye." Without another word, he pulls a blanket from his pack and uses it as a pillow where a promptly drops off to sleep with his back to the door.

"And that was the whistle-stop tour ladies and gentlemen," Reuben quips, causing the others to snicker quietly, trying not to disturb their companion. He then pulls his blanket out of his pack and hands it over to Ghorza who refuses it but thanks him all the same. She takes her wolf fur cloak off to cover herself with while using her pack as a pillow. He then calls softly to Conn and Kali. "Are you guys taking first watch then?"

"We will. Too much to look at right now," Kali whispers excitedly. "This tome has many spells that I can study while we have some time." She then focuses on studying.

"Well, alright then. Night guys." Reuben then settles his head on his pack, pulls out the cooking pot, then settles himself to soon drift off.

"Rest easy there," Conn answers him. He discovers a wooden box of holy symbols and even finds one for the Goddess of all Waters, Unda. Settling down while holding the wooden symbol, Conn reverently prays.

Conn sits down with the newly acquired holy symbol to Unda after lighting a fresh torch. As he examines the ripple effect on the symbol under the flame, the light makes the symbol seem to move and undulate much like the sea near his hometown. His mind falls under the apparent hypnotic effect where it is then set adrift to float beyond the boundaries of the Human Mind. At first, his journey is turbulent like a storm-wracked ocean, but the more he focuses, the calmer and more serene his voyage becomes to lands of new opportunities and discoveries.

Conn opens his eyes, more rested than he has ever felt before. He does not recall ever returning from his spiritual journey, but he does feel much more relaxed and energised. He even surprisingly notices that the small room has not filled up with smoke from the burning torches. It is only then that he realises the chill in the room.

Kali looks at the pages of the tome in her lap trying to force herself to understand the strange characters scratched on the sheets of parchment while they writhe and squirm around like snakes trapped in a pit. The harder she tries to read the strange script, the more they seem to move. *This must be why Lippio never let me truly help him when he worked on such pages.* She knows that she is the weakest member of the group and that they all will be required to step up at some point, but right now that just seems to be so impossible for her right now. While she knows she is smarter than most, she also knows that her current knowledge will not prevail over everything that her companions may have trouble with while they are stuck here. Instead of giving it up as a bad job, she settles into the meditative trance-like state of Elven rest her mother taught to her a few months prior to Kali leaving to study under Lippio.

When she comes round, Kali looks around to see Trystan, Ghorza, and Reuben all fast asleep. Conn seems to be meditating. Breathing a cleansing breath, she looks to the pages of the tome again as the characters keep writhing their way across the page. Letting her mind maintain the calm balance she found during her rest, the characters then seem to settle down into an ancient language that she has never seen before but finds that she can understand each word that the characters create when joined together in different ways. She even finds a meditative process that enables her to study the book more clearly. She studies the tome intently and tries to learn the spells that she hopes will help her and the group best with whatever they come across when escaping from this place.

Everyone in the room awakens or comes out of their trance-like states around the same time. The first thing Conn does is to check on Trystan and Ghorza's injuries and is relieved to see that both have virtually healed while they slept. They do not know how long they were asleep, but they tear into the first of their dried rations that Trystan found in the room next door. They then look around at the rest of the remaining items they did not bother with earlier. There is an ebony javelin with a golden yellow topaz inlay in the shape of a lightning bolt; a divine scroll that Kali hands to Conn since he is the more spiritual out of anyone in the group; and what looks like a stick that is about a foot long and a quarter of an inch thick.

Kali then discovers an inscription down part of the handle, which reads, *Deprehendere abscondita ostiola.*

"This wand can help us locate any more doors that are hidden from us," Kali says excitedly. She puts it into her map case to keep it safe and ensures that the stiff leather lid is properly secure since the map case is only slightly longer than the wand.

"Whoopee do. Now let's just get out of 'ere and 'ope that there ain't anyone waiting for us when we leave," Trystan snarls. He did need that sleep but now the need to leave and re-join his family is burning stronger than ever.

The others just nod, and Kali retrieves her dagger to open the door while Reuben repacks the cooking pot.

Ghorza stops her by pushing the Half-Elf away from the door saying that she will be the one to go through first. When Ghorza pushes the door, it does not move so she looks questioningly to the Half-Elf who indicates a section on the side of the door.

"You need to place your fingers inside of the door and give it a pull."

Ghorza nods and soon has the door open to re-enter the equipment room with her rhomphaia leading the way.

Reuben realises that she has forgotten her pack and quickly grabs it.

The room remains empty, so they head for the other door from the one they entered by to continue into the unknown. Trystan looks to the sacks of rings, axe heads, and ore before helping himself by filling his belt pouch with as many bronze rings that he can when he catches Kali's disapproving eye.

"What are you looking at?" he demands angrily. "This will 'elp me get some work done on my farm that I ain't been able ta sort out. Makes me feel better ripping that bloody Sorcerer off too. Besides, you'll all need some if yer ever get outta 'ere long enough ta live."

"If you want to be a Sorcerer too, then I believe that you will need a lot of silver, especially to start off with. Just think of it as Treorai is giving you the money to get started," Conn says to her, helping himself to a pouch of rings. She looks at him like he has just fatally stabbed her, unable to even speak for a change.

"Treorai be bloody well damned," Ghorza states vehemently grabbing half a dozen handfuls and shoving it in her backpack. "I need this to pay off some damned snooty bitch so I can actually return home without losing my life."

"You'll be killed if you go back to your home?" Reuben says to her in wonder. She nods and tells them about how Annest Wiliams bumped into her then starts screeching up a storm about how Ghorza got in her way before receiving a hard-right hook to her jaw from the Half-Orc. "Nicely done, though why you should fear for your safety because of her is not right." With that, he grabs another half dozen handfuls of silver nuggets for his backpack, just in case Ghorza has not got enough. Her mounting anger dissipates quickly, causing her to smile at the thought that someone she hardly knows could ever do anything so nice just for the sake of it. She starts wondering if Reuben has any ulterior motives.

Kali just looks at each of them, stunned at their actions and the justifications for their blatant theft. "You do know what you are doing is so wrong," she simply states. None of them seems to care.

"We're robbing a man who, more than likely, stole this from the other people he caught," Reuben comments.

"And who did he steal it from?" she asks in a challenge.

"From the other people he brought here," responds Ghorza, her annoyance mounting since Reuben already answered that one.

"And where are these people?" she asks them, her tone challenging.

"Dead!" snaps Trystan. "Now that's dealt with, let's go."

"Judging from what we saw on that list back in Skarmazh's room, I have to agree with Mr. Gibbs," Conn tells her.

She looks stunned by Trystan's blunt statement and starts to work through what Conn has just said. "Are you sure?" she asks him. After a few seconds of silence except for the impatient huff coming from Trystan who follows up with a semi-quiet curse, she decides to make a move for the exit.

"Finally. Now let's get outta 'ere," Trystan breathes, opening the door to lead on into the unknown.

"Oh, and Trystan," Conn calls to him. When the large man glares, Trystan wonders, *what now.* "The debt is paid in full, from all of us. Especially since each silver piece is worth more than what you tried to charge us for the questions back in the cell." Trystan just grunts his acknowledgement.

Finally leaving the room, they step through the door into another torchlit room.

Looking around, they worry that there may be something even worse here. They see that they are in some sort of dining hall from the looks of the arrangement of tables and benches. There is another door on the other side of the room. All the tables show signs of damage, spilled food, and food scraps, but they can find nothing else beyond the filth. Without another word, they head for the other door to keep moving.

CHAPTER 22

Gimil Tarik

They enter one end of a long and featureless rough-hewn corridor stretching away perpendicular to the room they just left. The only light source is the two they are carrying, though one of those will not last much longer. Making their way slowly forward with Ghorza and Reuben at the front with one torch and Trystan bringing up the rear with the other, their path comes to a corner with an extremely faint glow further down.

Reuben hands Ghorza his torch, then waves her back, where she notes that he has closed his eyes before glancing around the corner. When Reuben opens them again just after peaking around, he can just make out the outline of a couple more doors close by in the glow coming from a torch much further down this stretch of corridor. He then indicates for Kali to join him and slips quietly round the corner up to the first door where they put their ears against the rough wood.

They give each other a nod, then return to the rest.

"There is somebody in the next room from the sound that we heard," he pauses while looking to Kali who offers a confirming nod. "How many do you think are in there?"

"Just the one. Possibly another prisoner." She pauses for a second before continuing to look around at each of them. "I'll go in first while you four stay close outside."

"And why should it be you who goes in?" Trystan demands of her.

"Because, out of all of us, I am probably the least threatening," she retorts, thrusting her face up into his, her arms taut just behind her. Trystan glares at her, looks at her stance, smirks, and then nods in agreement. Before anyone else can respond, she opens the door and steps through. "Oh! Hello there," she says to the torchlit room's sole occupant. She notes that the very air in here smells foul and feels stagnated. In the corridor, at least the air was moving, even if only slightly.

"You are not my master?" says a surprised, aged voice. "Who are you?"

"I can't bloody well see," fumes a baritone voice from outside in the darkness. It seems Trystan is getting annoyed soon as Kali started talking to the occupant in the room.

"Welcome to my world," the old man says quietly to himself. "A simple light conjuration won't help my sight though," the old man tells her. She sees a copper bucket helm on his head, though there is a hinged plate covering his face to curl under his nose. The helm is secured to his head via a leather chin strap.

"I read up on that spell in case we ran out of torches. Also found a pouch of spell components by a tome I found," she rambles on to the old and wretched Human. She has an instinctive feeling about him. "Please excuse me for a second Sir," she says, then turning her back on him to face the doorway and beckons them all inside. The torchlit room only has a small chest, a table, chair, and a single bed by way of furnishings.

"Everyone, this is ... oh, I do not know your name Sir," she says in surprise to the old man.

"I am Gimil Tarik, Priest of the Great Mother Nádúr Mháthair and manservant to Treorak, Sorcerer of the Deepore settlement," the old man says proudly and rising to his feet. "Or, at least, I was," he recants more quietly, slouching back down.

"Which part?" Reuben asks with a smile.

"All of it I'm afraid," he tells them. "You see, I found a relic to the Nádúr Mháthair and wanted to return it to my shrine until my Master saw it. Then he forbade me from taking it anywhere, so I tried to steal it away. When the Master caught me, he kept me in this room and bid me to never leave here again."

"But how does he keep you in this room?" Conn enquires. Reuben nudges his arm and points to the man's head. Conn saw the helm but did not realise that was the problem, not a fashion statement. "Ah, that'll do it," he comments sheepishly.

"So, how many are you?" Gimil probes.

"Use your eyes old man," Trystan snaps at him, frustrated at yet another delay.

"He can't. He's blinded," Reuben tells him quietly.

"Yes, I am blind. Not deaf young man," Gimil admonishes softly with a smile. Reuben looks to his feet in embarrassment while Trystan just stammers an apology.

"We can always free you from Treorai's grip, that's if you want us to," Ghorza offers, wanting to help him.

"Treorai? That is his boy," Gimil exclaims.

"Who is his boy?" Ghorza requests.

"Treorak, of course!" Kali tells her irritably.

"Treorak? Treorak? I know that name," Ghorza says suddenly. "He had a tower just outside of the Deepore Settlement!"

"I already told you kids that. Ya don't listen too good, do ya!" Gimil scolds them irritably. He continues calmly before his annoyance flared at them. "What do you mean, had? Doesn't he have it anymore?"

"Treorai has it now," Ghorza tells him. "Treorak disappeared a few years ago, believed to be dead."

"Ouch! Can you put that any more brutally?" Kali says in shock. Nevertheless, when she looks to Gimil to apologise, he is smiling. "Are you okay Sir?"

"Oh, I'm fine young lady. Now, who is the husky one with that brutal honesty? I like her."

"That would be me," Ghorza says moving towards him a step. Reuben swears blind that she blushes.

"And what do they call you then dear?"

"Ghorza," she replies. "I was living in the Deepore Settlement when I was brought here."

"I see." He pauses briefly. "That's not a normal Human, Dwarf, or Elven name, is it?"

"I'm a Half-Orc, born to one of the tribes in the Strykejern Fjellene mountains before I fled to settle at Deepore."

"Ah, well, that explains your honesty. Those tribes may be many things, but liars they are not," he says before pausing briefly. "And much respect to your strength and resilience too. Being born to those tribes and surviving long enough to escape as a female and a half breed at that, is no mean feat. Not something I'm sure I could have done even in my younger days."

"Thank you, Sir," she responds, feeling further embarrassed by his compliment.

"Now Ghorza. Would you be a dear and release me as you just kindly offered just now?" he requests of her. She studies the leather chin strap that has no fastenings while he continues. "Do you know that the tower and the house attached to it at Deepore is called the Montem Turris?"

"I didn't, no," she replies as she tries to grab the strap with her large hands. "Can you lift your chin, Sir?"

"Of course, dear. Let me sit down first." Feeling behind him, he finds the seat of the chair in the room and places his hands on either side before sitting down with a grunt. After he raises his head, he rambles on. "That tower was created by Treorak purely by using the arcane arts." Ghorza tries again to get a grip on the strap with both hands, but her hands prove to be a little too large for such a short length of binding. The faceplate curves under and across his cheeks. *No wonder he can't see.*

"That tower was once a small mountain, but Treorak used his magic to mould it very carefully into the tower. He even turned the stone he did not need into mud, most of which wound up in his garden plot," he continues with his narrative. Then he quietly adds, "he did love his garden."

Ghorza gives up just trying to use her hands and asks Kali for her dagger in the hopes that that will work better. When the Half-Elf hands it to her, she decides to ask a question of her own for old Gimil. "Is that why the tower is so smooth to look at?"

"Exactly girl. The quarrymen were so few and far when he wanted to create his home that he only required carpenters for the door and window frames in the end," he answers her, happy to oblige someone who seemed to be taking an interest in his story. One he has not been able to tell for what seems to be an awfully long time. Ghorza is only listening in part and hears Trystan's quiet grumbling in the background. She grips the strap with one hand and places the point of the dagger under the leather with the other. She prepares to pull it out when the strap suddenly snaps, and the helm just falls to the floor. The dagger slices deeply across her thumb. "Ah, that is so much better," he says with a new strength coming into his voice and his eyes clearing to allow him to see again. "Now, those windows are the most impressive feature of all. Treorak had frames made for each of the windows, filled each with the earth that he compacted and smoothed over into framed slabs before turning all that mud into stone. Once he was satisfied with each of them, he then turned them invisible before having them placed exactly where he wanted them throughout the house and tower where he then sealed them into place. Well, that's my story for you, and thank you for freeing me Ghorza. I owe you my gratitude."

"It's fine. I am happy to help," she says quietly sucking her thumb and looking up to see him smiling kindly at her.

"The strap looks old and feeble," Reuben says after picking up the helm.

"Don't touch it!" Gimil shouts hurriedly.

"Crap it. What are these damned things?" Reuben screams in surprise, as the helm appears fully repaired on his head. "My eyes! I can't see," he wails.

"It's enchanted, you foolish boy!" snaps Gimil, who then breathes before finishing. "Hold it long enough and you wind up wearing it. Someone break the bloody strap for him."

"No worries. I can do it," Reuben says hurriedly. When he draws his dagger and grabs the leather with his free hand, the strap feels impossibly strong.

"No. You can't," Gimil tells the boy as the old Spiritualist struggles to remain calm. "The enchantment uses your own strength against you. The harder you try, the stronger it becomes. It also enfeebles your mind to prevent the casting of any magic and blinds you."

"Oh, crap. Can someone help me please?" Reuben groans. Kali then lets out a shriek as Trystan barges past her, takes the dagger from Reuben's hand, and places it against the inside of the strap where the helm falls to the floor once again.

"Now, can we get on with getting outta 'ere?" Trystan bellows, his frustration finally exploding.

"Just a couple of things quickly before you go," Gimil quickly interjects.

"What now?" he responses, quite a bit sharper than he intends. He holds no malice for the old man, but these kids are driving him flaming nuts.

"Ghorza, please take these two vials of liquid. They are healing potions should you need them in the future but use them wisely. Also, I would like to heal each of you if you will allow me?" he says hurriedly. When everyone agrees, Trystan even adding a quiet thank you, Gimil continues with his ritual. *"Nádúr Mháthair, slànaich na lotan aca."* When he finishes with his spell, those that were still hurt find that their physical injuries heal over and their bruises disappearing altogether.

They say thank you and offer to take him with them, but he politely refuses to say that he needs to rest before going anywhere. He also explains that he is unable to move as fast as they are anymore and will hate to be the one to slow them up. Leaving him to his rest, they then head back out into the corridor and head for the door next to his.

CHAPTER 23

The Dining Room

They open the door into a sparsely decorated room with a brass candleholder and two chairs beside a table with one of the chairs lying on its side, a simple unmade sleeping cot, with a small shelving unit over the table divided into small squares for the storing of scrolls, by Kali's best estimation. Lippio has many just like it in his shop, but these are empty. Reuben tells them that he believes someone has ransacked this room already. They decide against going in and head through the set of double doors further down the corridor to see where that one leads instead.

The doors open into a very dark and cool room. It must be a large room since their torches cannot even pierce the gloom to learn where the walls begin. Keeping their weapons ready and close together, they enter cautiously.

"This seems to be a dining room of some sort from what I can see," Ghorza quietly informs them from ahead of the group, her eyes already shifting to her greyscale sight where it takes over at the end of their torchlight for a little more detail than what their own eyes cannot pick out normally. Her vision can extend as far as a Human's in the daytime, though she can only see in varying shades of grey.

They take barely five steps into the room when they suddenly freeze with several torches instantly flaring to life to illuminate the largest room that they have ever seen in this complex so far. Columns appearing to be half-buried in the walls rising and forming arches towards the centre of the ceiling about twenty or so feet above their heads. It is what Ghorza said.

There is a large dining room table surrounded by several chairs dominating the centre of the room. Another set of double doors set in the wall along one side, a smaller door near a very scrubbed table in the corner nearest to them. And a strange stone-like effigy of some large creature that they have never seen before half-carved out of the wall at the far end of the dining room, probably when this room was mined out. The engravings all around the room show Dwarf-like people depicting the creation of this room and their lives here, but there is nothing about them creating such an effigy.

Now that they can see more clearly, they breathe a collective sigh of relief to find another empty room. Heading for the other double doors they are then surprised when the effigy, barely a head taller than Ghorza or Trystan, steps away from the wall and bars their progress. They are even more surprised when the creature speaks to them in a stone grating-on-stone voice.

"You are not permitted here. Lay down your weapons and await my master's return. You may be seated if you wish. Refreshments may also be provided. You need only to ask."

"What manner of creature are you?" Kali wonders aloud. She thought that she knew every creature from her surrounding area, but this one is new to her.

"I am a Golem. My Master has named me, Hobbes."

"A bloody speaking stone creature? By the gods, this is ridiculous," Trystan bellows.

"I am made from clay you belligerent Human. Master will have no need of you. I will kill you now to save my Master the time." With that, Hobbes starts heading towards the big man.

"You'll have to take us all down if you want him," Ghorza snarls.

"So be it," comes the detached response. Trystan gives the Half-Orc a look of surprise.

Conn is the first one to attack with his bronze-headed mace, but the weapon just bounces harmlessly off the creature's right leg.

Ghorza and Reuben attack at the same time, though while the young man misses due to avoiding a huge clay arm, Ghorza's strike with her rhomphaia manages to chip a ridiculously small piece from the creature's chest.

Conn notices this and starts thinking.

"*Alacritas iacula!*" Kali produces a single bolt of energy like the ones Treorai launched at them. She directs it at Hobbes' where a larger chunk of stone flies off its chest from the impact and even knocks it back a step.

Seeing this, Conn hurriedly begins to formulate a plan.

Trystan lances his spear out at the creature, but it deflects the blow with its arm right into Conn's waiting hands.

Conn's magical symbol glows when he says, "*Cumhachd a thoirt do armachd!*" before releasing the weapon.

Trystan looks confused.

Ghorza strikes out again to glance off the Golem's leg.

Reuben follows closely after and scrapes across its stomach, though Trystan's attack is more successful this time as he strikes the creature in the head to smash out a good-sized chunk. He quickly nods his thanks to the boy for whatever he did.

Kali casts another energy bolt to strike the Golem's chest a second time with another chunk flying off it and knocking it back a step.

Hobbes does not even wince at any of the attacks striking him. It catches Ghorza with a backhanded slap, launching her onto the table near where Conn is standing.

He checks on her to see a deep red mark forming rapidly along her jawline, though she looks angrier than hurt.

Trystan launches another attack at the damned creature's torso to succeed in damaging it further.

Ghorza is eager to get back into the fight but hesitates at Conn's request.

He casts his spell on her weapon.

Reuben goes into to attack again but the creature catches him with a clawed attack to his stomach and bites down on his left arm. He screams briefly before falling to the floor bleeding profusely.

Hobbes looks like it is about to finish the young man off when another energy bolt strikes it in the chest, knocking him back again.

Conn dives to the floor to drag Reuben away from the battle.

The Golem strikes Trystan across his chest, causing the man to miss with his own attack as a result.

Roaring in rage at what happened to her newfound friend; Ghorza brings her rhomphaia in an overhead attack to shatter through the creature's right arm. She is pleased with the new strength of her blade.

Almost in a panic with two of her companions down, Kali frantically recalls another spell. She screams out, "*Alacritas iacula!*" almost desperately, conjuring a third energy bolt to strike the Golem with.

Conn grabs out some herbs and places them on Reuben's injuries. He places his hands over them and saying, "baintighearna nan uisgeachan uile, slànaich na lotan sin." Under Conn's magic, Reuben's injuries cease bleeding at least and the herbs ensure that his wound will not get infected.

Trystan swings once again but Hobbes moves to strike at Ghorza.

The infernal creature catches Ghorza in the stomach with a clawed hand.

This only hastens her own overhead strike to come crashing down through Hobbes' head. The magic holding it together finally fails to cause it to shatter into little pieces.

"About bloody time," a sweating Trystan says, his breathing ragged.

"We all need to rest after this," Conn says bending over Reuben to examine how the unconscious young man is doing. He catches Ghorza's look before continuing. "His wounds are extensive, but he'll be alright once he has rested."

"We'd better get outta 'ere then and find somewhere safer," Trystan tells him. When Conn and Kali give him a quizzical look, he takes a tentative breath before continuing. "Ya never rest near ya last kill. Learnt that one from a 'unter I knew a couple of years back. If the noise of the fight don't attract anything, then the blood might."

They decide to head for the empty room that they found earlier. Even Trystan does not think about arguing against the idea of them going back for a while.

CHAPTER 24

The Potter

The Guildsman rides through the cold night following the fast-flowing river heading west towards the small settlement. He allows his horse to set the pace while he tries to figure out what is going on with this Half-Elven woman, the Reuben boy, and their connection with the others that this Salvia and Emlyn are seemingly a part of.

He pauses for a while so that his horse can eat some grass and shrubs while he makes a small fire to make some tea before continuing.

While he is sitting on a small boulder, he looks around to see poppy-covered rugged hills all around him with the fast-moving river cutting a swath through this part of the valley in the growing light of the dawn. He cannot see the rising sun through the overcast sky, but he is appeased to find a sheltered dell from the seemingly never-ceasing wind that blows through the mountains behind him in the east.

While some plants and trees have taken root, there are not as many as he thought there would be around here. It seems that the ground is only just recovering from the destruction wrought upon it by those inhabitants that came before.

With a sigh, he buries his small campfire, then remounts his horse after packing up and continues with his journey.

It is nearly midday when a arrives at the small settlement of about fifteen buildings, though he can see where there used to be more at some time. Mainly the indentations in the hills, though a few roundhouse ruins are remaining. He sees that many of the occupied buildings are roundhouses with extensions, separate shacks, or in the case of one building, what looks like three roundhouses that have been joined together.

On the other side of the river, not far from a stone bridge, he sees a middle-aged woman with fair hair kissing a brown haired and bearded man, presumably her husband. The man then takes their two young children towards some light red maple woods around a large pond-like area, carrying a bronze shovel and some wooden buckets between them. The woman enters the lean-to attached to their roundhouse.

She sits behind one table and scoops out what appears to be some mud from the bucket beside her where she then proceeds to roll it into a long worm on the wet tabletop. The Guildsman soon realises that she is rolling clay. Once she is satisfied, the woman then swiftly coils it around itself for a while, then works the coils up to form a rough bowl shape. She then proceeds to smooth out the base and sides to seal all the gaps and cracks. The woman then slides a thin cord under the bowl and places it on a second dryer table.

By this time, the Guildsman has crossed the bridge and is heading towards her home when she notices him.

"Greeting's stranger. And who might you be?" When she looks at the man on his horse, a cold chill inexplicably runs up her spine.

"I was looking for a friend of mine who was coming this way," he calls in that quiet slightly nasal tone of his. "I was hoping that someone here could help me."

"I haven't seen anyone coming this way," she tells him without even trying to sound apologetic while heading back to her worktable. "Very few ever do, except our visiting trader."

"I see." He looks thoughtful for a while. He then looks back at her with another thought. "I did find some goats wandering in the hills across the river. Are they native to this area?"

"Goats? No, they belong to Mr. Gibbs. He tends a good-sized flock out there. Wandering you say?"

"That's right. There was no one with them though."

Without another word, she races off in the direction her husband had wandered with their children with the Guildsman perplexingly watching her go. It does not take long for her to return with her husband hustling their daughter and him carrying their younger boy.

"Give me Caillin while you go see if you can learn what happened," she instructs him.

"I'll quickly stop by Mailse's place and get her to join me," he responds putting his son down to gently nudge him towards his mother. Once his wife has the lad's hand he races off for the bridge.

"Mailse is another herder?" he asks of the woman who starts to head back to her work area.

"She looks after the sheep across the way," she says turning her head towards him. "The herds are kept that side of the river to prevent them getting to the crops on this side. Why do you ask?"

"I was just taking an interest," he answers her nonchalantly.

I sure ya are, but I cannot for the life a me figure out why. She does not get a chance to say anything more due to her son piping up.

"My name is Caillin Ó Dobhailein, and I'm six," he tells their visitor. "Ah'm gonna be a potter like my mamaí." His older sister just looks at him and heads for their roundhouse where he then adds, "That's my sister Lann. She's 11."

"That's enough out of you, young man," she tells him before the stranger can respond. "Now get in there an help yer deirfiúr." She gives the boy a nudge towards their door. She then turns her attention back to the stranger in front of her. "As fer you, yer friend hasn't come to Spire, which is the end of the valley this way. Ah suggest that ya get on your way back from where ya came from an leave us quiet folk in our little bit of peace." She then turns on one clay-clogged shoe and heads for the house.

With no further forthcoming information, the Guildsman shrugs and heads back towards the bridge for the Dwarf Road.

He does contemplate speaking to her husband or this Mailse, but if their response is as forthcoming as that woman's then he will get nowhere with them too. To get those answers by more convincing methods may result in a trail of dead bodies and where such a small settlement is concerned that will begin to draw the wrong sort of attention for his liking.

He decides to return to Palovicus instead.

CHAPTER 25

Recovery

The empty room is about the same size as Gimil's. They decide to carry Reuben straight in and place him on the single bed since this room is slightly closer.

Conn then decides to look for the old Spiritualist and knocks on the room next door but gets no answer. Upon opening the door, he sees that Gimil has already gone so he begins looking for anything that may help him with his companions' recovery. Searching through the two drawers in the table and the small chest. Con finds a good supply of healing herbs and clean strips of rolled-up cloth. In hopes that Gimil does not return for them or object to his making use of them, Conn grabs what he can including a clay bowl and a pitcher of water.

Returning to the other room, he notices that Kali is resting in one of the chairs by the table. Her tome is in front of her, and a torch is lit to send flickering shadows into the far corners of the room.

Once he enters the room, Trystan closes the door and wearily sits down with his back to it.

Ghorza is sitting opposite looking extremely upset. When Conn goes to help Ghorza, she tells him directly that if he does not help Reuben out first, then she will kill him. The look in her yellow eyes causes him to gulp. He turns to see what he can do for the young man on the bed.

"Hey boy. I'm hurting too," Trystan says as he grabs at Conn's trousers.

"But not dying yet," he responds coldly. Trystan falls silent. Relieved by the uncharacteristic silence of the man Conn prays to his goddess for her aid. "Baintighearna nan uisgeachan uile, slànaich na lotan sin." Reuben's injuries begin to knit themselves together and the bruising and swelling goes down. After nearly ten minutes, the healing energies flowing through Conn and into Reuben ceases, leaving the young initiate virtually drained.

Heaving a long sigh, he checks on Trystan's injuries next and washes them before creating a poultice in the clay bowl to smear over his wounds, then bandaging them. Next, he moves to kneel next to Ghorza. He is about to work on her wounds when he sways dangerously before she grabs his arm to give him a little shake. Jerking awake, he quickly apologises and resumes what he sees as his duty to his companions.

"You're looking so tired that you're almost as pale as Kali. You must get some rest first," Ghorza tells him.

"I'll be okay once I've finished," he replies, though he does confess to himself that he really can do with some much-needed sleep. Using some of the water in the pitcher, he washes out the old poultice and pours some more water in to splash his face to help him finish off before he does collapse.

Examining her jaw, he tells her that there is truly little that he can do about that right now. "Rest will be the best remedy." Examining her other injury, he makes up a second poultice and bandages her as well. Without even clearing up, he falls right off to sleep against Ghorza who lowers his head onto her lap before she seeks her slumber.

She is grateful that Conn managed to work on her injuries before dropping off. The pain that she felt is so much more bearable now. She is also happier that Reuben is breathing so much better too. She allows herself a wistful smile before closing her eyes.

Kali comes back out of her meditation and sees that everyone is asleep. Feeling much refreshed, she then turns to her tome to see what she might need to memorise next. By the time she finishes, she is relieved to note that even Reuben is awake and looking so much healthier.

He is talking softly with Ghorza and Trystan. Conn awoke earlier and went straight into his meditative praying trance. Kali decides to break her fast with a handful of nuts and dried fruit from her rations while she waits for him to finish.

"Trystan is telling us about his goats and how he cares for them," Ghorza says to Kali when she realises that the Half-Elven maid is back with them. At least that is the way Ghorza sees it when Kali has her head stuck in her tome. "It's so much more involved than I thought."

Kali smiles and decides to join them once she finishes eating.

Once Conn finishes with his prayers, they decide to head out until Ghorza gets herself into knots with her pack. She had been carrying it in one hand and dropping it if there was a fight before, but now she has decided to try and wear it like the others are doing.

"What's wrong with this damned thing?" She looks up to see them looking at her.

Conn and Kali look at her in confusion while Trystan smirks.

Reuben openly chuckles before helping her.

"Ordinarily when wearing a cloak, you can just fold it between the straps of the pack, but you decided to wear a fur cloak. They are so much bulkier," he explains to her with a smile. "The only other way to wear your pack is to put it on under your cloak, which also has the advantage of protecting it from the worst of the weather."

"As well as making it look like yer got a 'ump back." Trystan roars with laughter at his own joke.

"Mr. Gibbs. That is enough from you," Kali scolds him now that she knows why Ghorza was looking like she was doing some strange dance. She was beginning to wonder if it was a tribal thing. When he looks at her, he just rolls up on the bed with tears streaming down his face from laughing so hard.

"Ignore him, he is just being an idiot," Kali tells her softly. "Reuben is absolutely right with what he tells you and I am going to put my pack on under my cloak too. The way Mr. Gibbs has his cloak between his pack straps is fine, but he is going to know it if we are caught out in bad weather. Especially with the way the weather can rapidly change around the Valle."

"Good point," Conn says in full agreement. He then takes his pack off and manoeuvres it under his cloak.

By the time they get sorted out, Trystan has calmed down enough to just snigger every time he looks at 'the hunchbacks.'

Upon leaving their sanctuary, they are relieved to find no one is waiting just outside. They head straight back to the dining hall. Upon going through the double doors, they are glad that the clay rubble of Hobbes is still in the middle of the floor. They decide to investigate the door nearest them only to find an extremely clean kitchen. Even the work surfaces have been scrubbed and the bronze knives and cleavers are glistening.

Compared to what some of them know of the Races they have encountered to this point, this surprises them. It is not until Ghorza suggests that maybe the dining hall is where Treorai has his meals. The cleanliness of this kitchen then begins to make more sense to the others.

Trystan takes the time to fill their water bottles from the hand pump in here after checking that the water is drinkable, if a little salty.

They leave the kitchen and then notice that there does not seem to be so many lumps now like there were after they defeated him. They look to each other worriedly, then move quickly to the double doors in the hopes of getting out with all due haste.

CHAPTER 26

Isolation

Quickly moving through the doors and closing them afterward, the companions find themselves in a long well-lit roughhewn corridor. After the virtual darkness of the others, this one almost seems blinding and there is less noticeable smoke from the pitch. What little there is rises to the ceiling and seems to dissipate there. There is a couple of wooden chests here half-filled with spare torches. Trystan grabs a couple.

Heading down quickly, they come to another set of double doors with another door further down. The single and the double doors are both bound in patinaed straps of metal.

Reuben slips in front of Ghorza and places his ear against the set of doors. He listens intently amongst the noises where he finally picks out voices and focuses on them. When he is satisfied, he then directs the others back the way they came a short way so he can tell them what he has heard.

"It sounds like there are four people just beyond the door in there. I can't say what they are as I don't recognise the language," he tells them while they crouch or kneel.

"So, what do you suggest?" Kali asks him.

"We go in 'ard and fast ta cut whatever is in there down afore they can warn anyone," Trystan responds in his brassy tone.

"How do we know that they are not friendly?" Conn reflects. "They could be trapped here just like us and Gimil was."

"We are not the blood-thirsty savages like you seem to think we are,"

Kali snaps quietly at the large man. "We have to know what they are and why they are there in the first place."

Abruptly, Ghorza snaps her short spear from her back, spins in a half-circle on the spot, and launches it straight down the passageway. Without a word, she just dives over those in front of her and charges through the double doors with her rhomphaia leading the way.

By the time the others recover enough from her sudden explosive action, they hastily follow with their own weapons at the ready. Ghorza is fending off three Goblins with her back to the wall. A table, chairs, and bone dice have been knocked flying.

Reuben, Trystan, and Conn soon come to her aid. Before the Goblins realise that anyone is behind them, they are all dead.

Reuben wipes the blood on their clothing after he quickly slit one's throat.

Conn delivered his mace to the back of another's skull.

Trystan withdraws his spear from the third one's back.

"That was fast," Kali says slowly in surprise, catching up.

"When I saw the Goblin look out of the door, I just reacted," Ghorza answers her by way of an explanation and an apology at the same time, looking to the floor she is toeing.

"Thank the gods that you did," Reuben tells her. "If anyone of them got the word out, then all of us would have been in serious trouble," he comments giving her a clap on the shoulder and a smile. She returns the smile nervously and walks over to the Goblin she threw the spear at and yanks it from the creature's chest to clean it.

"Nice shot," Trystan says in adoration, causing Ghorza to grimace with embarrassment.

With the excitement over, it is only now that a foul smell strikes them all, making each of them want to heave.

This part of the corridor goes in a short way before running parallel to the main passage to end in a single bound door. The far wall is lined with more doors spaced closely together. Moving further into the corridor, the obnoxious odour gets stronger. A closer examination of these doors shows that they have a thick sliding bar on each. A small square hole above containing a single crossbar to prevent anyone from putting their arm through. There are a dozen of the cells in total.

When they open the first door with their weapons at the ready, the space inside clearly defines it as a cell that is only slightly wider than the door but is otherwise empty. Spreading out, they each begin to open the other doors one by one.

They decide to take each cell in pairs, Reuben and Ghorza take the first door, then Conn and Kali take the next one in line, and so on. The closer to the end of the corridor they get the stronger that odour becomes.

Trystan just leans back against the wall thinking that these kids seem to be only too happy to waste even more time. *We should just keep moving. I may be a goat 'erder an' they can make a crap load of mess, but this place stinks so much worse than the goat's shelter ever could.*

It is Conn and Kali who get to explore the final cell.

There is a young Human woman in torn and bloody pale shirt and brown trousers. She is sitting against the back wall, holding her knees to her chest as if to comfort herself while glaring at him with pale malicious eyes. The smell of urine and excrement is so strong now that it makes their eyes stream and causes them to vomit against the back wall.

Once they recover enough, Conn only just has time to yank back the bolt when the prisoner barrels through the door. She briefly looks around with maddened amber eyes and bolts past them towards the single door, knocking Kali flying in the process. The others belatedly race over to Conn and Kali's assistance.

When she cannot get out through the door, she spins around on them. Snarling and salivating, she charges them.

Conn leans into his shield and holds his bronze mace at the ready, preparing for the impending impact.

Reuben swears that the woman looks at them like they are food and pulls his short sword and dagger.

Seeing his reaction, Ghorza gets her rhomphaia ready.

The woman closes the gap faster than many of them anticipates and swipes at Trystan's arm with one broken nailed hand only to catch air.

Conn and Reuben swing at her just a moment too late.

Ghorza brings her rhomphaia to the side of the creature's face, cutting deep, but this only serves to enrage the woman even more. Spinning her weapon full circle, Ghorza then catches their attacker straight across her thigh.

Conn jumps aside to avoid being struck by the woman, bumping into Trystan.

Trystan looks at the boy and gets bitten hard on his arm, causing him to cry out and drop his spear.

Without missing a beat, Kali casts one of her energy bolts at the woman who howls in pain.

Trystan yanks out his dagger with his left hand and catches the creature across her left arm. The weapon evokes a howl of agony. In retaliation, she lashes out at Trystan and just misses him.

Ghorza pierces the woman's chest with a desperate thrust.

She shrieks briefly before falling to the floor, looking so serene in death.

Conn realises that the foulness of the cell is much stronger with the door open, so he decides to close it again in the hopes of reducing the stench in some small way. He then drinks some water to rinse his mouth out. The water is warm and slightly salty but has no effect in making him feel better. At least his mouth does not taste so foul anymore.

They quietly debate why she was in one of these cells instead of in the main cell where they woke up, but Trystan soon ends that debate. "I don't care either way. Jus' want ta get outta 'ere," he says still smelling something foul in the air.

"I'm sorry that you got hurt Sir," Conn begins. "If you let me have a look at your injury, I might be able to heal it," he offers.

"Fine," Trystan growls by way of accepting the boy's apology. Besides, the bite hurts like all the nine levels of hell tore through it.

Conn examines the wound and cringes when he sees the tear of the bite marks. He casts a healing enchantment on the wound which stops the bleeding and heals the flesh, hoping that they find a powerful Spiritualist quickly once they get out.

"OK boy! What was that thing?" Trystan bellows as he catches Conn's look.

"I believe that she was afflicted with the wolf bite disease," he begins hastily. When the others look at him blankly or, in Trystan's case, with fury, Kali quickly interjects.

"What he means is that he believes the woman was bitten by a Werewolf who gave her the wolf bite disease." She did not recognise the creature, but when Conn was starting to explain, she then remembered some of the stories that Lippio and her mother had told her when she was growing up.

"That's it. Exactly …" he catches Trystan's glare and hurriedly stops talking.

"I am sure Conn did not mean for you to get hurt Mr. Gibbs," Kali tells him, sympathy in her melodic voice.

"Let's jus' get going," he snarls.

They leave via the single door and head back out into the main passage which turns a corner. They can see the corridor ending in another set of double doors and a single door just around the bend.

"Of all the bloody luck," Trystan curses.

CHAPTER 27

The Tool Crafters

They look to the single door closest to them, then the double doors at the end of the corridor debating which way they are to go next.

After their luck with going through, as Trystan puts it, *the damned double doors*, Reuben listens at the single door and hears some growling voices either arguing or conversing from somewhere close by on the other side. Cracking the door open to see if he can better understand what they are saying Ghorza quickly snaps a hand onto his shoulder. Snapping his head around, he sees that she has a finger pressed to her lips. Ghorza catches on to what the occupants are saying and indicates Reuben to close the door before whispering into his ear.

"Hobgoblins are counting and arguing over numbers," she husks.

"Hobgoblins can count?" Reuben whispers back in surprise until he sees her scowling at him.

"They may be brutal, but they are not stupid," she scolds him harshly, struggling to keep her own voice low. She then shrugs before adding, "They also have very good hearing."

It is then that Reuben suddenly realises that the conversation beyond the door has already ceased. He draws his short sword and dagger.

Ghorza readies her short spear for throwing.

Just then, Trystan demands what is damned well happening from behind them.

They turn their attention away from the door briefly and almost miss it being opened by one of the large, green-yellow creatures.

Ghorza quickly spots her target and throws her spear at the furthest Hobgoblin.

Reuben skips forward to cause the one to open the door to step back while still holding the handle and avoiding a dagger to his stomach. This aids the young man's sword to open his throat instead.

With both Hobgoblins down, they charge into the room to find that it was only the two of them. The room contains a selection of large stone mallets, bronze-headed flat picks, and square wooden shovels.

Ghorza walks over to the one she killed. She kicks him over onto his back only to find her spear tip buried in his chest and the broken shaft lying next to the body. Angrily, she kicks the Hobgoblin in the ribs with a curse, relishing in the crunch of bones.

Looking around the room properly, they find a small table with a piece of parchment, a wooden pen, and a vial of ink, though more of the ink seems to cover the table than the scrawl scratched on the parchment itself. They also see a second door at the end of the room where they can hear a metallic banging accompanied by the sound of heavy breathing. It is then the others join them in the room, led by a very impatient Trystan.

Ghorza pulls her rhomphaia out moves to listen for more Hobgoblins at the door while Reuben quietly warns Conn, Kali, and Trystan to be ready.

When he looks back to the Half-Orc, she gives him a shrug. He then replaces her and listens to a conversation going on amongst the heavy breathing and banging sounds before turning back to the group.

"Whoever they are, there are definitely more than two of them, but I can't understand a word they are saying," he whispers.

"Well, let's just get in there an' figure it out," Trystan whispers aggressively, sweat starting to bead on his forehead.

Reuben nods and quietly slides the thick wooden bolt back on the door indicating for Ghorza to go in first.

She kicks the door and charges into the room, causing it to bounce back off her arm, though she barely notices it. Reuben follows closely on her heels and quickly takes stock of the room. He notes that the heavy breathing has stopped soon as the door flew open.

"Stop!" he shouts to Ghorza just before she lances a short, grey-bearded man. She angles the blade over the unflinching man's head at the last moment, while skidding to a halt and looking at her friend quizzically. The short man just glares at her silently, the promise of death filling his grey eyes despite his current situation.

"They're prisoners just as we were," he explains hastily, indicating the chains linking them to respectively assigned stations.

"Were?" Trystan growls at him from the doorway. "We still ain't outta this stinkin' place yet!"

Reuben flickers a smile at one edge of his mouth briefly. He then takes a deep breath before returning his attention to the short men. All of them wear a full-length metal spattered leather apron over blackened trousers and aged boots; one of them is also wearing a bandage around their chest and has a shorter beard than the rest.

Conn enters the stiflingly hot room while each group watches the other to see what they will do next. He sees that each of them is at one of three work areas. A forge where one of them was working the bellows while a second was hammering a point onto the flat-headed pick in his hands, a woodworking bench where a third was fitting a handle to the head of a hammer, and the fourth stands by a smelter against the opposite wall to the other work areas. All look as powerfully built as each other. Despite the heat from the flames in here, there is extraordinarily little smoke in this room.

"You're hurt? I'm a Spiritualist with the art of healing wounds," Conn says, approaching the short bearded one with the bandages at the smithy area. They look at him in confusion until the young man goes to undo the injured man's wrappings before he receives a hard slap, knocking his hands away. He is rubbing his hands when the offended one speaks.

"I'm not bloody injured ya damned simpleton! I'm just protecting my tits from splashing metal and flying sparks! Do ya know how much it hurts when yer tits get burned ya bloody stupid shingle head!" She then looks to the others. "Stupid Human's got too much bloody rubble for brains." The other three nod quietly, still watching the others stoically while Conn stammers out an apology through sheer embarrassment.

"How about you wait outside while I find out what's what," Reuben suggests quietly to Conn.

He wholeheartedly nods his agreement and rapidly leaves them to it, frowning at Kali when she gives him a smirk. "You knew?" Conn accuses her harshly when they are back in the tool store.

"I only realised when you moved towards her. That allowed me to see the obnoxious one more clearly," she tells him with a little musical chuckle. When she sees him still glaring at her, she calms down. "Look Conn, it is natural to confuse the different genders where Dwarfs are concerned if you do not have much to do with them. Unlike male Dwarfs, who take great pride in the length of their beards, the females can only grow short beards. There are even a few who shave them off, though that is more frequent when they reside amongst non-Dwarf folk. Those keep their chins clear to better fit in with the societies of other races, some even prefer it that way. I do not know of any other race that is like the Dwarfs where facial hair is concerned."

"Please forgive my friend, but he has led a rather sheltered life growing up with the Spiritualists in his hometown," Reuben explains to the four of them after Conn leaves the workroom.

"Still no excuse for being so bloody touchy-feely around those he don't know," the short red-bearded Dwarf fumes, though Reuben notes that at least she has calmed down some.

"This is getting us nowhere," Trystan chimes in. "Let's just get the flock outta 'ere ta where we can be free of this blasted 'ellhole in the ground."

Five pairs of eyes turn towards the large man. With the look the Dwarfs give him, Trystan suddenly feels that it would be safer if he never left the cell in the first place, though he is momentarily stunned when he realises that even Ghorza gives him that look too. He uncomfortably mutters something about waiting in the other room and for Reuben to be quick about it before shambling out. When he passes through the door, he straightens up as if nothing were amiss.

"You too?" Kali asks with a knowing smile. Trystan harrumphs and slumps into a corner.

"It definitely would be safer in the salt mine than it would be in there. I don't rate the chances of your two friends."

"I know what he said to offend you all," Ghorza blurts out.

"Ye can bloody well piss off an' all," the female Dwarf tells her.

"Now just you wait a minute," Reuben jumps in when Ghorza scowls and starts to move towards her till she bumps into his arm. "They are my friends that you're insulting, and you are definitely in no position to go name-calling. Now apologise to my friend," he demands of the Dwarf.

"Like bloody hell I-"

"Bu sizdan yetarli, Beata," the leanest of the Dwarfs, the one at the smelter tells her. He also has red hair though his beard is plaited.

"Ya can belt up an all lil brother," she snaps at him. "If it weren't fer yer falling asleep, we wouldn't even be 'ere."

"Leiulf is right Beata. That is more than enough from you," the Dwarf by the woodwork bench snaps back at her while keeping his eyes fixed on Ghorza. "Just remember that if it was not for you and Waldemar here who went charging in after Leiulf was captured when we needed a plan, then none of us would be here at all, especially against those five."

The most powerfully built-looking one standing next to Beata by the forge hangs his head shamefully, his singed brown beard falling below his stomach. Beata just mutters something about not being the one to fall first.

"So, I ain't a fighter much like you two are, but that is why I use my wits instead. And I still maintain that if we planned it properly, then we would not be here now," he says angrily.

Three of them break down into a shouting match in a dialect that not even Kali can begin to decipher. Reuben tries to attract their attention, but it is not until Ghorza shrills out a sharp whistle that they stop and look at her and Reuben. The young man rubs his ear clear of the aftereffects, then nods his thanks to Ghorza for the now silent room.

"Now sir," he says looking to the woodworker. "May I know your name please?"

"An Odam with manners," he responds in happy surprise. "Certainly, young man. I am called Oddmund. Oddmund Bjerke, historian, and woodworker. Dwarven historian, of course. May I know yer name young man?"

"It's Reuben Sir. Reuben Bunner."

"An interesting name to be sure," Oddmund says thoughtfully.

"My adopted parents are bakers in Brackston. I took on their name when they took care of me and put me to work," he explains to the Dwarf.

"You are adopted? What do you mean by adopted? Do you not have ota-ona of your own?" enquires Oddmund. Reuben looks at him quizzically where Oddmund then realises his mistake. "Apologises. I mean, parents."

"I don't know my parents, Sir. I had an accident when I was younger and the Bunners took care of me ever since."

"Do you remember anything of your past?"

"Not much Sir. I have skills that I never knew I had till I got here, but not much else," Reuben answers him. *What a nosey Dwarf this one is.*

"Oh, ya poor little boy," Beata says walking towards him only to be stopped by the length of chain. "Come to Beata," she tells him as she holds up her arms to him. Reuben looks quizzically to Oddmund who half shrugs and half tilts his head in her direction. Almost hesitantly, Reuben moves towards her where she yanks him down more to her level and proceeds to give him a powerful hug. He is then further surprised when a second Dwarf also gives him an equally powerful hug. "It's okay young one. Me and Leiulf also lost our parents when we were younger."

"We lost our father in a Troll ambush and our mother in a cave-in around the same time. It was Waldemar's oila who took us in and took care of us," the one called Leiulf explains. Waldemar just nods.

"It's alright now. That happened several years ago and it's not like I can miss them since I don't remember them," he says to the two Dwarfs.

"Damn, these shingle heads sure get over things fast," Beata says, looking to the others.

"Odamlar do not tend to live as long as we do," responds Oddmund. "Besides, if he has suffered xotira yo'qotish, then it is not surprising that he does not miss his ota-ona."

"I suppose." She then looks to Reuben. "So, what are we to do now? What is it that you want from us?"

"We will free you from your chains if that is your wish," Ghorza says quietly. Then she quietly adds, "despite your rudeness."

"Ghorza," cautions Reuben quietly.

"Do'zax ning chatishma va uning so'z bilan!" Beata fumes.

"You'd throw the chance of freedom back into the face of those who offer it freely?" demands Leiulf glaring at her,

"U Orc tug'ilgan yotipti. Ular yolg'onchi tasdiqlangan qilyapmiz."

"Then trust in the young man if not the half-breed," he admonishes her. "What say you, young man, do you wish to free us as well?"

"Urm. We can't promise you safe passage, but we will release you from your chains," Reuben stammers out.

"That's good enough for us young man," Oddmund says to him before smiling smugly at Beata.

"But only if she apologises for her rudeness and asks us herself," Ghorza chimes in quickly.

"Ghorza. What in the nine hells are you playing at?" Reuben whispers to her harshly.

"U bir damlatas o'tirib borish mumkin!"

"Beata!" Oddmund and Leiulf scream at her. Waldemar just scowls.

"This is our one chance for freedom. If that is the only cost to us, then it is a really cheap price to pay," her brother shouts at her. Ghorza, Reuben, and the others in the storeroom begin to worry that all the noise will start to attract some unwanted attention. Trystan and Conn even move over to the door leading out into the hallway to listen for anyone approaching.

"Whatever! Okay!" she says angrily. Turning her attention more towards the young man than the half-breed, she takes a deep calming breath. "I apologise for my rudeness. Now could ya release us from these damned chains so that we may go free," she says through barely gritted teeth. *I'll remember this one bitch*, she promises silently.

After Reuben tells Conn, Kali, and Trystan what is happening, the large sweaty man finds a key on one of the dead Hobgoblins and hands it over after learning that they cannot break the chains.

The chains proved resistant when they try to use a bronze pickaxe. Even when they banged it with a hammer.

Reuben then takes the key and releases the Dwarfs' ankle cuffs, where he is told that these were designed by Dwarfs over a hundred years ago. Once they are free, they grab a heavy mallet or a pick each before heading out after learning where the young man and his friends came from.

"Are we flaming well ready now?" Trystan demands when Reuben and Ghorza leave the workroom. The Dwarfs leave the storeroom.

"Yeah," Reuben answers with a big sigh of relief. "Let's find our own way out of here."

"And about time too," comes the growled response.

They head out after hearing a door open and close. Conn throws the visibly perspiring man a concerned look.

CHAPTER 28

Slave Quarters

Returning to the main corridor, they find themselves outside of the double doors that they were hoping to avoid after their fight with Conn's Werewolf. With a twitch of his shoulder and a brief one-sided smile to the others, Reuben takes a brief listen at the door. He stands back and looks quizzically back to his companions.

"It sounds like there is a fight going on in there," he says keeping his voice low. "Should we go in or let it die down first?"

"Oh, let them kill each other an' we'll figure it out after," Trystan declares to draw surprised glances from the others. "What? It saves us having to sort it out now!"

"The Dwarfs may be the ones in trouble!" Conn fumes. "If it is them, then we have to help them!"

"Why! Cos ya feel responsible!" he roars back.

"We are the ones who released them to walk free," Kali says calmly. "We have to ensure that we can all get out of here, including those we free along the way."

"I'm going in," Ghorza bluntly says. "Even if they don't like me," she finishes, throwing open the double doors into a long filthy dimly lit room where the Dwarfs are besieged by six Goblins. One of them is distracted by the opening of the doors, to provide Leiulf the time to bury his pick into its head.

The Dwarf tries to get his pick back but winds up exposing himself to another Goblin who opens his throat with a bloody meat cleaver.

Beata screams out her brother's name.

The Half-Orc charges into the room.

Reuben and the others follow in her wake when Leiulf falls to the floor.

Oddmund tries to get to their fallen comrade but the Goblin he is facing forces him hard into a series of frantic parries.

The Goblin manages to slice his knife deep into Oddmund's arm, causing him to drop his heavy wooden hammer.

Waldemar's attacks become more furious. His attacks put two of the Goblins on the back foot before burying his bronze pick in one Goblin's chest. He then swings back into the other Goblin's throat.

Ghorza then crashes through the battle lines to cleave Leiulf's attacker almost in two.

Conn races in to get Leiulf out of the fight now Ghorza has gone past the fallen Dwarf.

Skidding to a halt off to one side, Reuben snatches his bow off his shoulder and pulls an arrow before releasing it at Oddmund's sneering foe. The arrow flies past the Dwarf's ear and strikes his opponent's shoulder.

Trystan barrels the wounded Goblin straight into the wall before slamming a dagger deep into the creature's eye.

The final Goblin looks at Beata's hate-filled face and that of her companions. Deciding that the better part of valour is to beat a hasty retreat, he drops his knife while he backs off and spins on his heel to spring for the double doors at the far end.

Beata sees Reuben readying his bow with another arrow and snatches them off him. Before Reuben can protest, she releases the arrow and then throws the bow down at his feet.

The arrow buries itself in the Goblin's spine. The creature flops to the floor, unsure what has happened to prevent his mobility.

Beata looks to Conn, who is kneeling beside Leiulf. The young man just looks at her and shakes his head sadly. With a scream of rage, she rips Leiulf's pick out of his Goblin's head and strides over to the floundering Goblin where she kicks the creature over onto his back. It sees the full fury in her face before she buries the pick right between his eyes to cut off its final scream. She then proceeds to destroy the corpse.

Kali almost vomits at Beata's sheer brutality and the subsequent spray of blood decorating the floor and ceiling with each swing.

Reuben folds her into his arms while Conn walks over to heal Oddmund's arm.

Beata finally stops and returns to hold her brother in her arms. When she looks at Conn's back, unadulterated rage suddenly replaces her grief. Confusion races through her mind. Her brother cannot be gone. Squeezing him tightly, air escapes his lips to blow across her cheek.

"What do you think that you are doing?" she yells at him. "You're supposed to be helping my brother! He's not dead yet!"

"I'm sorry, but there is nothing I can do for him," Conn says softly with a deep sadness in his tearing eyes.

"If you can heal, then heal him!"

"I can only treat the injuries," he says regretfully, barely keeping himself from bursting into tears. No matter how hard he tries to keep emotionally steady, Conn cannot keep his voice from cracking as he continues. "I am not powerful enough to bring back the dead." He turns away from her so that she does not see the tears starting to fall from his eyes.

Angered even further, she drops Leiulf back onto the floor and storms over to Conn. Spinning him around by his arm, she slams a right fist into his jaw screaming at him. "Heal him!" repeatedly. Conn's head explodes in a blinding pain.

Oddmund yells at her "No!"

Waldemar races over.

Fortunately for Conn, the pain does not last long.

Waldemar barrels right into Beata, throwing his powerful arms around her to keep her from fighting back, and pins her to the floor.

Ghorza roars and goes to charge the female Dwarf but Trystan clotheslines her; landing on her back where he then sits across her and keeps her arms down on the floor.

Reuben releases Kali and tells her to check Conn. He races over to the downed Half-Orc.

"Let's stop this nonsense right now!" Oddmund calls out to the room. "This has to stop now before anyone else turns up!"

"Maybe someone should," Trystan calls back. "It might give 'em something more ta focus their rage on." He then yelps. Ghorza has manoeuvred one knee to crack him between the legs. Clutching his groin, he rolls off her when Reuben slides down beside her. He grabs a shoulder with one hand and forces her to look at him with the other while shaking his head.

"That bitch killed Conn," she tells him in a threateningly low husky tone. "I'm going to kill her."

"Hold it right there," he orders her. Keeping Ghorza in sight from the corner of his eye, he then calls out. "Kali. How is Conn?"

"He is alive," she answers him. "He is just knocked out."

"See," he says returning his full attention to the fuming Half-Orc. "He's alive. Not dead. Now let us keep this as calm as possible." When she finally nods, he can see that she is slowly calming down. He then eventually lets her go and they stand up together. He motions to her to stay where she is and heads over to the struggling Beata who Oddmund is reprimanding. At least, that is what Reuben thinks judging from the tone. After a minute or two, Beata breaks down into tears where Waldemar lets her go to allow her to crawl to her brother's side.

"We need to get outta 'ere and now," Trystan stresses. "Else we might all be caught."

"Too late," Ghorza and Reuben answer him simultaneously looking to the set of double doors the Goblin tried to make a break for.

"We already have company coming," Reuben finishes with a smile at Ghorza. Just when he finishes speaking, the double doors burst open to admit nearly a dozen greenish-yellow skinned humanoids. "Ghorza. Now's the time to get angry!"

"Obara! Ndi mhporo ahu na-agapu," says the first one readying a large club. "Kwusi ha tupu onyeisi ahu akwusi anyi!"

The Hobgoblins charge en masse. One of them is surprised to find a short sword ending its charge. Its belly is sliced open to pour its stomach out through the gash in his leather armour.

Trystan thrusts out with his spear to catch a second with a glancing blow when the Hobgoblin tries to duck to one side.

With a roar of unbridled rage, Ghorza brings her rhomphaia down through another's shoulder into his chest. The blade of her weapon punches out through its back due to his own charge. She boots the Hobgoblin off her weapon.

Kali uses one of her energy bolts to take down a third.

Finding their initial charge floundering so quickly, they stall. Their attempts to strike at the Half-Orc and Human barricade is easily avoided or premature.

The three Dwarfs race up from the rear of the defensive line in a mad rush.

Reuben goes for a double thrust only for his target to jump back out of his reach.

The Hobgoblin retaliates to crack Reuben hard across his leg, almost breaking it in two with his club. The young man loses his short sword and falls back from the line.

Ghorza spins the long weapon 360 degrees to slice the top of another's skull.

A Hobgoblin sees Beata reach them. He fails to parry her attack when she swings her pick up to catch it under his chin and launching him a couple of feet backwards into the air, ripping off its lower jaw.

Kali releases an energy bolt and catches another, though the Goblinoid manages to carry on with his own offensive.

Waldemar takes Reuben's place next to the Half-Orc.

The young man pulls his bow off his shoulder and leans against the wall for additional support.

Ghorza spears another Hobgoblin through his chest.

A Hobgoblin clubs Trystan under his ribs, a second one drops Beata under his club to her thick skull. When Beata falls, Oddmund yanks her backward to take her place.

Kali catches the same one she hit before with a second energy bolt and Waldemar smashes the Hobgoblin straight across his hip. It drops shock-eyed on the floor, the light of his life fades into the eternal darkness.

Taking deep breaths, Reuben shoots an arrow straight into another's chest to blast the life from him.

Kali throws a dagger into the melee, only to miss everyone.

Trystan spears a Hobgoblin in the ribs.

While it remains standing his breathing starts becoming ragged. The Hobgoblin still manages to smash the large man's left arm against his chest causing Trystan to lose his breath and severely winding him.

Ghorza catches another Hobgoblin on the inside of his upper thigh and leaves him to bleed out.

Oddmund slams his hammer into another's chest, splintering the rib cage under the two-handed blow.

Waldemar accidentally dodges straight into one Hobgoblin's attack, leaving him on the floor struggling for breath.

Ghorza's rage starts flagging as a deep weariness begins to overtake her, missing her chance against Waldemar's aggressor.

Reuben replaces his eye with an arrow.

The last one catches Oddmund across the side of the skull. The Dwarf falls to the Hobgoblin's savage blow.

Kali throws a second dagger, piercing the Hobgoblin's heart to cause his yellow eyes to widen in surprise.

With no more opponents to fight, Ghorza looks around as if in a daze before falling to the floor, feeling absolutely drained.

Kali looks around to see Conn getting up off the floor from where Beata had knocked him out and stare at the devastation in the room.

The young Spiritualist sees Ghorza on her hands and knees breathing heavily, Reuben looking deathly pale trying to use a wall to keep him upright though he is sliding down it slowly, and Trystan and the Dwarfs have fallen amongst loads of dead Goblinoids. All but Kali is covered in blood, though he cannot begin to sort out whose blood belongs to whom. Especially not with the pounding headache resulting from that Dwarf woman's attack on his person earlier.

"What in the nine hells happened here?" he asks of no one in particular.

"I would have thought that was obvious," Kali snipes.

He looks at her in surprise, then realises that she looks even paler than normal.

Seeing his expression turn to one of concern, she then looks apologetic and dismisses his countenance. "It is alright. I am just exhausted from such a concentrated use of magic in so short a time. I will be fine, but if you can, then take care of the others first."

"Don't worry about me either." Reuben quietly tells him when Conn heads towards him. "I'm still awake but those that aren't should be seen to first." Conn nods, causing his head to throb. He winces then turns his attention to Trystan and the Dwarfs.

"Kali, I think it will be best if we get everyone back to the storeroom." Kali looks at Conn quizzically, but Reuben soon catches on to his thinking.

"A place to rest up and recover that can be defensible if need be. Good idea."

Kali goes to Reuben where he leans heavily against her while they go out the way they came in.

Conn then asks a weary Ghorza to help him move Trystan and the Dwarfs. It takes them nearly a full five minutes or so. No sooner than they close the double doors with the last of the Dwarfs between them, they hear sounds of fear, surprise, and anger.

CHAPTER 29

The Calm ...

Conn works his way through the unconscious and injured, casting a little healing magic to prevent any further blood loss. He then returns to those with broken or shattered bones to use more focused magic before resorting to his herbs and poultices.

Reuben smiles gratefully at him for repairing his shattered leg. The young Spiritualist even expresses his shock at Reuben being able to move at all, let alone remain standing for however long he did. After Conn moves on, Reuben stands up gingerly to ensure that his leg can support his weight properly. He quickly whispers to Ghorza before disappearing out into the short corridor with a pick.

Conn looks on in confusion at Reuben's disappearing back and then a subsequent scraping on the door. With a shrug of his shoulder, Conn returns to his duties, wondering if healing the young rogue first was such a great idea. While he works, he looks forward to getting some rest for himself if only to shift his headache.

Kali, despite Ghorza's rumbling snores, truly falls asleep soon after she sits down in one corner of the room next to the equally weary Half-Orc.

When Reuben returns, he has a self-satisfied smile to accompany his private thoughts. He then asks Conn to aid him in moving the table in front of the storeroom door. They then stack as many mining tools as possible on it for additional weight. He even jambs a dagger under the door as Kali did with that secret door earlier. When they finish, they both settle down secure in the knowledge that they have done everything they can to secure the room.

What is quickly becoming the norm for the group, Kali is the first one to be awake and immediately begins to study her tome after breaking her fast on some dried berries and nuts. When Conn leaves the comforting embrace of sleep, Kali looks up and smiles briefly where she then returns to her study thinking, not for the last time that this way of storing parchment is so much more convenient than trying to store so many scrolls.

After grabbing a strip of jerky from his rations, Conn then checks on his wounded charges while he chews away and holding the jerky in his teeth whenever he needs to check under their wrappings. He notes that Trystan is still sweating profusely and is feeling hot to the touch. It looks to the young man like Trystan is suffering from a fever. The young Spiritualist grows anxious. He also notes that Trystan's snores are sounding like faint growls and one of his legs twitch spasmodically. He has only ever known dogs to do that in their slumber.

He goes to ensure that Reuben has not overdone it from before they rested.

Ghorza suddenly jerks awake with wide yellow eyes and a sharp intake of breath making Conn jump and nearly drop the remains of his breakfast onto the grimy floor.

Reuben wakes up just as fast, turning immediately to the Half-Orc with concern etching his forehead.

"What is it?" Conn asks once he removes the jerky.

"Dark dream," she starts breathlessly. "My head hurts."

"Chew on these bay leaves. It should help some," he tells her. "Just wish I could do something for Mr Gibbs."

"What's up with him?" Reuben wonders looking over to the profusely sweating man.

"He has a fever, though I'm really hoping that it is nothing worse than that," Conn tells him quietly. "Unfortunately, I don't have any coriander to try and bring that fever down."

"And if it is not just a fever?"

"Then we could all be in for a major headache of our own," he tells them warily.

"He got hurt when we fought the mad bitch," Ghorza utters around chews.

"She bit him," Conn clarifies.

"And …" Reuben probes.

Conn just looks to the floor before mumbling about needing to check on the others. He silently wishes that he did not feel the need to tell anyone at all. The only drawback to that idea is he will have to tell someone at some point. He knows that this is way beyond his current capabilities to even attempt to heal the Goatherder. *Even to keep Mr. Gibbs' condition quiet for this long is dangerous in itself.* His thoughts are interrupted rudely.

"Where is that Yarim nasl bitch?" Beata screeches as soon as she wakes up, sitting bolt upright. "I'm gonna kill her!"

"Oh, shut the hell up Beata," Oddmund orders her quietly, only just waking up himself and in no mood to deal with her nonsense.

"If it wasn't for that … aah!"

Waldemar just reaches up from where he is laying and yanks her back to the floor before rising himself, kneeling on her stomach and glaring into her eyes with muscular arms folded across his thick chest.

"You was asleep," she struggles to say in denial as he slowly increases the pressure on her torso.

He just grins darkly at her.

"I believe he's trying to say-" Oddmund starts before Beata interrupts him.

"I know what he's trying to say," she wheezes where Waldermar then finally eases the pressure.

"So, what is he trying to say?" Oddmund asks her with a grin, noticing that the others are watching them with quiet interest despite knowing that this is none of their business.

"That I'm not to do anything, as you well know you ablah!" she fumes at him. Oddmund grins at her, angering Beata further and making her mood worse when Waldemar mirrors his expression. She just sits up when Waldemar moves and fumes quietly to herself. "Ahmoq eshaklar. Yarim zotli fohishadan intiqom olishimga xalaqit beryapsizmi?"

"Heard that," Oddmund informs her quietly and finishes just as quietly with. "And quit talking in our tongue as well. We do not want

Chet elliklar learning our dialect which is why we use theirs when we're amongst them. You know why from our histories."

"What was that all about?" Reuben whispers to Kali.

"Most of the other Races, except the Elves, are excluded from learning their tongue due to a disaster in their history during the days when the world was still waking up," she whispers, looking over her shoulder to ensure that the Dwarfs do not hear her. "It was around the time of The Splicing when they adopted a new tongue and kept it to themselves and the Elves."

"Alright then!" Trystan bellows as he wakes up finally, a thin film of sweat still clinging to him. "It's about time we moved on, don't ya think?"

"When you have broken your fast," Kali tells him coldly.

The feverish man just looks at her in mute surprise before muttering to himself. "Ah, goats' balls! She sounds just like ma bloody wife. Those two will probably get on like a flaming roundhouse on fire," he growls quietly grabbing a jerky from his pouch to chew on. Kali's sensitive hearing picks it up clear enough to make her look away and grin in amusement.

The group spends another hour or so with the Dwarfs ensuring that all their weapons are sharp while Waldemar and Oddmund keep a close eye on Beata as they work. Once they all finish, the whole group head out into the passageway.

Oddmund, being the last to enter the wide corridor and closing the door behind him, startles everyone by suddenly chuckling.

"What's with you now?" Beata snaps at him seeing that he visibly must pull himself together before he can answer.

"I was wondering why we didn't get disturbed," he says pointing to a strange mark in the door.

"I do not understand. They just look like two parallel lines of scratches in the wood joined by a line bent downwards in the middle," Kali responds when she looks closer at them.

"This is a Goblinoid mark meaning great danger or death," Oddmund explains with a smirk. "Or close enough to be interpreted as such." Beata glares evilly at Ghorza, drawing the others to look her way when Reuben chimes in.

"Actually, that was me."

"You, my boy?" Oddmund questions, looking on in admiration at the young man appraisingly and at his quick wit.

"Reuben asked me if there was a dire warning to Hobgoblins that would make them fear an area before I crashed," Ghorza says quietly. "That was the only one to come to mind. I don't understand much of their tongue though. Just snatches here and there,"

"I'm impressed," Oddmund says with another brief chuckle. "That's one mark that can keep out a whole tribe."

"What does it mean?" Kali asks him directly, but he just waves her question aside.

"I'm afraid that that is a question for another time since there is no easy answer. Right now, we have to keep moving since even that mark will not work forever."

"Agreed," Trystan rumbles impatiently.

"Now," Oddmund says his face all serious and spotting Waldemar holding onto Beata's arm. She continues to glare at the Half-Orc. "I suggest we split up from here. We'll go find ourselves some equipment from what you told us earlier and see if we can hunt us some Goblins while you kids try to find a way to get out of here as fast as you can." Conn tries to object, but Oddmund cuts him off with an upraised hand. He knows that if Beata stays with the group for too long, then the hot-headed Dwarf will cause trouble with Ghorza which could bring about the end of them all. Not that he feels any fondness towards the Half-breed. With some distance, Waldemar and he might be able to help bring her back down. "No, young Spiritualist. It needs to be done; otherwise, those buggers might catch us all from behind."

Conn nods his head quietly at the sense of the older Dwarf, though even he is aware of something else going on than just the fear of an ambush. He then realises that Oddmund flickers a glance between Beata and Ghorza while he was speaking. He nods again to the Dwarf; feeling more assured that he finally understands the significance of what Oddmund is saying and pleasing the Dwarf at how fast these kids catch on. "We need to get back to that area where we fought the Goblinoids to see what lies beyond."

Trystan snaps off a nod in solid agreement and heads through the double doors. Oddmund and Waldemar almost drag Beata in the opposite direction.

CHAPTER 30

Before ...

Trystan lights a torch and walks straight into the long dimly lit room with the young folks in his wake, rubbing his forearm with the base of the torch irritably. The air smells of stale sweat, personal waste, and rotting meat. He notices Kali scrunch up her narrow nose, so he knows that it is not just him that is affected by it. The others are too, but to a lesser extent, probably because their sense of smell is not so acute, or they have smelt something akin to it before. The first thing he does notice is that someone has removed the bodies from here, including the fallen Dwarf. *I'm glad that the others ain't 'ere. They would go nuts, especially that red-'aired mouthy one.*

Now they have a chance to notice the room properly, they see that the walls are engraved with images of Dwarfs in worship to their gods. Conn notes that there are only three of the four Elemental deities. It takes him a little while, but then he finally sees a tiny image of the Dwarf version of his Unda, the Goddess of All Waters, though their representation has 'him' with a scowling beardless visage. It is only the similarities between the Dwarfs version and his own like the water instead of legs that gave him any clue as to who their God of Water was or is. He is not entirely sure since he knows nothing about Dwarf religion. He is just theorising.

Halfway towards the double doors at the other end of the room, Trystan sees a door off to the side. He opens it to reveal a torchlit kitchen in the state opposite to the one attached to the dining hall. He walks in without hesitation. The others call to him, but he just ignores their 'whiny voices.'

There is a smouldering fire pit in one corner with a cauldron hanging over it that contains some watery brown liquid with a fatty scum forming across the surface. In the middle of the opposite wall, there is a bowl shape depression lined with copper in an alcove. This is being constantly filled to overflowing by the trickle of water from the rocks above it, then draining out the back through a hole that leads to a second one in the floor. Supporting this basin is a stone column with a small, rusted metal door about midway to the floor.

Above the depression is a carving of three religious-looking figures behind and flanking a Dwarf in a throne-like seat with what appears to be rays of light shining out of his head. The Dwarf is holding a rod in one hand and a stone in the other.

There are a couple of tables with various wood, stone, and flint tools and utensils used for preparing food, pieces of which also cover the surfaces amongst the implements and the surrounding floor. None of the implements look as if they have had a decent wash in ages.

Trystan looks around briefly before noticing that an odour emanates through a door in the wall off to one side. He walks into the room only to stop abruptly. There are various types and cuts of meat lying or hanging around in various states of decay, some salted, some smoked but most of them have not even been preserved. Trystan spies all the meat stored here and takes an involuntary shuddering deep breath. The effect on his feverish state makes his stomach churn so badly that he stumbles back out of the meat store, straight into Ghorza's waiting arms where she then lowers him to the ground.

"That's rank. The sight of the meat … especially the … the other meat. Well, it just … makes me feel sick ta see it … just hanging there." Every time he pauses to draw breath, his stomach convulses violently.

"How do you mean Mr. Gibbs?" Conn responds. "The other meat?" Conn looks in confusion at the others.

"I will go and see what he means," Kali volunteers. When she walks past Trystan, he tries to stop her only to find that the experience has virtually sapped his entire strength from him. Conn turns his attention to Reuben and Ghorza who are sifting through the clay and wooden pots and bowls.

"What are you two up to?" he calls to them.

"Looking for something clean enough to get him some water," Reuben answers quietly.

"We will need to wash something out and fill it," Ghorza says. She then drops a clay cup to break on the floor after seeing a maggot wriggling out of the thick detritus stuck to the inside. "Though most of these are beyond any attempts of scrubbing out whatever is in them," she adds with disgust.

"I found a bowl," declares Reuben. "Though, it is still going to need to be washed out first." He then finds a thick but short length of stick with one end spliced into bristles to scrub the wooden heavily stained bowl and fills it with fresh water. Kali gags as soon as she exits the meat store, her ivory complexion turning green.

"Are you alright?" Conn almost freaks at seeing her.

"I have just thrown up after what I saw," Kali answers him quietly. Conn takes the bowl from Reuben and supports her while she takes sips of the slightly salty water.

Reuben looks at Ghorza, who sighs and finds another bowl to scrub out with the stick brush to fill it for Trystan.

When Kali finally recovers enough, she begins to tell them what she found. "It is absolutely awful in there." She shudders before being able to continue between sips. "There is deer, boar, goat, and horse meat hanging up next to Elf, Human and Dwarf remains. There is even some Orc, Goblin, and Hobgoblin hanging in there."

"And they were feeding that to whoever is here?" Conn breathes in wonder.

"That's gross," comments Reuben in disgust.

"It's actually a common practice amongst some of them, such as the Goblinoid races and even some Orc tribes," Ghorza tells them nonchalantly causing them to look at her in surprise. "The animal meat is probably reserved for the Sorcerer and his friends while everyone else gets the rest." Kali and Trystan heave threateningly, making the others step back quickly.

"I'm going to echo Reuben. That **is** gross," Conn says, his stomach churning at the thought. Ghorza just shrugs by way of a response.

"Hold on," Kali says weakly. "The Hobgoblins came through the doors, but the Dwarfs were fighting Goblins when we joined them."

"That's true," Conn agrees. "But I don't know what you're driving at."

"The Goblins must have been working in the kitchen," Reuben says, thinking that he has Kali's train of thought.

"You said that me and Trystan were to be sent to the kitchens," Ghorza adds vaguely to the Half-Elf.

Kali nods with a grimace.

"OK! We really need to get out of here," Reuben declares not feeling too well himself at the new thought. "From Trystan's trembling and feverish look and Kali's face, distance sounds like the best medicine for them." He then finishes quietly with, "and for me."

"Agreed. If you and Ghorza can support Trystan, I'll help Kali," Conn says wholeheartedly. Reuben and Ghorza find that they need to sidestep through the door to get Trystan out of the kitchen where they head towards the set of double doors the Hobgoblins charged through what seems like days ago.

Taking a chance on what lies beyond, they walk straight into the next room to find the doors partially open across from them, though this room is no wider than the other corridors they already walked through.

After a quick look and a sigh of relief to find that they are indeed the only occupants here they set Kali and Trystan down. They then close both sets of doors. Now they have a chance to look around properly, the solitary torch in this room reveals stone benches against either length of the room and more religious-inspired carvings in the walls.

With the distance from the meat store, Kali and Trystan soon begin to recover. Conn checks on Kali first who nods that she is feeling much better. He then turns his attention to Mr. Gibbs. He notes that the man is really starting to burn up. Sweat visibly beads his forehead and soaks through his clothing.

Trystan tries to push the fussing young man away from him but Conn notes how feeble the effort is with some surprise. The man then starts scratching his arm where he was bitten furiously.

He leads the others away to another corner where he then voices some of his concerns. "We can delay no longer. Whatever happens now we need to get out of here and fast."

"Now is the time that you need to tell us what is going on Conn." Kali looks directly at him and notes that he is hiding something from them. Reuben also notes Conn's expression but ascertains what he means from when they spoke earlier in the tool store. The young man sighs in resignation.

"Mr. Gibbs is extremely ill and is way beyond my capabilities to heal him," he tells them in the hope beyond all hope that they leave it at that. He notices Ghorza subconsciously resting her hand on her bronze sword and tries not to think of the possible horrendous inevitability. "I think we should make a move and now."

"Alright." Reuben looks at him suspiciously. He knows that Conn is not being entirely honest with them and he can see it in Ghorza and Kali's expressions. *He's not just got a fever, but a wolf bite fever,* he suddenly realises. Now he understands why Ghorza is almost caressing the short sword. When everyone is ready, Reuben supports Trystan and heads out of the door down a wide torchlit corridor.

Walking down, they notice a brighter-lit room through an arched doorway at the far end. Disregarding the first double doors to their left, they head towards the far room in the hopes that it will lead them out so much faster than stopping to explore the rooms they pass. Halfway down the corridor, a section of the wall on the opposing side and in the middle of the two double doors slides back and to the side. They freeze on the spot for a couple of seconds before seeing a stunned Dwarf in scaled leather armour carrying a bronze-headed hand axe and a small shield, a second Dwarf also wears scaled leather armour with a short bow with a bronze-headed heavy mace hanging off her belt, while the third is wearing leather armour covered in bronze metallic rings and carrying a mattock.

"Oddmund! By the gods, you startled us." Reuben splutters quietly before breaking into a smile at the recovering Dwarf's broadening grin.

"Where did you come from?" Kali exclaims with a quiet squeak almost at the same time.

"Well met to you all too," he answers happily. "Secret doors create great shortcuts through complexes. Found one in the large dining hall you spoke of, though that was originally a courtroom. No sign of the moving statue you spoke of though."

"There are no secret doors in that room," Kali declares indignantly. "These fools cannot make a secret door that will deceive these eyes," she finishes with a sniff to the air. She notes with some surprise that it smells fresher here.

"You're certainly right there girlie," Beata snorts in agreement. Then adding, "Stupid shingle-heads."

"But that door is Dwarf-made," Oddmund finishes smugly.

"Dwarf?" Conn's expression echoes the confusion in his tone.

"Aye," Oddmund answers proudly as if he made it himself. He then points out the ceiling of the corridor they are standing in. For the first time ever, they suddenly realise that the ceiling is only half arched here where all the others were fully arched.

Waldemar then draws a stone across the wall to get their attention. When they face him, he shows them the palm-sized rock and lobs it to the top of the wall where it then just disappears. Looking on in confusion, the party look from him to Oddmund for an explanation.

"There is actually a walkway up there which doubles as a shooting gallery if they are ever attacked. That is accessed from somewhere else. This was definitely a Dwarf-made Mine. Any more explanations will have to wait for later." His face then turns serious. "We need to get out of here and fast judging from the looks of your friend."

"That's what we have been discussing before you turned up again," Kali tells him distractedly.

They hurry on down the long corridor until they see the second set of double doors off to their left just ahead of them. When they get there, everyone stands quietly while Reuben has a quick listen before leading them back a little way to tell them what he has heard. What sounded like multiple tools of wood and metal banging on stone.

"That sounds like the mine," Oddmund says, noticing Kali's distraction and choosing to ignore it for now. He already knows the source of it, though the surprising thing is that Trystan also seems to have picked up on it too. Humans are just not that sensitive. That concerns him more than he thought it would.

Waldemar taps Beata's arm and smiles at her as he nods at their direction of travel down the empty corridor where she sniffs the air herself and smiles back at him.

"We're not far from the exit Oddmund," Beata informs him.

"That will explain the temperature drop since we entered this corridor," Kali comments. While she feels it, it does not bother her.

"How would a shingle-head like yerself ever know that?" Beata scoffs.

"Because she's Half-Elven," Oddmund informs her quietly. "Let's see how close we can get."

"What about those behind the door?" Reuben asks him. "They may need our help."

The Dwarf smiles at the young man before answering him. "Your heart is in the right place, but we need to ensure that we can get them out without losing anyone, including your friend there," he finishes with a wave of his hand in the profusely sweating and shivering Trystan's direction.

Reuben nods and they continue back down the corridor to the first set of double doors in the right-hand wall. The young Scout listens at these doors and nods to confirm that he can still hear the same rhythmic sounds, only slightly louder. Oddmund then gathers them into a rough ring before saying anything of his thoughts.

"Right. Here's the plan as I see it, though if any of you have any different thoughts, then I will hear them," he begins, looking to each in turn. Not surprisingly *the kids are hanging off my every word while Beata and Waldemar have already decided to go with whatever plan I come up with. That's Beat Bop and Rockwall all over. So long as they get to hit something, they don't really care either way.* "We know that we are nearly out of this place. You young folk concentrate on getting your Mr. Gibbs out of here while us three will get those in the mine." He watches Reuben about to protest when he is talking but then falls quiet again once Oddmund finishes. "Everyone knows what they are doing?" He nods when they nod.

Oddmund does not bother to ask for questions since he knows that time is of the essence, especially if Trystan Gibbs is suffering from what he thinks the man is suffering from. He has never experienced it himself, but he has read various parchments about similar ailments. *First comes the fever, then the bloodlust, then the first change.* Shaking his head, he then tells them that it is time to move. He is pleasantly surprised that the now pale-looking Trystan even manages to stand on his own two feet using his spear for support so that he does not hamper any of the others, though that also concerns him at the same time.

The companions then get into position to be ready for Oddmund's signal.

CHAPTER 31

The Storm

Reuben stands near the arched doorway next to Ghorza. She watches four Dwarfs and two Humans in a large torchlit room bashing chunks of white rock into granules on a long table. A couple of the Dwarfs look up briefly but have give no indication that they have seen them.

Two of the largest greenish-yellow complexioned Hobgoblins they have seen keep watch on the slaves as they circle the room in a clockwise rotation. Fortunately, neither of them shows any concern for the corridor the companions are hiding in.

Behind him is Trystan, who is drenched through and shivering while holding his spear overly tight as he leans on it, with Conn and Kali behind him.

Reuben can see that the young Spiritualist is keeping a surreptitious eye on the big man. He divides his attention from the room in front of them and Oddmund standing near the closest set of double doors. Beata stands beside him and Waldemar beside her.

Oddmund looks around to each of them and nods where they nod back upon catching his eye. He looks to Reuben while Beata slowly slides the quietly grinding bolt handle back in preparation. He then holds up three stubby fingers and drops each one in turn. One of the Hobgoblins passes the crushing room entrance, turning his muscular back to them on his circuit.

With the fall of the third finger, Kali casts a spell finishing with the words *"Partum clypeus."* A brief yet faint glow flickers around her while Ghorza and Reuben race into the crushing room with the others following.

Beata shoves open the double doors where the Dwarfs charge through into a dimly lit cavern.

Ghorza and Reuben race to take on the first Hobgoblin from behind. The Half-Orc spins her rhomphaia in a tight arc to gash the Ogre across one leg who twists, roaring in surprise and pain. The roar is cut short when Reuben slashes his sword across the large creature's throat when it reaches down to grab his leg.

Seeing his comrade in trouble does not concern the second muscle-bound Hobgoblin. He just charges down the other side of the crushing room only to be hit by two of the Dwarfs with their small hammers. He then finds his way retarded by a pale-faced and trembling Trystan.

Conn races into the room and stops to assess the situation quickly before deciding to aid the big man.

Kali enters to see Trystan facing one of the creatures on his own while Conn moves to support him. She shoots a couple of energy bolts at the Hobgoblin. She is concerned at how enfeebled Trystan is looking despite his insistence on helping them.

The Goblinoid facing Trystan swings a mighty mattock and catches the man across the ribs to try and bury him in the wall.

Kali screeches Trystan's name catching Ghorza and Conn's attention. They must race around the long table to get to the second guard.

Conn reaches Trystan with a sliding stop. The Hobgoblin has already begun his swing and smashes his mattock against the wall right where the young man's head should have been.

Kali launches a second pair of energy bolts at the guard standing over Trystan and Conn in the hopes of distracting the creature long enough for the young Spiritualist to work his own magic.

Reuben finally manages to cut around the table to charge the hide-armoured Hobgoblin from behind with Ghorza close behind him.

Conn begins gathering the energies necessary to help Trystan. The mattock descends to shatter the young man's forearm. Screaming in agony, he barely keeps control of the mystic forces flowing through him through sheer force of will long enough for the large man's injuries to begin to knit together.

Before the Hobgoblin can follow up, a Dwarf behind him swings his hammer to shatter his knee, causing it to spin in a blind rage and a howl on the trapped Dwarf. Raising his mattock to pulp the audacious Dwarf, he does not realise its own danger. A spear punches straight through the back of its neck and out of an eye.

The Hobgoblin looks stunned for a moment, his one remaining yellow eye staring vacantly before his body catches up to what has just happened. He falls to the floor taking Trystan's spear with him.

Reuben has to jump quickly back to avoid being crushed by the falling Goblinoid.

Kali and Reuben search the bodies to find a key on each of them and release the slaves from the workstations they were chained to. Conn casts enough healing on himself to reduce the pain. He just finishes repairing his arm when Oddmund and Beata carry Waldemar through. All three of them are soaked in blood and water. While Conn helps Waldemar, Ghorza and Reuben leave to free the miners after they speak to Oddmund.

Looking around to those around him and receiving a quick nod from each of them in answer to his own, Oddmund then holds up three stubby fingers. Beata begins to slide back the handle in the door attached to an internal bolt that slides surprisingly smoothly, only a faint grinding of salt dust to mar its passage. Oddmund folds his last finger where the youths then race into the salt-crushing room.

Beata pushes the doors wide to reveal a cavernous salt mine sloping down slightly containing the surviving slave miners of various Races, gender, and ages. The mine is primarily supported by stalactite/stalagmite pillars.

The three Dwarfs charge in to get a greeting roar of surprise which rapidly changes to one of pure hatred resonating throughout the area. Beata stops immediately to swiftly look round. Two muscular-looking Hobgoblins in hide armour and carrying large mattocks in their fists charge through the shallow puddles toward the Dwarfs, one further behind the other. She quickly notches an arrow and shoots, only for the flying missile to graze off the leading creature's skull.

Oddmund and Waldemar take up their position several feet in front of Beata and ready their weapons.

Both Hobgoblins charge straight at the two steadfast Dwarfs where the first one receives a crack from Waldemar's mattock across its knee and a fast strike from Oddmund's underhanded axe strike straight to its groin. A screeching howl erupts from it as the Hobgoblin doubles over, staggering it back a step to narrowly avoid another arrow.

The second one races into the battle and almost catches Oddmund, who deftly dodges aside of a blow that winds up splashing salty water over him.

Waldemar swings a second time at the first Hobgoblin's other knee and smiles at a second satisfactory crack. He smiles even wider at seeing the Goblinoid's shattered kneecaps and hearing its cry of sheer agony.

Oddmund is too busy dodging the second creature's potentially devastating weapon that is slapping up a lot of water and rock dust with each crash on the ground.

Waldemar goes to avoid an attack from the first pain blinded Hobgoblin, only to slip on some shingle as the offending mattock swings wildly above him. An arrow punches through its armour and chest to pierce its heart.

The last Hobgoblin keeps swinging, though it misses the constantly evading pair.

Beata maintains a steady rate of bow fire. To ensure that she does not hit her friends, she keeps her shots high, though not one hits the Hobgoblin. She notches another arrow but when she pulls back intending to go for the kill shot when the bone bow cracks. Cursing the stupid weapon, she flings it to one side and charges forward pulling her heavy mace.

The Hobgoblin brings its mattock down on Waldemar only to strike the floor in a splash once again. He then bellows in agony as Beata and Oddmund smash their mace and hammer against the Ogre's right and left hip almost simultaneously. The pain-stricken creature lashes out blindly and causes Beata to duck while tracking the swinging weapon.

Waldemar, seeing the wildly swinging mattock coming his way, is too slow to jump out of the way. Pain explodes across his chest, the sensation of flight, then a second bone-jarring crash on his back.

Oddmund, too intent on seeing an opening, swings his axe into the creature's forehead where it drops his weapon.

A cold fear seizes Beata, and everything seems to move in slow motion after the mattock caught Waldemar. She watches her friend get launched backwards to crash against the cavern wall. Then sliding down and almost piling up on a dry patch of floor. Screaming out Waldemar's name and forcing Oddmund's attention to their friend for a second, a blind rage surge through them.

Snapping round on the Hobgoblin trying to nurse his numerous injuries, they both swing their weapons with almost supernatural strength on either side of his temples.

The guard does not even have a chance to realise that its life is just about to end. It just ends.

Without saying a word to the other, they walk over to Waldemar and carry him out of the salt mine cavern gently while the slave miners just look solemnly on.

Oddmund and Beata carry Waldemar into the salt-crushing room where the other now free slaves sweep a space clear on the salt grounding table for them to lay their comrade down.

Reuben speaks briefly to Oddmund, then nudges Ghorza and indicates with a wave of his head towards the mine where the two Dwarfs just came from. Without a word, they leave the room while a weary Conn moves over to where Waldemar is lying.

When the young Spiritualist is about to say a prayer for their fallen companion, he notices a slight fluttering of Waldemar's ruined chest. Leaning down close to listen, he looks at Oddmund and Beata in surprise. He then prays to the divine powers with all his heart and soul. Faintly at first but growing in intensity, the healing energies begin flowing through him and into the Dwarf. Although it takes virtually everything he has left, he sees Waldemar's chest begin to regain its proper shape when the ribs knit together and his breathing gains strength. Then the healing energies cease, Conn falls to the floor with waves of exhaustion washing over him.

Reuben and Ghorza return from the salt-crushing room ahead of six terrified slaves. Just after, Waldemar manages to sit up and slide off the table into the waiting arms of his friends.

CHAPTER 32

Reunion

While the Dwarfs greet each other, being long-separated comrades, the Humans working with the Dwarfs retreat to a corner to distance themselves from everyone.

The six slaves from the salt mine meekly follow Reuben and Ghorza into the salt-crushing room. They look around like they are wondering what horror is to come next or if this is just an elaborate game arranged by the Sorcerer and his friends for their vile amusement.

Kali looks across at the new arrivals to see what she thinks is a Human girl until she spies the hairy-topped sandaled feet and sloped forehead. It is then that she realises that this girl is a Hauflin woman, though she is very thin in comparison to Marroc Mugwort, the Palovicus apothecary. She always did wonder if Marroc ever stopped eating; he even ate when treating his patients.

The next three are Human. A young boy with almond-shaped eyes, a young olive-complexioned girl almost coming into womanhood if she has not done so already, and the third being quite a bit older than Trystan Gibbs with a wildly bushy greying beard and pale blue eyes.

The final two are Elven.

It takes Kali a few seconds to recognise them through the mess they are covered in. "Eloen? Tarron?" whispers Kali, wondering if they are actually who she thinks they are.

With their sensitive hearing, they look directly at her where she realises that she is right. With a hesitant smile, in case they do not recognise her, she slowly stands up after making sure that Conn is resting comfortably. She moves towards them with tears beginning to sting her eyes. She calls to them again. When the two Elves from her mother's city acknowledge her, they breathe a sigh of relief, understanding that this is no Sorcerer's joke, and begin talking quietly with Kali, though Tarron is more reticent.

The young girl holding the younger boy around the shoulders sees a weary, shivering, and sweat-soaked man. He is leaning against a dead creature like one of those that guarded them in the mine before the Dwarfs arrived and killed them. Looking around, she spots a young man resting on the floor against the salt crushing table; the Dwarfs congregating together in a huddle, including the one sent flying against the wall, though the girl has no idea how he survived, let alone be up and conversing with the others; the Elves speaking to another while the male throws venomous looks at the Dwarfs, and the two that unlocked their bindings are having an argument with the old man from the mine. The Hauflin woman they know as Ana, rests in a nearby corner just quietly watching everything.

Reuben and Ghorza check on the miners to ensure that they are all right. None of them will be up for a fight any time soon, but at least they are out of the mine. When Conn feels more up to it, he will check on their cuts and scrapes, they tell them. They go to the old man where he glares at Ghorza before turning his attention to the young man with a barely controlled rage.

"You are working with them," he snarls accusingly.

"Working with them? We just freed you," Reuben retorts hotly. The man's words clearly confuse Ghorza as well.

"Not that cursed Stafa and his ilk," the man rasps, though Reuben cannot figure out if that is the man's age or the effects from working in the salt mine. "Them!" he says with a vicious shake of his head at Ghorza.

"Ghorza? She's our friend and companion," Reuben responds hotly in the larger-built man's face with the understanding of the old man's accusation sinking in. "She has helped us get to you so that you can be freed with the chance of us getting you all out of here." Reuben knows he is messing up his words, but he does not care right now. He is just so infuriated at this person's reaction to his liberators.

"Heimskur rass bara fattar paf ekki!" The man looks to Reuben who clearly does not understand him. "Because they can't be trusted!"

"I trust Ghorza with my life, more than I ever can with anyone else," Reuben rages in response.

Ghorza must look away at her friend's words when a tear begins to form in the corner of her eye.

"Then more fool you, strákur!" the man retorts. He then drops to the floor and leans back against the wall, refusing to say anything more to them.

The young girl looks back to the shivering man lying against the dead creature. His filthy shirt around the edges of the leather cuirass looks soaked, the full scruffy beard covers most of his pale face but there remains something familiar about him to her dry and sorely tired eyes. Walking towards him with her arm still protective around the young boy's shoulders the man finally becomes clearer to her. "Papa?"

Hearing the small voice of the frightened girl, he turns his head towards her. He looks at them with blank brown eyes not understanding who he is seeing. He then sits bolt upright as he looks at them quizzically. "Lianhua, Tudi?" He blinks again. *How can they be here?* "What are yer doing 'ere? Where's ya mama?" He then looks frantically around the room as he staggers up using the wall to support him. "Where's ya mama?" his demand rising in volume which draws everyone's attention and jolting Conn awake enough to look over.

Instead of answering him, the two children race into his arms where they begin crying against him. He kneels back down so that he is at the same level as them and holds onto them tightly.

"What is it, Mr. Gibbs?" Kali calls, rising to walk towards him and leaving the Elves she was speaking to.

"They're ma kids," Trystan tells her. He then prises them from him so he can see their faces properly before speaking to them again. "Now, where is yer mama?" He demands of them again with a slight growl of irritation that his wife would ever let their children be brought to a place like this. He then begins to shake them as his volume begins to rise again. "Why aren't ya safe at 'ome with yer mama?"

"Stop that, Mr. Gibbs!" Conn calls over him, though he looks as pale as an Elf. Trystan stops shaking them and starts to stride over to him when Reuben and Ghorza move swiftly to get between the Goatherder and the young Spiritualist.

Kali reaches his children and moves them to the opposite side of the long table, trying to think of a spell she can use to stop him if she must. She was surprised to learn that he was married. Now she is absolutely stunned that he has children. Though it does explain his overwhelming desire to get out. *I just thought he was being mule-headed about it.*

"She's dead papa. Mama's dead," Lianhua says, her voice breaking. The simple words are like a sledgehammer blow that stuns him as he turns to face his daughter. He looks to Tudi for confirmation though the boy can barely whisper, "it's true papa," through his tears.

"You need to calm down Mr. Gibbs," Conn tells him in a quiet and reasonable tone. "You're scaring your children when they need you the most right now."

"Where do ya get off telling me ta calm down!" he growls at the young man while staggering to his feet though every muscle in his body screams in agony. He uses that pain to fuel his anger and his strength.

Conn cannot help but see the anger in the big man's eyes between Ghorza and Reuben, despite his feverish state.

Trystan glares first at Ghorza, but when he turns his attention to Reuben, Ghorza snaps into motion.

She slams his head against the wall beside him with one hand to disorientate him. When he bounces off the wall, she spins him half circle and brings her other arm around the back of his neck. With the back of her hand forcing Trystan's chin up while being bent forward almost double, she forces him to look at his terrified children.

Trystan struggles against the Half-Orc's grip for a little while, but the sight of his children cowering and crying behind Kali's dress while they watch him soon saps what little strength he felt from his efforts.

With no other option but to look at his children, the realisation hits Trystan like that Hobgoblin's heavy club. Tears begin to sting his own eyes. *What in the damnation am I doing? What is 'appening to me? My 'ead 'urts like 'ell. So warm, so cold, gut churning. My babies. They need me and I feel like I'm losing it with them. It's not their fault. Jus' feel so tired all the time. They need me and I need them. More so now than ever.*

With a nod from Reuben, Ghorza lets the man go where he then falls to his knees, tears streaming down his cheeks.

Trystan struggles to hold up his arms for his children.

They tentatively come out of hiding at Kali's smile of encouragement and fall into their father's embrace and cry with him.

"Told ya they couldn't be trusted," the old man mutters from beside Conn.

"And who are you?" Conn counters as he looks at the old man.

"Dragoslav Wolinski of the Tribe of the Dire Wolf," he proclaims proudly. "Was, of the Tribe of the Dire Wolf," he says much more quietly.

"What do you mean by that?" Conn wearily looks askance at Dragoslav while his forehead creases.

"When a man is considered too old to provide for his family, then he's expelled from the tribe where he is to wander off and die," he explains to the Spiritualist. He then takes a deep breath before continuing. "I was wounded on a hunt and couldn't keep up with the others anymore, so I was thrown out." He then shudders before he continues. "That was when I bumped into that damned spellcaster and his half-breed sidekick before winding up here," he finishes miserably.

"I was actually asking who can't be trusted," Conn responds, even more confused now. Kali joins them now the situation with Mr. Gibbs has been dealt with.

"The Half-Orc attacked him for no other reason than he is upset," Dragoslav answers indignantly.

"She was not attacking him," Kali retorts heatedly. "Ghorza subdued him long enough to help calm him down quickly for the sake of his kids."

"What does this … subdued … mean?" It is clear to Kali and Conn that Dragoslav has no understanding of the very concept.

"A conversation for another time," Oddmund interrupts. "It's high time we all got outta here."

"Ha. Says the Dwarf who got us all caught in the first place," the male Elf snarls musically at him. Both Elves have the same slate colour hair that Kali has, though their complexion is more porcelain with darker grey highlights along their cheekbones, nose, and brow.

"You got them captured with you?" Kali explodes at Oddmund. The musical lilt to her voice does little to diminish her tone.

"Well, it was like this-" Oddmund begins sheepishly.

"Oh, this should be good," Tarron sneers.

"Not right now Tarron," Kali snaps, realising that it is not going to be a quick explanation if there is any worth hearing. "Let us get out of this infernal mine first at least. Eloen," she looks to the female Elf. "Please do not let them start this now."

"Elf, you're just lucky-"

"Enough Beata!" Kali warns.

Ghorza moves to stop them, but Reuben stops her and places himself between the Elves and the Dwarfs.

"If you want to keep this up then you are quite welcome to do so," Reuben says loudly enough to get himself heard. He then continues in a dangerously quiet tone. "But you will do so once we have got the children safely out of here first. If you do not agree to this, then I will ensure that you will not leave here alive. Is that understood?"

Ghorza looks at her closest friend with concern when she almost sees a darkness wash over him briefly.

The Elves look at the upstart boy with light grey eyes as hard as granite though it is more Oddmund's response that surprises them.

"Aye lad, you got the right of it. Let us all get out of here in one piece."

"The prisoners should stay here until we ensure that the way is clear before bringing them with us," Ghorza suggests.

"I'm staying with ma kids," Trystan declares abruptly. The Goatherder really wants to join them, but his hands are too painful, and do not have the strength to hold his spear now.

Conn nods after he stands up to ensure that the salt miners' and the salt crusher captives' injuries are as clean as he can get them at this time. *Some of them have begun to turn infectious, but there is nothing I can do right now.* He needs the time to rest and pray for he has little enough mana strength right now.

Ghorza hands Conn the two clear potions Gimil had given her. "You look tired. Could you use these to regain your energy?"

He looks at her in surprise and smiles gratefully. "It doesn't work that way, but I'm sure that I can use them if I need to." He then hugs the Half-Orc in thanks. Conn is then surprised when the female Elf Kali called Eloen suddenly moves to his side and flickers a smile upon catching his eye.

"I will help you," she tells him regally with a smile. Tarron is about to object until she throws him a threatening look of her own.

When they are ready, Reuben and Ghorza stand at the double doors out of this room where even the tough hide of the Half-Orc can feel the sharpness of the wind blowing through the cracks in the door.

Kali and Conn take up position behind them with the now seven Dwarfs bringing up the rear.

The Hauflin woman walks up to Reuben as silently as a ghost, causing the young man to jump in surprise.

"I apologise for scaring you," she says softly.

Reuben then realises that her abrupt appearance by his side is not the only thing that causes his sudden fright. It is the memory of another one of these folks who sat in an alley cradling her knee before the back of his head exploded in a flash of pain.

"I am Ana. Ana Lightouch."

However, that one had auburn hair, whereas this one is sandy. Before he can talk, he has to swallow at the lump that has suddenly formed in his throat. "It's okay," he says to her trying to be as genuine as he can with a smile. "How can I help you?"

"Do I look so fearsome to your young eyes?" When he shakes his head, Ana looks askance at him briefly before Ghorza pipes up about his first encounter with another Hauflin woman which causes this one to nod a couple of times. "Ah, now I understand. You've met Salvia. Yes, she is good at what she does."

"Sounds like you admire her," Reuben says looking at her suspiciously.

"I admire her skills," she answers him with a nod. "Not what she does with those skills. But that is not why I disturb you."

"Then why do you?" husks Ghorza sharply and receiving a warning look from Reuben. "What? We're probably about to have yet another fight before we get out of here as it is."

"Your friend is quite correct, but I do disturb you for a good reason," Ana says quickly. She does not want them degenerating into an argument before she can make her request. When she sees them looking down at her quizzically, she decides to continue. "I notice that you have spare blades in your boots. Would you mind if I borrow them? I have some skill with their use and can help you should there be another battle."

"Erm, yeah. Sure," Reuben stammers. He sheaths his weapons and bends down enough to retrieve them. He hands her the daggers before drawing his short sword and dagger. When he looks to a confused Ghorza, he just shrugs nonplussed himself.

Ana thanks him as she then checks their balance and flips them around in her hands a couple of times before walking back to stand beside Kali at the doorway.

Reuben gives Ghorza a twist of a smile before they reach for the door handles in preparation.

CHAPTER 33

Dark Battle

With a nod to each other, Reuben and Ghorza each push on a door just before hearing "Gbaa!", Oddmund bellowing out "No!", Ana yelling "Bows!" and Beata screaming "Down!" in rapid succession. Reuben jumps back, pulling the door with him before falling to the floor. Ghorza snaps her door shut and holds them both while several thuds reverberate through them. Reuben's vehement curse then draws everyone's attention to the arrow sticking in his thigh.

Conn moves up and kneels beside the young scout to examine the arrow's position. With a relieved sigh, he finds that the arrow went straight into the side of his thigh, stopped only by Reuben's leather trousers on exit. Conn finds that the tip of the arrowhead exited the young man's leg cleanly. His idea of 'cleanly' being that the whole arrowhead punched through.

He calls for help in getting Reuben to the table and instructs them to hold him in place. With an apologetic twist of a smile, Conn makes a small incision in Reuben's trousers. He snaps off the feathers then alternately pushes and pulls the arrow straight through where the young man screams in agony with each motion. The young Spiritualist uncorks one of Ghorza's vials and drizzles a little potion on either side of the wounded leg where it stops bleeding. He then covers the fragile wounds with a poultice.

"Do you feel any better?" Conn asks knowing that the leg is not fully healed. He would like to do more, but he also has a feeling that he is going to need the potions and his energies for what is to come.

"It still hurts like hell," Reuben says with a wince when he puts his weight on it.

"It will," Conn explains apologetically. "This is all I can do until we get a chance to rest."

"It's fine Conn," Reuben tells him with a tap on his shoulder. "At least I can still move on it." He takes a few tentative steps and winds up limping until he can master the twinges of pain with each step.

"Did either of you get a chance to see who attacked us?" Kali asks them.

"Couldn't see a thing," Ghorza tells her. "But we were kind of distracted by all your shouting." Kali then looks to the two Dwarfs and the Hauflin.

"When I heard the command, I knew what was coming. Didn't get a chance to see anything though I fear," the Hauflin volunteers.

"When I hear bows as a warning, my instinct is to hit the ground," Beata admits.

"I saw people ready to attack, but could not see who properly," Oddmund tells them.

"The room went totally dark soon after we opened the doors," Reuben adds. "I don't think even the light from this room could penetrate it."

"I wonder if the darkness is an evocation?" Kali says looking to Conn. She does not know why she turns to him, but *he seems as adept with the knowledge of the magical arts as I am.* She then remembers a conversation with another Spiritualist, Gimil Tarik.

"It is possible," he answers her thoughtfully. "Though, it is not one known to the Goddess Unda that I have heard of. One of the other faiths may have access to such magic, through their worship of Ignis or Gaiea for example."

"Unless it is not divine but more arcane based," Kali suggests.

"Are ya going ta get going, or not," Trystan calls weakly. "I gotta get my kids outta 'ere!"

"Unfortunately, your friend is quite correct. Rudely put, but correct all the same," Tarron tells them with a melodic snort of contempt at the large Human with his children. "If he really cares for them, then he would be more involved in aiding their freedom too."

"It is plain to anyone that Mr. Gibbs is very poorly," Conn tells the Elf quietly.

"And what's yer problem Elf?" Trystan snaps back at him, "Standing there like ya gotta support post shoved up yer arse!"

"I totally agree with our Mr. Gibbs. We really do need to get moving," Oddmund says quickly and loudly enough to attract their attention from each other. *While I have no love for these Elves of the mountains, fighting amongst ourselves will be a sure way for none of us to get out.*

"Me too," Ghorza husks while glaring at Trystan and Tarron threateningly. "Let's get in there and take the fight to them hard and fast."

"Tsk. That is such a typical Orc tactic," Tarron mutters to Eloen.

"I may only be a Half-breed, but my hearing is still good enough to catch your words," Ghorza snarls at him.

"Yep," Reuben chips in before any aggressive hostilities break out. "It's definitely time to move. Everybody, back into position. Now!"

Between them, Ghorza and Reuben agree that only one of the doors needs to be open, which might offer some protection to those following behind. Reuben shoves open the door and switches places with Ghorza who slips into the room with her back against the closed half and crouches.

With the door open, Kali summons the arcane energies she requires to illuminate the dark room finishing with a "obtestārī lūx". The resulting spell sends a globe of bright light about a foot in diameter from her hand only for the darkness to swallow her attempt. "The darkness is magically created but I am not powerful enough right now to banish it," she tells them forlornly.

Beata bellows a curse in her own language and charges into the darkness. Waldemar and Oddmund, suddenly grasping that Beata has rushed off yet again, give chase with the other four closing in from behind.

It is in their rush to catch up to Beata when the Dwarfs hear the guttural "Gbaa!" where Waldemar involuntarily catches someone in his arms.

Some of the arrows fly out almost hitting Kali.

Staggering backward just out of the darkness, Waldemar then realises that he is holding Beata with an arrow in her chest and a second in her right arm. Her weapon? He has no idea where that is, though he does know that she is going to be highly upset for losing it.

Oddmund brings his shield up in front of him and crouches to cover their retreat with the other four Dwarfs from the salt-crushing room, so

Waldemar can focus on dragging her out. One of them even stumbles over something and scoops it up. When the Dwarf looks at what he has got after returning to the light, it is Beata's mace.

Conn sighs with the realisation of what his job is going to be in this fight. Fortunately, he knows that he is not alone since the Elf, Eloen is with him to help those who will be hurt in the coming struggle. She is working up another poultice with his pestle and mortar for those who are injured by using the herds he has placed on the table. *If only we could defeat the darkness.* He then focuses on pulling the arrows lodged in the unconscious red-haired Dwarf. He is only just too glad that neither arrow struck any vital areas.

Once the arrows are removed, Eloen presses poultice-smeared rags against the injuries. Conn uses the last of one vial to stop the bleeding, but there is nothing more he can do for Beata, or anybody else for that matter. He knows that he will need his energies for the next victims coming out of that room.

Kali picks herself up after diving out of the doorway and tries to figure out her next move just before more arrows skitter out of the darkness. Coming awfully close to being an arrow's target is the fearful reality that strikes her, numbing her thoughts for a few seconds. It is only the knowledge that the others are relying on her to help them that allows her to begin to focus again.

"Gbaa!"

Oddmund is almost out when he falls with a couple of the missiles catching him near his eye and in his arm. He does not even realise due to the oblivion of unconsciousness taking him down. Blood pours profusely from both wounds. A couple of the crushing room Dwarfs drag him out with them from the hellish room.

Reuben knows that the room continues to open out to both sides once through the door, though he cannot see much beyond that. Glancing quickly round the door, he sees Ghorza vanishing into the darkness, stabbing the rhomphaia ahead of her with each step forward while keeping her back to the roughhewn wall. He slips into the room where Ghorza was crouching. Taking a deep breath, he launches himself to the opposite side where the darkness swallows him completely. Three thuds strike the closed half of the double doors, though another three flies out through the open half.

Waldemar helps the Dwarfs by grabbing Oddmund by his leather scale armour with one hand and dragging his bleeding friend to the young spiritualist when an arrow catches him in the leg, causing him to stumble. Using his mattock for additional leverage, the stubborn and silent Dwarf slowly continues with his self-appointed task to get Oddmund back to the healers.

Ana is just about to move in after Reuben when she hears the word, "gbaa!" before more arrows fly out of the darkness and strike the other side of the closed door. *That is a Goblinoid dialect, though it is too guttural for just Goblins.* She needs those arrows to stop flying out before she can do anything, otherwise, they will likely strike her before she can even get close in her weakened state. Despite this, she also knows that they could do with her in that room to help locate their aggressors since each attack is proceeded by that single command. She decides to dive into the room to follow the young man to help him. She feels that it is her responsibility to show him that not all Hauflins are like Salvia, despite knowing how unreasonable that is at the same time.

Ghorza, cursing quietly to herself that even her second sight is failing her, stabs again into the darkness with each step. She grunts when she feels a sting against her arm, though she just shrugs it off while continuing her stabbing exploration. This darkness is frustrating and angering her at the same time.

They hear another command from the darkness. "N'ihu n'okwa. Gbanye!" This is followed by some clatters on the stone floor.

Reuben steadies himself before feeling his way silently around the room, his ears twitching for any and every noise around him. He feels another wall that he believes is running parallel to Ghorza's. He waits and listens, mentally praying to whatever gods are listening that they will not notice him too soon.

Ana also listens intently. She hears the Half-Orc grunt at one point while continuing to move into the room. Then the realisation hits her. *Bugbears! Damn them all to the nine hells!* A heavy bestial grunt of pain follows shortly after the sound of metal striking stone. She then hears an odd thud sound and nods in satisfaction. She decides to dive into the room.

Ghorza grunts when something slams into her chest and knocks her back a step. In pure anger, she swings her weapon in an overhead arc and is satisfied by the sudden restriction of motion before continuing to strike through to the floor. Something heavy hitting the floor follows soon after.

Reuben stabs out with his short sword just as Ghorza was doing with her rhomphaia but feels nothing but air. He then hears that command before bowstrings vibrate to release their deadly barrage, though not so many as before. He realises that he is quite safe where he is. But he also knows that his new friends need him to do more than hide.

Conn and Eloen help Waldemar move Oddmund to the heavy table. The young Spiritualist fears for the old Dwarf's survival when he sees the pale pallor around his forehead and cheeks.

Ana maintains her crouch to make her a foot shorter than her three-foot stature where she then finds a corner in the room. Another Goblinoid command resonates out of the darkness, "Azu n'okwa. Gbanye!" *They are dropping their bows.* A second clattering of what sounds like bones being dropped seems to confirm her thoughts.

Ghorza and Reuben both feel a rush of air near them. Without knowing it, they both swing out with their weapons. Only Ghorza smiles when she catches someone with the bite of her weapon. This is followed by a guttural cry of what she hopes, is their agony.

Conn and Eloen remove the brass-headed arrow from Waldemar's leg and bandages him to try and prevent further blood loss. He decides not to call upon Unda at present. He knows that his ability to heal multiple wounds is limited at best. There are still people in there that will need his divine magic more. He does promise Waldemar that if there is anything he can do afterward, then he will surely try. The silent Dwarf just nods in understanding.

Reuben almost loses his sword when his shoulder explodes in pain after something heavy crashes against it. He stabs out with his dagger to no avail.

Ana continues to sneak her way into the room, following a similar path she saw Reuben take before he disappeared into the darkness. She soon discovers the boy. He nearly knocks her over when he stumbles backward after being struck. "Boy," she whispers. "High attacks only."

"Got it," he answers. Then he feels a crashing blow against his left arm that does make him lose his dagger.

Ghorza feels the rushing of air pass her from a couple of heavy objects. She retaliates with a powerful strike of her own, making contact to result in another howl of pain. She decides to strike in the same area again, but this time she misses it. She feels the breeze when one of her attackers fail to land a blow against her.

Reuben lances out with his sword and finally cuts deeply into his foe, though he receives a heavy blow to his chest for his troubles. The winded young man falls to the floor after feeling his chest cave-in, though he remembers little after that.

Ghorza stabs out with her rhomphaia in sheer anger. She only just holds on to her weapon when her victim falls backward, grabbing it in hopes of wresting it from her grasp.

She does not know how, but Ana feels that the young man who lent her his daggers is in serious trouble. She lashes out and catches a creature with the resulting curse convincing her that her supposition is correct. She is definitely fighting Bugbears. She goes on the attack with even more ferocity.

Ghorza, for all her troubles, gets another whack to her stomach to enrage her further.

To everyone's surprise, the darkness suddenly drops to reveal two dead Bugbears near Ghorza with another two standing near her. There are two more bleeding from multiple cuts near Ana in front of an evilly smiling Treorai.

In her enraged state, Ghorza buries her weapon deep into the stunned Bugbear's chest.

Ana slices another open across their leather-covered hirsute stomach in a sudden flash of movement, then dancing away to avoid the worst of the attack from the other one.

Conn, not even thinking about why the darkness fell, charges into the room with Eloen beside him. Quickly taking stock, they grab Reuben away from the fight.

Kali races in to help Ghorza.

The Half-Orc receives a club to her chest to infuriate her further still.

Then Treorai pulls his hand out from under his robe. The darkness falls over them once again.

Ghorza slashes out again to kill another Bugbear.

Ana manages to drop another.

Conn grabs up Reuben's short sword and only just manages to block an attack while Eloen stays with Reuben.

Ana howls briefly in pain before she falls silent.

Then the darkness disappears from the room once again. This allows Ghorza to gut the last Bugbear facing off against her. Kali is the first to notice why the darkness has disappeared this time. Treorai has gone.

Ghorza charges in with an almighty overhead strike that cleaves the last Bugbear's head in two. She finally loses her grip on the blood-soaked haft of the weapon when the dead creature falls, this one finally dragging it out of her hands.

Without hesitation, Conn turns to Reuben and uses the second potion while noticing Eloen race over to Ana and bandaging the mortally wounded Hauflin.

Ghorza's anger finally abates. She drops to her knees, then promptly falls to the floor, unconscious.

Conn uses the last of their bandages to stem the flow of blood from the Half-Orc's multiple injuries. There is absolutely no way she should have been able to continue fighting with that many wounds and bruising across her arms and torso. When he finishes, he finally drops to the floor in exhaustion. *None of us are going anywhere right now, it seems.*

CHAPTER 34

What Came Before

A purple glowing outline of a doorway appears in the wall of the dining hall. Lusha is sipping at the full-bodied red wine while waiting for Treorai's return. When he steps through from somewhere else in the complex, she sees some of their newest captives struggling to get out of a purple ropey mesh and the Goatherder firing an arrow at her Master before the fading portal turns back into a solid wall.

She had helped him seal the fine thread net against the wall and watched him hide it behind a blending spell. That was after that diseased woman escaped, causing them to lose many of the Goblins that they had to watch over the prisoners they captured. The net trap can be activated in one of two ways: when the targets pass it; or by an activation word. Her Master, having a vindictive streak, went with the activation command just so he could see his victims struggle before adding additional insults to his victims.

The first time they sought miners, they used Goblins for the work and Treorai thought that Orcs would make good guards for the slaves. Unfortunately, the Orcs proved too restive, and many Goblins were lost.

It does not help that Orcs and Goblins generally do not mix well and barely make contact unless it is to trade. The Goblins tried to employ some Hobgoblins to protect their wares until their larger cousins began to dominate them to serve instead. Then they made their own trade negotiations with the Orcs.

"Master," she wonders, giving him a quizzical look. She knows full well how nasty Treorai can quickly turn if he thinks anyone is trying to play him. She has seen how far he will go to brutalise someone only on a couple of occasions and it scared her almost to death.

The targets of Treorai's cruelty were beyond anything that the Slaver Lords from the Southern States could ever devise. She remembers one man, who tried to play Treorai when the Sorcerer had an extremely bad day, was charmed into walking through a pride of lions. Another occasion was when Treorai was in a jubilant mood until a stupid Hauflin wanted to renegotiate his price for some information. Treorai hypnotised the Hauflin into swallowing half a Salamander only for the Salamander to regrow inside of them. *It took months for the suffering Hauflin to die before his stomach erupted.* That thought still makes her want to heave, but she manages to force it down with a large swallow of wine.

Fortunately, Treorai does not notice her preoccupation. He is sorting through scrolls he produces from his cloak until he finds the one he needs.

"Too much, too soon. That Herder is the one at fault here beyond my own desire to remain concealed," he tells her tapping his staff twice on the floor to create another doorway before looking back to Lusha. "He has managed to get our captives to work together against us. Come and I'll tell you what happened."

"Yes, Master."

"Hobbes, you are to make sure that no-one leaves this room alive or die in the trying. Then return to Montem Turris." The stone creature rumbles its affirmative where Treorai then steps through with the golden-skinned woman in his wake. When the doorway begins vanishing, he hears Hobbes clearing up the dining hall table and smiles wistfully. *As if anyone can defeat Hobbes without magic.*

Creating a simple light, Treorai illuminates a small room with no door, lined with shelves of different items. He continues talking while both fill a sack with what they can carry. He looks at his first tome, shrugs, then puts it back on the shelf. "You know; I really did underestimate that Herder. He managed to get those four kids from different parts of the Collis Valle with vastly different backgrounds to work together so that they could escape Skarmazh and his cells. It is quite unbelievable what he has managed to do. That is the first and last time I will never gather so many together again." He places his hand in part of the wall and gives a little tug to cause part of it to open, revealing a room of miscellaneous items and sacks of silver, copper, and tin ore. There is a door to his left and right. Looking briefly to the wealth in this room, he reluctantly goes through the left door with due haste. Treorai continues straight through a vulgar-looking room where his Goblinoids have their meals provided for them by the slaver kitchen and heads through the door opposite. *Disgusting creatures.*

"Are you sure that he is the organiser in their escape?" she wonders softly.

Turning a corner, he heads halfway up the corridor before opening a secret door. They glance briefly back the way they came when they hear the squeal of hinges. He then continues through the passage beyond to another secret door.

"Who else? Do you really think that that drunken angry sot is going to listen to four children who have barely reached adulthood?"

She nods in silent agreement, though she does wonder. It was one of the reasons she chose Conn in the first place. Deep in thought, she keeps up with the Sorcerer.

The secret door slides shut behind them where they continue up a parallel corridor.

"No. He is much more resourceful than I gave him credit for. He has got them armour and weapons from the armouries of those we captured and stripped, as well as breaking through the careful ambush and trap I had set in place for just such an eventuality."

She snaps a wary look at his back when he turns the corner at the end of the passage and strides through a room with six slaves pounding down chunks of rock salt on a heavy table. They then brush the granules into sacks beside each of them under the watchful eyes of two of his strongest Hobgoblins.

"Of course, I have planned for this contingency as well and have already begun to make the necessary preparations," he continues casually.

They pass through a set of double doors into another room containing less than half a dozen sacks of crushed salt. At the other end of the room is an alcove next to a flight of stone spiral steps heading up. *I really wish I could've gotten through that door to the Dwarf stronghold,* he thinks wistfully while glancing towards the alcove.

Lusha continues to say nothing as she follows him up the stairs into the first level of a tower.

"Tell me what you learned from your research," he tells her where he then begins drawing a pair of concentric circles on the floor between which he writes intricate runes from memory.

"Krilge is seeking a weapon of a metal as yet unknown to this region which has only been found in the wild-lands to the south. An ore they have called iron. This metal is in a Goblinoid stronghold in the hills to the south-east of a town called Lakeside. The stronghold has strong defences. I believe that their best chance will present itself if they wait until someone leaves the stronghold who is carrying these weapons before they hit or trade with them. I believe Salvia will be the most crucial at locating and making the necessary plans to ensure Krilge gets hold of them. It will take them quite some time to get back to us."

"This iron," Treorai asks distractedly continuing to write his runes. "Tell me the properties of it."

"Iron is an ore that is extremely soft to mine but is much harder than our existing weapons once it has been smelted and shaped, though they will be much heavier. They are even looking at using it for armour. If Krilge listens to Salvia properly, he may even walk away with some as well which will be of great benefit when facing off against his father for the control of the tribe." While she speaks, Lusha spies a pair of sacks filled with silver ore and gems. *He has been busy. Or has he gained the knowledge of foresight?*

"Uh-hum. And the other matter we discussed?" She sees that he is finishing the last of the runes and is double-checking that he has not missed a thing or made a single error. Once he finishes rechecking his work, he pulls a small piece of parchment, ink, and a writing stick. He then proceeds to write down a short message.

"The shapeshifters are located along the north-facing range of the Hamo Montes about five days away as the crow flies. It will probably be nearer 20 days before we can get to them and make our negotiations."

When she finishes talking, he mentally summons his familiar. Within the space of a couple of breaths, the largest blackest raven she has ever seen flies down the stairwell to them and lands on the Wizard's shoulder. It listens intently when Treorai speaks to him and ties the small scroll around one leg. Upon finishing, the bird squawks and then flutters off back up the stairs to the upper levels and out to complete his instructions.

Treorai shudders. He hates the idea of using his familiar for such long-distance work, though Krilge and Salvia should not have got so far since they are less than a day away. It makes him feel vulnerable and he fears that his bird may come to harm. If that ever happens, then it will leave him weakened for a while, maybe for too long if certain people find out. *They will not hesitate to steal or even kill me if they ever find out what I am truly up to, garnering the secret that is behind that solitary door in the room below.* Familiars tend to be smarter than the average of their breed, and his raven is no exception.

He then instructs Lusha to get some rest before leaving for her crucial mission. He also notes that she does not say anything about the two sacks at the foot of the slope even though he knows that she has seen them. He nods appreciatively at her discretion. *She might work out better than I hoped after all. If only she could get on better with the others when they are around, then she would be a real marvel to work with.*

He meditates to organise his thoughts and thinking over the past day before casting the summoning. He had a bad feeling when they captured Trystan Gibbs, which only intensified once he heard about the jailbreak. Of course, he punished Skarmazh by sending him on an errand from which the Hobgoblin and his four guards has not managed to return from, but that is by the by.

They are young men and women who spent all their lives in their respective settlements. That is why he chose them in the first place. The other benefit was that they did not know each other, which often makes those types of people easier to manipulate since they should not have been able to trust each other. Planning to dispose of the Half-Orc and the Goatherder to the meat locker was a stroke of genius. They would have kept the other slaves alive while also disposing of two strong, and now troubling, individuals. The additional irony was that the Herder's kids would have been feasting on their father to keep their strength up and not even realise it.

However, they did work together. *This is worth further study.*

He wonders if Skarmazh is very much to blame. The Hobgoblin is the one to put this Gibbs into the cell with them, but only under his instruction. Skarmazh did wonder if the solitary confinement cells would have been a better place, but it was the Sorcerer who dismissed the idea. If Treorai had thought about it sooner, he realises that the Hobgoblin actually had the right of it. It was too soon for the Herder to go to the mines due to his naturally aggressive nature and they did have his kids soon after, though he was not to know that at the time. This meant that the man would have to go into the meat locker either way Treorai looked at it, or he was likely to cause more trouble than it was worth. Like now. The Goatherder is the group leader here. He is positive of that. For the slaves to get the drop on Skarmazh so quickly, he had to be the one organising the entire escape.

Upon hearing what had happened, Treorai made a concerted effort to grab as much as he could carry in sacks so that he could get them back to his home at the first opportunity. Whatever he did leave behind would be of no benefit to them. Besides, he may be able to return once all this has died down. He still wants to get through that trapdoor in the alcove next to the stairs.

He comes out of his meditation and takes a deep steadying breath and ensures that he is in the centre of the circle before reaching out with his mind.

In a cavern overlooking a coniferous forest of redwoods on the east face of the Hamo Montes range, a mottled grey-furred Bugbear Shaman is meditating in front of his private shrine. His bearlike face is raised slightly, and his eyes are closed while sitting on the rock floor of his chapel.

In the adjoining cavern is his solitary residence before joining the cavern complex proper. There, a female version of his race whimpers on the stone-framed bed with a thin cord tying her hands to the stalagmite column at the headend that cuts in whenever she moves too much. Krashak is in a particularly brutal mood today, ever since that run-in with those Lizardmen. Now she is there to suffer for it.

He is a Shaman of the Bugbear clan Mgbuntu with his own people under him, though he is not the Chief. Not yet at least. The clan is divided into three groups. Chief Grashnik has one, Gashnik the Sneaky has a second and is the Chief's brother from the same litter, and he has the third group.

He knows that they are only allowed to remain in the cavern since they provide free additional security for the Lizardmen's Master, to prevent them from escaping with any treasure that takes their fancy. Even though they do like to try every now and then by attempting to slip past the guards. This time it was his group's turn to watch the cavern entrance which is concealed by a pair of alpine laburnum and the accessway to the lair beneath them. However, he lost one of his own this time and another two were injured. Such losses would not be so bad since they have a few females with young about to come of age right now, but that also means that it will be harder to beat Chief Grashnik's evening hunt score for food and their own share of the treasure. The competition between the three leaders can be fierce and has even led to bloodshed on a few occasions.

I am really going to have to push them this even ... what the ...? Krashak's meditation abruptly ends when he feels an insistent push onto his mind. "Who dares?" he barks aggressively. The female on his bed whimpers in fear thinking that he is about to continue his assault on her.

"Not you bitch!" he growls at her as he strides past to the entrance of his private sanctum. He stops a warrior trying to avoid his gaze by staring intently at a stalactite/stalagmite column while walking past it. He jumps when the Shaman growls at him. "You, call my crew together to meet me here fully armed and ready to go immediately!" *They are not going to be happy with being forced to move this early, but who cares about that.*

The warrior nods with a hard gulp and then hurries away. Within a minute, Krashak has fourteen Bugbears waiting outside his private chambers. He walks out fully armed and armoured in a rigid leather cuirass and a Tenebrae armour skirt over his mottled grey hairy legs. He even spots one of the injured from that earlier encounter.

"Runerunner, fall out!" he growls at the warrior. Krashak marches up to him, then barks into his face. "You can't pull your weight on the hunt; then you ain't no use to me! Clear off back to the nursery!" The wounded warrior, Runerunner, yelps fearfully and starts to scamper away.

He has no reason to know that he has just impressed his superior. *No need to either, else they would all do it. Besides, he has the makings of a good Shamanic Adept from his early studies, so it will be a waste to bring him along before he has a chance to heal.* Runerunner is not his actual name but is one given to those who desire to become a Clan Shaman.

"Runerunner! Get the bitch from my chamber and take her back too." Runerunner snaps off an affirmative and disappears to his duty. It would not surprise him if the young Shaman Adept had his way before releasing her. He would have done.

Krashak then leads his group out of the cavern and heads north along the east face of the mountains. It only takes him about fifteen minutes to follow the mountain pass to a peak where the pass then weaves its way down to a fast-moving river. He orders the other Bugbears to hold until he returns, then moves around the peak to an almost hidden thick wooden door and enters.

Thirty minutes after Treorai sent out his call, a Bugbear wearing a rigid leather cuirass with a tenebra armour skirt over his mottled grey hairy body opens the door above, and calmly walks into where he is waiting.

"Ekele, Nnukwu Onye Nchuàjà nke ugwu, Krashak," he begins in the creature's tongue warmly. "And welcome to my humble tower."

"Cut the crap Sorcerer," the Bugbear snarls back. "It ain't your tower. You didn't build it. We know the ancient ones did. Now, what do you want?"

I did not expect that. This one is more intelligent than he looks. "Straight to the point. Good," Treorai says coldly, more to cover his surprise at this Bugbear's response. Showing respect to this folk is not working out so well in this instance.

"Listen up Sorcerer," Krashak snarls again. "You know I can't get to you because of your circle, but your bitch over there ain't so lucky. She'll make an interesting addition to our clan." He opens his bear-like jaws and licks his sharp teeth to emphasise his point, though both Lusha and Treorai know exactly what the loathsome creature means.

If they did not decide to eat her straight away, then they might toy with her first. Treorai glances over briefly at Lusha. *Though it would be fascinating to see what a Half-Bugbear would look like if she could survive their brutally savage desires.* He catches her questioning look at him before taking a breath and turning his attention back to the Shaman.

"I need some of your warriors to work with me for a little while," he tells Krashak.

"Why?" the tribal high priest snaps. "How many?"

"I find that I have a little problem downstairs that they should have no problem helping me with. Ten should be sufficient."

"For a little problem, you need ten of my warriors?" Krashak sneers. "Some little problem you have there. Payment?"

Treorai is more than ready for this. Taking something out of a belt pouch, he throws it to the Shaman, the protective barrier fizzes briefly, as it passes through. Krashak snatches it out of the air and looks at a religious icon of some deity in his sharp-clawed hands.

"What is this? Metal?" he says in wonder.

"Gold," Treorai readily answers. "A rare enough metal in these parts, but I know where I can get hold of more. A lot more."

"Tell me and we deal," Krashak demands sharply.

"Give me your warriors and I will tell you when the problem is resolved."

"I'll give you six. No more." The finality of Krashak's statement leaves Treorai no room for further debate. When the Sorcerer nods, Krashak barks out an order whilst still watching him very carefully. "Isii mbu, na-ala n'ebe a. Ugbu a!" He does know a spell that will shatter the Human's feeble magical protection, though it is better not to let on unless the Sorcerer is stupid enough to betray them.

It only takes a short amount of time for another six Bugbears to walk into the tower, each one standing to attention in front of their leader, their bear-like heads turned towards him. Krashak walks over to them and talks rapidly to them as he gives them their orders.

"I thank you, High Priest Krashak of the Mountains. May your faith in Ugwu never falter?"

Without another word and barely a backward glance, Krashak heads on up and back out of the tower. Now he will need to get his people working extra hard tonight with the loss of so many. He just hopes that they will only be gone temporarily.

Treorai looks to the Bugbears and greets them before ordering them to follow him down a spiral staircase. They enter a faintly torchlit room with a set of double doors in the far wall and sacks of crushed salt against another. He then turns to face them.

"I am expecting some hostile visitors to come charging through those doors," he says pointing in that general direction. "What you are to do is to stop them by whatever means are necessary. Do you understand that?"

"Of course, we understand you," one of them snaps at him. Then he adds with a leer, "We aren't stupid Hobgoblins."

The corner of Treorai's mouth twitches briefly as he grasps the Bugbear's meaning. He begins to stroke his close-cropped beard while he thinks about what the best way is to use these Goblinoids to his advantage. After all, he only really needs them long enough to ensure that his disappearance goes unnoticed, or until they defeat the troublemakers for the last time.

He could use his staff to help him get away very easily. However, he has relied on his staff quite a few times over the past couple of days and it does have a limit to the magical energies it contains. Especially if it runs out of energy before he can find someone who will recharge it for him. Then the staff will be just that. A staff.

"Your problem?" the Bugbear calls breaking into Treorai's train of thought. When he looks to the speaker, the creature continues. "What are we dealing with here?"

"Three humans, a half-elf and a half-orc," he answers with an edge of irritation to his tone.

"That all?" he responds in mocking surprise. "By Ugwu, this should not be a problem," he finishes with a smirk.

"What do they call you?" Treorai demands, his baritone voice dripping with contempt at the creature's arrogance.

"Bleddynn. Elder son of Grashnik, Chief of the Clan."

"Alright, Bleddynn. What do you suggest?"

"Two rows near the stairs with our bows with the front three kneeling. When the door opens, the front rank will shoot through the right half, the rear through the left. That way, anyone in front of those doors will be easily caught under the rain of arrows, making it that much harder for anyone behind them to get through," he casually tells Treorai before finishing with a snarl. "Like shooting Goblins in a pit."

Treorai does not find the analogy so surprising since Bugbears of all the Goblinoid races are the most intelligent and brutal individually, let alone when they are in a group. The Hobgoblins prefer strength in arms whereas Goblins prefer to overwhelm their opponents by sheer numbers. He cannot help but be impressed by the speed and cunning of the plan Bleddynn just reeled off. He nods thoughtfully before saying anything, though, in truth, he already knows what he is about to say. "And I can conceal you all in darkness for as long as possible,"

"That won't be necessary," Bleddynn tells him. "We'll be better if we can use our eyes in such a vile-smelling place as this." He refers to the stink of Dwarfs, Humans, and Hobgoblins in the next room, which easily permeates through the door of the salt-crushing room to their sensitive noses.

"Nonsense. I have every faith in your abilities. I will provide you with the cover of darkness." *Besides, that darkness is more to ensure that I get away than helping them.* He leaves them to make their final arrangements. When he heads up to the basement of the tower, he finds Lusha is still there and waiting for him.

"Now they are in place Master," she says once she is certain that none of them are following. "Is now the chance for you to leave here?"

"Not yet Lusha," he answers with a smug grin. "I need to know that they are going to be able to cause enough harm, that there will be no chance for that troublesome lot to follow me. Therefore, I will need to ask you to take these items down to the old boathouse before leaving for your own duties."

"Yes, Master." She gives him a look of concern first, then leaves with two of his sacks.

The only other thing on his mind is what those runes are that he found in the alcove. They looked Dwarven, but they were not of the dialect that the Dwarfs of Spire used. Has he found the ancient one's mine, or did the Dwarfs of Spire develop their own variant?

CHAPTER 35

Aftermath

Kali looks around at the devastation of fallen friends and foes alike. Her heart pounds painfully in her chest at the cost of their freedom. She was unable to even imagine that life could be so brutal, not even when Lippio told her stories about his adventuring life with her mother. The young Half-Elf sees that Conn and Eloen are doing what they can to make their comrades comfortable though that seems extraordinarily little right now. While none of them lost their lives in the fight this time, Kali fears that it is only a matter of time before any one of them could die from their injuries. Conn already looks dead on his feet. Not from any injuries sustained in the fight, but from sheer exhaustion.

Eloen's cousin, Tarron just looks through their dead foes' pouches, throwing the contents away in disgust and gives the unconscious Ghorza a kick as he goes past. He even has no respect for her friend, even though the Half-Orc risked her life in the mere hopes of helping everyone get out alive. Though it looks like it may have cost her dearly when her strength failed her, from the multiple injuries she sustained in doing so.

Kali knows she should say something, but her voice fails her. Tears begin to sting the corners of her almond-shaped eyes.

She looks around to a noise behind her. The Dwarfs from the crushing room enter with that Northerner, Dragoslav, a feverish Trystan, and his children. She then realises that someone must take charge. She takes a long deep breath to control her emotional turmoil. Even then, it still takes her a little while before she manages to speak properly and clearly enough while struggling to keep her voice steady.

"It does not look like that we are not able to go much further right now, so I suggest that we clear this room of those creatures to allow ourselves the chance to be able to rest in some resemblance of comfort."

Tarron looks at her with disdain, Eloen, and the Dwarfs nod, and Conn just smiles at her wearily in thanks.

Trystan collapses against a wall keeping his children close. His fever seems to be getting worse.

The Dwarfs immediately start to remove the Bugbears. The Dwarfs wanted to remove the corpses from the salt-crushing room, thinking it would be easier on the young Spiritualist if they could make use of the heavy table for the more severely injured. But the thought of resting in the room they were imprisoned in made each of them feel sick to their very core.

Tarron literally looks down his nose at Kali's instructions. He starts to suggest about leaving the others to their fate and going, until he catches Eloen's warning glare before grumbling his way to helping. He may not like being around the Half-Orc and the Dwarfs, but he is not so arrogant to realise that navigating his way through the mountains on his own, *especially since my cousin has decided to stay and help, damn her soft heart,* is not the smartest of decisions that he could make.

The wahaikas, a short bone club-like weapon, and heavy maces that the Bugbears were using are now in the hands of the Dwarfs in place of the small wooden mallets that they were using to break the salt rocks. Beata, Tarron, and Eloen pick up a bone bow each and gather the remaining arrows. Kali just looks on in shock at their total disregard for the taking of property of others where she then raises her objection.

"Sweet, innocent, Kali," Eloen says with no mocking tone or harshness in her melodic voice. "In this world, you use whatever you can to survive, even if that means taking from the dead or from those who mean you harm. There is no shame in that. It is just survival. Taking purely for the sake of it? Now that is wrong, but there are those who do it anyway. We are not taking anything out of greed; we are taking them for need, so it is fine."

"That goes for the weapons and armour, but what about money and gems?" she asks the woman.

"Depends on where you found it. If it is in this place where that Sorcerer has decided to take from those he enslaved, then I for one will rest easier knowing that we have reduced his wealth. If it is a lair the Hobgoblins are using? That is fine too. It is our survival against theirs and we will need to replenish our supplies, repair our armour, and sharpen our blades at some point." Kali nods thoughtfully, though her concerns still clearly etch her face. "Let us put it this way. Would you rather those that would mean you harm to have the better armour, the stronger weapons because you are worried about taking what they have from them?"

"No, I would not, but..." Kali, says slowly.

"Well then. Do not be so hard on yourself. Whatever you took from back in there is yours by right." She pauses long enough to tap Kali's tome, reminding and embarrassing the girl. "You have no cause for concern there, sweet Kali." Eloen then looks up with her own worry. "Conn, settle down and get some rest or you will be no good to anyone. We can watch over you while we take our respite, as will the Dwarfs." The young man nods at her gratefully. He ignores Tarron's huff and is asleep soon as he puts his head down onto his backpack.

Conn wakes up feeling extremely refreshed. The usual tempestuous dreams were calm for the first time since he woke up in the cell with three other strangers. He takes a deep cleansing breath of the cool rank air and looks around at who is also awake.

Not surprisingly, Kali and Eloen are quietly talking in their language.

Ana and Tarron are with them, though the Elf moves towards Conn once he notices the young Spiritualist is awake.

Oddmund and the other Dwarfs seem to be trying to snore in direct competition with Ghorza. Reuben is lying beside her. Beata's head is in Waldemar's lap where he rests fitfully, and Trystan is looking slightly better than he has ever been since the 'Werewolf' bit him. He notes that someone seems to have taken off Trystan's armour judging from the pile next to his two children and covered him in a cloak which has shifted to reveal his still soaking back. It is only then that Conn notices someone has found some torches to light the room and there are a couple of spent torches below each wall mount.

"I trust that you are feeling better. Your pallor has improved at least,"

Tarron says quietly in his own deeper yet no less melodic voice as he crouches next to the young man. Conn nods gratefully.

"How long have I been asleep?"

"About half a day. While you slept, most of the rock delvers kept an eye on you all and the Humans left with the savage. Eloen and the half-breed came with me to find out where we are." Conn immediately looks to Ghorza, but it soon becomes obvious whom Tarron is referring to. "We are under an ancient tower built inside the peak of a mountain, though the top has been worked with discrete outlets to prevent flooding."

"You don't like anyone of mixed race, do you?" Conn says looking askance at Tarron. "If it was not for those two, we may not have been able to get out of here as whole as we are. The only reason Kali did not get into this last battle is that she needs to see where she is directing her magic, which you already know. But once the darkness went, she did not hesitate to stand shoulder-to-shoulder with Ghorza and the rest of us." Tarron looks to the salt dusty floor for a second before looking into Conn's eyes.

"You did not go into the darkness to fight beside your comrades either," the Elf observes.

"My role in the battle became abundantly clear within the opening stages. When the darkness lifted, I was in there pulling our friends out of the fighting and using the last remnants of Unda's power and the herbs available to me to keep them alive. To prevent them from bleeding out at the very least. While we were protected from the fighting your friend was with me and willing to help with the wounded. You? Well, you did nothing and just stood there with that 'this whole thing is beneath me' look despite the fact it that it was **my** friends who risked **their** lives to ensure that **you** can leave whenever you want to," the young man said with increasing heat towards the end.

"That is so." Tarron falls quiet in contemplation for a short while and then looks Conn directly in his blue eyes. "She will never be with you, you know that."

"What?" Conn says incredulously, flustered and slightly louder and higher pitched than he intends, wondering where that statement came from.

Kali and Eloen look over.

"Tarron, leave him alone," Eloen says standing up and approaching them. Conn watches her walk towards them which makes him think of a rippling stream. "He needs to meditate so that he can have the strength to aid the fallen."

"I have seen the way you look at her," is the whispered response in the young man's ear before Tarron then glares at her and walks away from him.

"What was he saying to make you so upset?" Eloen says to Conn. Sitting down beside him. She watches Tarron's departing back.

"I'm rather embarrassed to say," Conn tells her quietly with a slight reddening of the cheeks. She turns to face him but does not immediately respond. He looks at her to find Eloen looking at him musingly. He gets the feeling that she already knows the answer to her question, or at least suspects that she does.

"Actually, I find that the strength in your faith for one so young really impressive," she begins changing the subject. "But … you never know what the future may bring," she says with a mischievous look and nudging his arm with her elbow. "For now, you get on with your prayers so we can finally leave this place and I will do the same," she finishes with a smile, then chuckles at how red Conn has gone.

It takes them the best part of a few hours by working together to help the injured.

They converse together but must agree that there is nothing either of them can do for Trystan. All Eloen can do is to confirm that it looks like the man is in the throes of wolf bite fever. The victims are usually stuck in this feverish state until the first full moon after they have contracted the disease. After the first change, the victim can then lead a relatively, if wandering, normal life. However, she tells him that it will be virtually impossible for the children to be safe enough if left alone with him. The best-case scenario would be that he kills them when the change comes over him, though that would also destroy his soul. Fortuitously, she does know of a Druid nearby who may be able to help the goat herder.

She decides to send Tarron out to see what type of night it is though this does mean that they will have to spend yet another night in the tower.

This does not please him at all, but when she tells him what is going on, he reluctantly agrees. He suggests that they go up into the tower properly where it might be more comfortable for them all. And where the air is much clearer.

Kali and Reuben are very agreeable to his suggestion.

Oddmund leads the Dwarfs in an exploration, and all are impressed at the craftsmanship that went into its construction. The entire peak has been hollowed out, and arrow-slit windows are expertly disguised as natural formations within the thick rock walls, just as the solitary door on the first level is well hidden, though not so much that they can see it has been used recently.

The stairs head up from the tower basement to the first level, then continue to the four upper levels, and the flattened roof is all part of the original peak where two people can walk abreast at the top. The second and third levels of this tower each have two rooms and there is another room on the fourth level with a spacious corridor connecting the stairs.

Inside these levels, the Dwarfs find sturdy stone framed beds that also look to be part of the design of the overall tower. From what Oddmund can figure out, the planning for this entire venture began in such meticulous detail before even the first chisel struck. There is not one stone block throughout the entire construction and the quality far exceeds anything that they have ever worked on in recent years. Recent years to a Dwarf being within the last thousand. Any other furniture that may have been here has probably been taken by the passage of time. However, they do find it curious that the doors have remained surprisingly intact.

On the roof where crenulations would be on a constructed tower, the natural formation of the stone provides great hiding places and protection from those coming up, which also has a great view of a fast-flowing river that splits the Hāmō Montes range in half. On this side of the river, the remains of a small roundhouse are precariously perched at the base of the mountain, hard up against the waterline.

They had also explored an alcove with a slight circular depression in the floor, and some runes on the far wall beside the spiral staircase where Treorai fled from the companions' fight against the Bugbears. While the runes look of Dwarf origin, even the highly intelligent Oddmund cannot read them. He then begins to wonder if these runes were created from before the splicing of the races. He writes them down in charcoal on a piece of parchment that Kali rips out, reluctantly, from her tome to research them later when he gets a chance.

When night falls, Tarron heads up to the roof and relishes in the chill night air while watching the waning moon skittering amongst the clouds. He also learns that Trystan's fever has abated slightly when he returns to report his findings.

"With luck, that means we will have time to get him to Adenor before the next full moon then," Eloen says hopefully when she meets him on the first level. The Dwarfs have taken up occupancy on the second floor, Ghorza, Reuben, and Trystan's children on the third, and Kali with the Hauflin, Ana on the fourth. Conn refuses to take a room since he does not want to leave Trystan on his own. The beds may not be comfortable without some sort of mattress on them, but they are more comfortable than struggling up off the salt-dusted floor when they wake up. Ghorza decides to sleep on her cloak when she wants to sleep which, considering her extensive injuries, is quite a lot.

"Of course, we will have the time," Tarron snaps at Eloen. He cannot understand why she is wasting her time with these people. If it were up to him, they would have left once the fighting was all over. Though he still cannot stop mulling over that boy Spiritualist's words.

"It can take a while since we do not know where she will be at any given time. Even her meetings at the Thorpe are not that regular," she snaps back.

Conn can hear them quite clearly and is amused at how such a soft melodic voice sounds when the speaker is angry, though he in no way likes to hear Eloen arguing with her cousin.

He is confused with who this Adenor is that they keep talking about. He decides to ask Eloen at the first opportunity. She tells him that Adenor Le Floch is the local Druid who helps at a small settlement called Spire when they need it. She is also their spiritual leader.

CHAPTER 36

Return to Spire

With the coming of a pale cloudy dawn, they all meet on the first level where Trystan is being supported by a much-rested Ghorza. His fever has gotten worse again.

They make their way down to the stone roundhouse which takes them half of the morning with all the switchbacks. There is no door in the doorway and much of the roof has long gone. The wall on the riverside does not exist and half of the floor area is in the river. A couple of boat docks stretch out into the water with a riverboat on either side of one.

Eloen remembers that there used to be four here at one point though she has no idea where the last one went.

It is Kali who voices Treorai's name.

"I shouldn't worry none," Oddmund tells them. "From what I read; the Spiritualists in the Halls of Spire enchanted them to return to this dock if they were ever used. I'm just impressed that the magic could still be working on them."

The Dwarfs directly refuse to step into the boats and insist on working their way around the mountain instead.

Tarron recalls the fabled Dwarf's fear of water and smirks, while Conn remembers seeing the small representation of a water deity in the long hall, where they fought the Goblinoids and lost Leiulf. The Elf decides that it will be better to show the Dwarfs the quickest way, though only if they agree to keep their mouths shut.

They grumble but they agree. Oddmund and Waldemar glare at Beata as if daring her to say just one word. For once, she refrains from retorting, though she will not forget either.

The Elf's mood does not improve after losing another argument with Eloen when he orders her to come with him before he leads the Dwarfs out of the mountains.

The rest of the group decide that Conn, Eloen, Trystan, Tudi, and Lianhua take the first boat and Reuben, Ghorza, Kali, and Ana in the second. It is not like they could pry the children from Trystan's encompassing arms anyway.

Even with the rapid river, it still takes them about an hour to leave the mountain range into a rough hilly valley. Soon several roundhouse buildings first line the south bank and then both sides of the river, at a point where a stone bridge crosses it and just beyond. While the river still flows fast, the current is not so strong compared to when they were racing through the mountains. The boats seem to avoid the jutting rocks on their own. Conn and Kali believe that is part of their enchantment.

All the buildings are a mix of single-level roundhouses half stone and wattle and daub, or wholly wattle and daub. There are even some ruins amongst the buildings.

Lianhua tells Conn that they have come to the settlement of Spire.

Tudi expertly guides them towards the bridge after finally working his way from one of his father's arms. Where they beach the craft, Lianhua informs them that they are by their drinking hall, though there is no signage advertising its purpose. It is the size of the building on the north bank that more than makes up for it. Their tavern is a building that looks like three roundhouses have been joined with straight wattle and daub walls to create an L-shaped building.

Ana guides the second boat to follow them, and they all disembark the long crafts.

When they bang on the door, the hall keeper is introduced as Barhan Ó Méalóidv and his wife Saorla, by the children who greet them. Saorla apologises that they are not open. When they see the state of Trystan and his children, they quickly change their minds. Barhan is a plump, balding man in his late fifties, and Saorla is a matronly looking woman with silvery hair slightly shorter than her husband's five-and-a-half-foot stature.

Once everyone is settled, Reuben and Ghorza leave with Eloen and Ana to help find the Druid.

Conn decides to stay with Trystan in case there is anything he can do to help the man fight his fever. He then asks Barhan if they have any coriander, but it is Saorla who tells him that they are waiting for Fortinbras to bring some. Even Nóra, their Herbalist has currently run out.

When questioned further about Fortinbras, Conn learns that he is a Hauflin trader who visits them twice a year, every year. The trader even takes those children who are coming of age with him to help them learn more worldly skills than they can learn in the small settlement. Some of them return on their own, some with partners, though more are leaving never to return. Some of the latter either die on the dangerous roads or decide to settle down elsewhere. As a result of the latter, Barhan voices his concern for the fate of Spire.

Kali also remains behind so she can study her newly acquired tome of arcane lore, with only a slight twinge of guilt at using the stolen book after what Eloen said to her. She also feels that she should go with them, but with all the upheaval earlier, she never really got time to study. Eloen gives her a warm smile of encouragement, which helps the Half-Elf feel a little better. She also believes that Nóra may be the one to help her help Lippio, though she needs to get hold of his recipe first somehow.

When leaving the tavern, Ana takes the lead and follows the northern bank of the swiftly flowing river along an old stone road. The going is surprisingly level and brisk despite many of the slabs being broken with weeds growing through the cracks.

While they search for the Druid, Eloen explains that there used to be a Dwarf Citadel over a century ago in the highest peak of the west face near the settlement they just left. She even points out the great double doors that is the entrance that is now behind them. Keeping on the road, she tells them that the Dwarfs built the road to facilitate the merchant caravans who visited them regularly.

At that time, the small settlement grew quickly to become the largest and most prosperous place in the whole Collis Valle while Seaton and Brackston were still small family-run areas. Then a three-fold disaster struck the area. The wealth of the Dwarven Halls became so legendary that greed became rife and grew even more so with each retelling wherever the traders travelled.

The first to try to plunder the Halls came in the form of the many merchants trying to take more than was their due, according to the Dwarfs. This led the Dwarfs to approach the people of Spire to try to vet the merchants at the settlement before allowing them access onto the Halls. This proved successful for a time though some still slipped through. Those the Dwarfs caught were never heard of again.

Despite regular patrols throughout the box valley from the settlement and the Halls, the Goblinoids and the Orcs still made regular raiding incursions. Since these were done in small raiding parties, they were more of an irritant than any serious threat, albeit an irregular irritant to both peoples and the merchant caravans.

Then the Druid, Aona Ó Fin arrived at the Saltus in Valle, a forest on the southern end of the west-facing spur of the mountain range, where they are heading for now and who later became Adenor's mentor. Within a few months, these raids began to desist to the point that everyone thought that the Goblinoids and Orcs had moved on to easier pickings.

Then the second disaster and first devastating step before the actual fall of the Halls came in the form of an extremely rare collaboration of Goblinoid and Orc forces. While the Dwarfs worked hard with the settlement to ensure there were no such tribes or clans about, these forces seemed to come from nowhere. The attack on the Halls also led to the fall of the great settlement, in part due to help from the Half-Orcs hiding within Spire. When Eloen mentions the Half-Orc involvement, she throws Ghorza an apologetic look.

This battle saw approximately half of the settlement destroyed and the Dwarfs barely managed to survive. While the battle raged, the defenders of the settlement heard several rumbles deep within the mountain which gave them cause for concern. Then the King of the Halls, Anskar Vagen, emerged to send out a call for aid in sheer stubborn defiance. Dwarf builders and engineers arrived approximately fourteen days later with the promise of an armed force ten days behind them. This first group had charged ahead of the main force to begin working on repairs immediately. Then the third and final disaster befell the region.

Soon after the arrival of the builders and engineers, a family of Dragons, dark as night came and attacked the region. While the settlement was still licking their wounds from the first attack, the Dragons assaulted them from the river before moving onto the Halls and the wealth contained therein. "It is said that a couple of these Dragons were felled by the inhabitants of the settlement," Eloen adds.

This battle lasted a day and a night. The Dwarfs fought a valiant effort to protect their already damaged home. The result being was that the main entrance to the Halls was closed for the last time with refugees pouring around the mountain along hidden goat tracks. Many of these were too young and too old to fight. Some were just too severely injured. Compared to the number of Dwarfs that were inside when the Dragons attacked, these were the lucky few. A couple of days later, the armed Dwarven reinforcements arrived earlier than expected only to find that their duties had rapidly changed. Apart from a boy and his grandpapa, they escorted the refugees of the Halls back to their own home. The Dragons never left.

"And that is the hurricane tour of the history of the valley of Spire," Ana says with a chuckle.

"Didn't you know any of this Ana?" Reuben asks her, intimately aware that he is trying hard to not look down at her like an adult to a child or like someone trying to look down her top. Considering she is only about three feet tall; he finds this difficult, but he is more comfortable around her now that he knows her a little better. She has even promised to help him understand his skills and how she believes that they are more akin to those of a Scout, like a Ranger of a settlement whereas she is more of a wilderness Ranger. She does confess that there are few differences between the two as she understands them.

"Some, not all," Ana openly admits. "That is why I love meeting with the Elves as they have such great stories to tell if you are willing to listen to them properly."

Ghorza glances over to Eloen and can almost swear that the Elf maiden blushes briefly when she smiles. She returns her gaze to the sun-kissed hills and the birds in flight. She even smiles wistfully at seeing a couple of squirrels chittering away and chasing each other around a hawthorn bush. Reuben, who is wondering why she is so quiet, breaks her from her reverie by asking if she is alright.

"Oh, I don't know," Ghorza responds like she is somewhere else. "After everything that has happened, I believe this is the first time that I have truly been at peace. It just seems that my life up till now has been one long continuous battle."

"I, for one, hope you have many more days like this," Eloen tells her. Ghorza looks at the Elf suspiciously, but when she can find no falsehood reflected in Eloen's face she then smiles and nods her thanks before returning her gaze to the scenery with a sigh.

It takes them three days to find Adenor, or, more precisely for her to find them. The young dark-haired muscular woman dismounts from a large, grey-furred wolf with shimmering green eyes when they catch sight of them heading towards the Saltus in Valle woods. Eloen and Ana are putting down stone patterns periodically to indicate that she is needed.

After sending her wolf off she then reaches them to see what is afoot. It takes Reuben, Eloen, and Ana everything they can do to prevent the Druid from starting a fight with Ghorza when she catches sight of the Half-Orc. They soon realise that Adenor has little tolerance for any of that breed, so the journey back seems to take an age for Ghorza who is upset at losing that earlier peacefulness so quickly, instead of the two days it does take them.

After Adenor clears the tavern of everyone except Conn and Eloen. It is then they learn that Trystan is infected with Mad Dog Fever and not Wolf Bite Fever. Mad Dog Fever is a disease contracted by being bitten by a diseased animal or Human. After making a tincture of ground mad stone and rye whiskey, they finally emerge an hour later with a grateful Trystan Gibbs behind them; with a promise from the Druid that she will check on Trystan at the tavern over the next few days to ensure that he has no lingering side effects. With a distrustful glance at Ghorza, the Druid makes her excuses and leaves them to return to her grove.

"I don't think I've managed to make a friend there," Ghorza says sadly. Eloen and Reuben smile at her in sympathy.

"Ah, don't ya worry 'bout 'er," Trystan booms, his brassy voice back to full strength. "Ya always got a friend in me an' me kids." Ghorza smiles gratefully at the big man who claps her shoulder. "Ya all 'ave, but right now, I got me some goats ta 'erd an see ta, so ah'll catch ya'll laters."

ABOUT THE AUTHOR

AJ has always had a great love of fantasy novels and Fighting Fantasy gamebooks before he got into Role-Playing Games properly. When he was playing the games, he found more enjoyment in creating scenarios set in different worlds rather than using the printed versions. Many of the games he ran were enjoyed by the players, but there was still something lacking for him.

As he gained more experience, his scenarios became campaigns with ever more involved storylines. These became the predecessors for the types of stories that he wanted to read. He also read everything he could find from the fantasy literature as written by the late greats of JRR Tolkien, Terry Pratchett and those by R A Salvatore and Terry Brooks.

This all evolved into the world he now calls Pangaiea. When he was creating this world, the missing element from his past attempts came to light when he started thinking of the origin of this world. This then extended into the Gods of Pangaiea, overseen by the All-Mother, Gaiea, and her Elementum.

From one scenario boxset produced by TSR came a campaign idea. He was modifying it for a new set of rules for a new group of players when he was testing each element of these rule changes. This is where Conn Bruis, Ghorza, Kali Celaeno, Reuben Bunner and Trystan Gibbs were born along with the major villains. He was filling in their background details to give them lives of their own when the first novel idea came to mind with a supporting cast. His creation of additional scenarios for the campaign became ideas for additional novels. The first scenario in the campaign is now the culminated work for the first novel, with more novels to come involving the heroes' continuing adventures.

Printed and bound by CPI Group (UK) Ltd, Croydon, CR0 4YY